CURSED

L. R. W. Lee

Paperback ISBN: 979-8-950333-08-8
Hardcover ISBN: 978-1-0879-1685-9
Woodgate Publishing

Table of Contents

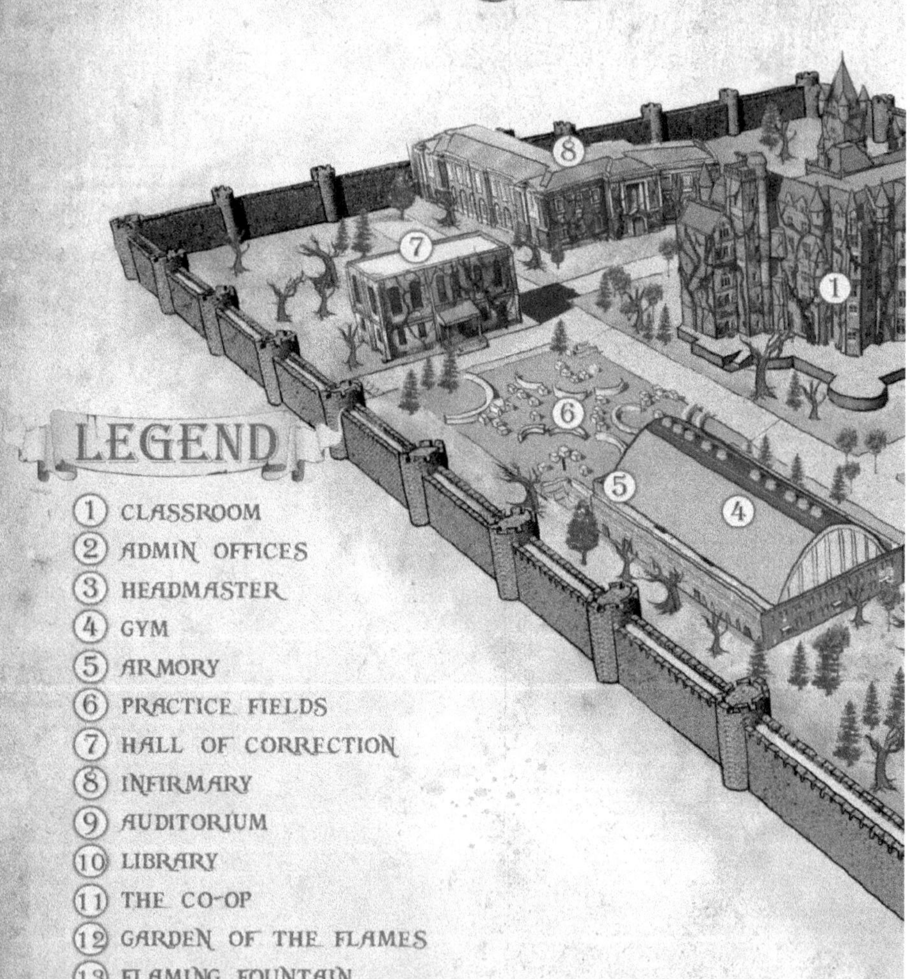

MORNINGSTA
LEGEND
1 CLASSROOM
2 ADMIN OFFICES
3 HEADMASTER
4 GYM
5 ARMORY
6 PRACTICE FIELDS
7 HALL OF CORRECTION
8 INFIRMARY
9 AUDITORIUM
10 LIBRARY
11 THE CO-OP
12 GARDEN OF THE FLAMES
13 FLAMING FOUNTAIN

AR ACADEMY
9
10
11
3
2
13
12

Chapter One

A siren screams past on the 101 Freeway not far from where I'm perched atop the South San Francisco Conference Center. Lights at night reflecting off the San Francisco Bay usually make it feel magical, but it feels anything but that at the moment. I'm on high alert and shift to stretch one leg then the other, glad only that I can disappear my wings when not in use since we've been in these tight confines for way too long.

"Be still, Gladriel. You'll give us away," Astread, my partner and BFF, warns in a hushed tone, crouching beside me.

I harrumph. My back's stiff, and my legs are practically numb from hunching in this position beneath a large metal vent. It rises a good four feet from the roof, then curves forward, affording us aerial cover from passing enemy but offering zero comforts. I may be immortal, but that doesn't mean my body enjoys this treatment.

Angelic brightness dimmed because we're in enemy territory, we've been surveilling the area for the last five hours.

As part of the cherubim army, I swore an oath to guard and protect all that is the Almighty's from the Enemy, and that includes humans. But daylight fled and darkness fell and nothing remotely resembling a threat has materialized despite intelligence reports cautioning us to the contrary.

The other four members of our squadron are paired up and scattered across the area, but none of them has communicated they've spotted danger either.

With nothing of interest to focus on, I allow my mind to wander to events from this morning, and I feel my stomach flutter. I can't help but smile.

"What a fake, Gladriel! Well done."

The deep, masculine bellow comes from the wooden benches surrounding the fresh, sawdust-covered sparring circle, from Kessien, my muscled squadron leader who just bolted up, followed by his raucous clapping.

His beautiful, beaming face makes my stomach flutter— it's so annoying—despite attempting to focus on Astread and what she's cooking up next to try on me. I've never allowed myself to have feelings for someone I work so closely with, and I'm not about to start; it would make things weird for the whole squad. If only my body had gotten the memo.

"Way to go!" Aliyah, a teammate, shouts encouragement, bouncing on the balls of her booted feet beside our leader.

One of another pair going at it in the next ring over barks as he lunges forward, connecting with his opponent's blade. The female beats her wings, skittering sideways to avoid his follow-up. Looks like they're evenly matched.

"You can do it, Astread," Jael calls from beside Aliyah.

Issra, on Kessien's other side, adds a two-fingered whistle for good measure to bolster my competition. What a male.

Kessien's still clapping. He's toned, not bulky, but definitely built, and in his black leathers… Gabriel, help me. I don't want "a relationship," but I appreciate eye candy when I see it. And I don't deny myself.

He sends me a wink, to which my body again responds, this time by dispatching a quiver that races through my gut. Stupid, fickle body, get with the program.

Astread increases my angst when—her back to our cheerleaders—she laughs, then feigns several kisses. Blast her.

I lick my lips, quashing the smile that's begging to erupt. I've tried to shut down her kidding, but it's only encouraged her further. There's nothing going on between Kessien and me, now or ever.

Why won't she believe me? Why won't my stomach?

Standing on the balls of my feet, I force myself to focus on honing my skills—it is why we're here, after all—flitting my gaze between her eyes and feet as I tighten the grip on Phantom, my sword. I will the flame of my celestial blade hotter, from dull red to orange, just to make things more interesting.

She grins, then mimics in response with Decimation, her blade. The look in her eyes shifts from playful to intense as she clenches her jaw.

Game on.

Holding my blade steady, I wait until she turns her toes left in response to seeing me glance over the top of her left wing, toward our cheerleaders. She always gives herself away.

I feint right, but she's not buying it this time. At the last second, she pivots and lunges right, barely blocking.

The flames of our blades clash in a flash of white light, and a wave of blazing heat races in all directions.

Humans will probably think there's been another solar flare. It's a safe bet considering the distance between here in the third heaven and Earth.

Regrettably, the heat will make my long, golden locks a frizzy mess, but the sacrifice will have been worth it, because she's off-balance.

I capitalize on the opportunity, slicing up and left. She lets out a howl when Phantom finds purchase in her side.

"I yield." She holds up a hand before bending forward and grabbing the wound.

Our cheerleaders race to her aid—Aliyah will heal her and have her good as new in no time—but before they reach us, she presses on her wound, straightening with a wince, and says in a hushed tone, "There's a picture for you."

I furrow my brow.

"… of what you and Kessien could be… if you'd let it." She grins before grimacing.

"What, a flash in the solar flare pan?" I joke.

She shifts, moving close. "No, fiery, passionate lovers."

I snort, then roll my eyes.

A seagull screeches overhead, bringing me back. I wish it hadn't because I was enjoying my reverie. I chuckle to myself.

Fluffy clouds drift across the almost full moon, but the smell of Chinese food from King Sun Buffet next door makes me wrinkle my nose. It smells like a mixture of lard and sweat in an old basement, and it's getting more pungent the longer we're here. I'll take Indian any day. The fragrance—yes, *fragrance*—of sautéing onions, curry, and other complex spices… I barely staunch a moan. It's divine. My heavenly body doesn't need such sustenance, but hey, it's fine cuisine, and I'll indulge every time. Enough said.

Astread nudges me before I can revel in my food fantasy further, and I turn to watch a couple emerge from the Holiday Inn on the other side of the conference center.

I scan the skies, looking for the pack of squalid, mangy menaces we've been expecting. Where are they? When will they strike?

The man takes the female's hand—ah, amore. Chivalry's not dead with this one—and they head for the sidewalk that stretches beside the four-lane road running in front of the conference center. No doubt they're heading for the restaurant. It's the only place to eat within walking distance.

The woman laughs at something her companion says, and I smile at how cute they are.

A disturbance forces me to tear my gaze away from their easy banter and focus instead on a vehicle several blocks away that's approaching from behind them at high speed, heavy-metal music blaring out the open windows.

Human senses aren't nearly as acute as that of spiritual beings, and I know they won't hear it until it's nearly on them.

My sore muscles scream as I tense, readying to unfurl my four wings in an instant if I need to. Astread turns her head as she notices but otherwise doesn't flinch. If we intervene, it'll blow our cover—not that the humans will see us, because they won't, but who knows who else might. Regardless, I won't allow this couple to come to harm, if it comes to that.

The man laughs as they stroll past a streetlight.

My pulse speeds as the car continues careening toward them, running a red light two blocks away and cutting off a pickup truck entering the intersection. The driver of the pickup screeches to a stop and lays on the horn, but the sound does nothing to stop the maniac.

"Demon. Has to be," I whisper.

Astread bobs her head. I draw my celestial dagger, readying as the threat nears. Always the controlled one, my partner, again, doesn't otherwise react.

Eyes wide, the strolling couple whirls around when the sounds of the commotion reach them. Turning back, they hurry inside the restaurant.

I exhale when the door closes behind them.

"See, nothing to worry about." A corner of Astread's mouth hitches as she continues watching the errant car. "Oh, ye of little faith."

I shake my head. "I may be an overprotective worrywart, but don't say I lack faith. Them's fightin' words."

She chuckles.

But the sound of a revving engine and screeching tires has me pivoting my head again, and I suck in a breath because that car swerves into oncoming traffic to get around a vehicle in its way.

Beastly demons! Too bad guardian angels aren't real.

I spot the repulsive, leather-skinned demon, that's the size of a terrier, latched onto the neck of the rogue car's passenger as he makes a profane gesture out the window when they're even with the driver of the offending vehicle. That demon has him under its control, and it's not about to release him; it's having way too much fun, judging by the loud cackle the thing lets loose.

If only humans could sense these bastards!

Demons roam in packs, so I guarantee there are more than one in that vehicle, and I again ready to launch.

"Hold. Don't ruin the mission," Astread says, grabbing my arm.

She's always better than me at detaching herself from the drama and staying focused on our orders. I can't help it. I hate situations like this. The notion that we're supposed to let these mangy misfits wreak havoc "for the good of the mission" always grates on me. Those demons will get humans killed at this rate—it'll look like the humans are nothing more than a victim of drunk driving. I huff to myself. *Hardly.*

Is that really "God's will"? No, it can't be. It's capricious, and God's not that… is he? I pause to consider. I'm hardly an expert. I've only seen him when he reviews the troops. A shiver runs down my back as memories of those times flash through my mind. In his white suit and tie, he's so bright, it's blinding… and intense… and, I'll admit it, a bit scary. No one so much as flinches. I've no delusions he couldn't whup our butts if we stepped out of line, but who'd be stupid enough to test him? No, he's powerful enough that I can't see him needing to stoop to being capricious. It would be petty for someone like him. Right?

I shake my head. I'm a warrior, not some brainiac, powerful archangel. That's above my pay grade.

Refocusing, I only barely squelch a squeak as, still in the wrong lane, another car approaches, heading their way.

I can't look, but I can't tear my gaze away either, and my heart again accelerates. We have to do something.

"How do you know this isn't the threat we were warned about? There are demons involved," I growl, not taking care to keep my voice low.

Astread glances over. "How do you know it is? The warning said to watch for a 'significant' conflict involving the enemy. This is hardly that."

I barely bite my tongue. *It is to the humans involved.*

The driver's will to live must be strong because it's the only way he regains control from his tormentor for a split second and darts back into the proper lane just before they would have collided head-on. Unsurprisingly, the other driver lays on her horn.

You tell 'em, lady!

My breathing slows as the car careens on, leaving a cacophony of horns in its wake.

I return my dagger to its holster and draw a hand to my leathered chest. I may not be "old" in immortal terms, but I'm too old for this crap.

Before my heart fully returns to its normal pace, a telepathic alarm sounds in my ear. I plug one ear with my finger to better hear the voice of the heavenly dispatcher. *"We've got a code 666 on Coast Highway 1 near Pacifica."* Astread, plugging an ear, tenses beside me. *"Demonic activity is behind a massive mudslide burying multiple vehicles. The enemy, including Fallen warriors, have been spotted. Multiple humans down. Proceed with extreme caution."*

This is bad. It's really bad. But fallen angels are there too. That's odd. Led by Lucifer himself, fallen angels are nothing but pompous, deluded scum. Seems the Enemy is pulling out all the stops.

"Squadrons 427, 132, 698, 546, and 336 report for duty," she finishes.

Squadron 132, that's us. Pacifica is just south of here. We were so close, but not close enough when it mattered. I wish we could have stopped this before it started.

I clench my teeth as I duck out from under cover, unfold as I stand, then hands on hips, extend my wings. "Guess we found the 'significant' threat," I murmur.

"Understatement, much?" Astread's tone is light as she stretches, pushing feeling back in her extremities too.

"I hope you gave it your best shot, fallen pretty boys, because you're going down," I growl, tightening the band that's keeping my hair confined.

Kinks worked out and blood flow restored a minute later, we high-five. Astread looks south and grins, a glint in her eyes as we launch.

Chapter Two

My fingers twitch on Phantom's hilt as we slow, far enough away from the scene of devastation so as not to be seen but close enough to take it in. In the light of the nearly full moon, my stomach drops.

Demons and Fallen warriors have converged, and through a cloud of them, I can make out a huge rockslide. What clearly used to be a section of the coast highway is just gone. Soil above the sheer cliff, along which the road ran, has come loose, and like lava from an erupting volcano, it's left a trail of devastation all the way to where it plunges into the ocean below.

I swallow hard. How many humans have lost their lives? I can only hope, due to the hour, not many were on this stretch of road. My shoulders curl forward. Who am I kidding? Demons wouldn't have created this chaos if they hadn't extinguished a good number of humans in the process. It's what they do.

Blighters.

Astread stops beside me, hovering. An unnatural calm and focus has replaced the glint in her eyes. She's downright scary when she gets this way, and rightly so with the sight before us. She's definitely a force to be reckoned with.

It's a good thing too, because I want nothing more than to kick some demon butt, then get to the humans.

The host of Fallen warrior angels stretches out between us and the cloud of swirling demons, no doubt to slow us down from rescuing the humans. They may slow us, but they're undisciplined idiots, and we'll dispatch them soon enough. Like Lucifer, these pretty boys and girls indulged their vanity and the Almighty clipped their bottom wings, then kicked them out of heaven before they could contaminate the place.

Darn right.

Clearly someone higher up planned their mission because they're not that smart. Gesturing with their drawn swords, they don't scare me or any self-respecting cherubim. I've never found it hard to discover and exploit their weaknesses. They'll soon feel our wrath and abandon their objective.

"Yip. Yip. Yip. Yip. Yip."

"Screech."

"Caw. Caw."

Their noise is deafening as they swoop and dive, celebrating their mischief. It amps up my impatience, but we need the rest of our ranks and a plan before we can whack some feathered butts.

I jiggle a wing—it's a nervous habit—trying to control myself as I scan the area, searching for friendlies but spot none. It's taking too long. I purse my lips. Those humans won't have long. We need to get to them before it's too late.

I need to move. Once I'm fighting, I'll be fine, but I'm no good at waiting, especially when human lives are on the line.

Seconds later, I spot the other four of our squad approaching fast.

Kessien and Jael halt and hover beside us, catching their breath. Kessien's strong jaw is set, and Jael opens and closes his fists, his steel-blue eyes focused, in battle mode. Aliyah and Issra, the other two members of our squadron, are nearly here.

Our squadron is the first to arrive, and with our angelic brilliance dimmed, our enemy hasn't spotted us yet or they'd be attacking. I just hope the rest of our forces arrive soon.

A plume of lingering dust from the rockslide reaches us, and I grab for my nose, but I'm not fast enough. Despite taking a deep breath through my mouth, I can't suppress a sneeze. I catch it against the inside of my elbow, doing my best to keep it quiet.

Jael doesn't react, just studies the scene before us, and I exhale. But Astread shakes her head, frowning.

I throw up my hands and roll my eyes, to which she gives me another shake of her head, but a corner of her mouth hitches as she returns her gaze to the roiling minions.

Kessien winks, making my stomach quiver.

Knock it off. Stupid stomach.

Fingering the hilt of my sword, I study the legion of demons. They're all larger than the menace in the car earlier; roughly the size of wolves, they no doubt weigh a good 200 pounds each. Moonlight shines off their bald heads. Between that and their pointed ears, crude, protruding canine teeth, and leathery skin that has hardened into a tough, black coat, they're as fierce and hideous as the zombies humans fear, only with wings.

Every time I see these things, my skin crawls. I've been a warrior for eons, but some things are just… nope, nope, nope.

It's not long before Zerell, leader of Squadron 427, Adellum, Squadron 546 leader, Tubiel of 698, and Esme of 336, along with their warriors, arrive.

Kessien alone turns his back to the chaos—he knows we have his back if the situation changes in the slightest—as he motions the leaders to gather.

In a low murmur, he says, "I propose we hit the middle of the Fallen with three of our squads as a distraction while the other two each attack a flank. Penetrate the flank, permeate the debris, and start checking for the living. It should be the fastest way. Once the Fallen and legion bug out"—because they always do—"we'll all help with rescue efforts."

Heads bob, and Zerell, eyes studying the chaos, brings his hands up to his lips. "We'll take a flank."

"So will we," agrees Esme, flipping her blonde ponytail over a shoulder. I'm not surprised she volunteered. Like me, she has a particular affinity for humans.

"Very well. Then the rest of us will hit the middle." Kessien's golden hair ripples in the slight breeze as he draws his blade and turns to face the enemy. Broad shoulders pushing back, he's wholly focused, and I have to say I love that look on him.

Astread bumps my shoulder when I'm still looking at him, and a corner of her mouth rises, to which I wrinkle my nose.

She holds out a fist to start our pre-mission ritual. I bring mine down on it. Habit has me reciprocate, extending my fisted hand, and she brings hers down. No matter how big or seemingly small the assignment, it's what we do. I don't even remember how it started, but we've done it for as long as I can remember.

Zerell's and Esme's squads separate, keeping their brilliance muted, and head toward the breech points on either side. I silently draw my sword, along with Astread and the rest of my comrades. Then we spread out in a v-formation, ready to drive a wedge through the middle of their lines.

Once everyone is in position, Kessien raises an arm, and we kill the dampening on our celestial brilliance and let ourselves shine as we charge forward. The white light from our blades adds yet more awe to our presence. With only the light of the nearly full moon before, the contrast is shocking to be sure. Exactly what we want.

Astread and I share a smile as the legion of demons stutters in flight for half a second and the Fallen warriors visibly balk.

We're on them in seconds. My BFF at my back, I reach a fallen angel warrior, and it takes me all of seconds to feint left, then run my blade through his right side. He doesn't see Phantom coming. He bellows in pain, then winks out of sight, hauling it to their infirmary in second heaven, no doubt.

Astread's having equal success as I hear another pained exclamation, and then she laughs a maniacally resonant sound behind me. It'd send a chill through me if I didn't know her.

I'm on to my next victim. This female's nostrils flare, no doubt pissed, as soon as she sets eyes on me. But being emotional will only impair any skill she has—one more confirmation they really don't teach them anything down there.

I feint left. Surprisingly she mirrors, and I easily block her blade. But she's left her side open.

I choose not to overthink it as I've been known to do and go with my gut, beating my wings and pivoting. My blade finds purchase, slicing through her black leathers like butter. A second later, she snarls at me before disappearing.

What? Are you a cat? Please, have some self-respect.

The instant the fallen angels realize our strategy, they swarm, trying to surround us.

Yeah, good luck with that.

Just before my next opponent reaches me, I spot Kessien and Jael at the tip of our formation, mowing down the enemy like harvesting wheat. Their blades are white blurs, their expressions fierce, and something in my heart stirs. They're both beautiful in action.

I take out my next two opponents with Astread at my back, meeting equal success.

It's not long before we hack our way through the fallen angel enemy line and start attacking them from behind. Zerell's squadron flows like water through the hole we create. It's all I can do not to shout my excitement, but I'm more disciplined than that.

The writhing flock of demons that's been insulated by their fallen brothers must decide they've had enough because we're nearly on them and they beat a hasty retreat.

Good riddance.

But once again, the Fallen prove how half-witted they are. The warrior across from me bares his teeth and rolls his shoulders, locking eyes with me. *Idiot.* They haven't yet given up the fight.

Fine. Bring it.

He beats his wings and charges me.

I raise my sword, letting the flame blaze white as I give him my best smile. It only angers him more. Mission accomplished.

He's within a yard of me, committed and unable to change directions, and our swords collide. Once, twice, thrice. I let him think I'm struggling just a little, let him think he's gaining an edge. Let him grow cocky. Then I wink.

With four wings, I have the advantage when it comes to maneuverability, over his two. His eyes bulge as I beat my wings, jetting around to his side before he can react. Phantom slices through his hip, and he disappears.

I dispatch my next opponent, a pretty male, then turn to see my partner playing with another Fallen warrior. I know she's playing because she's not in his face. Sorry to ruin her fun, but I'm wearying of this. Humans need rescuing.

I beat my wings, lowering myself slightly, then pivot around her and land a roundhouse kick to her opponent's groin.

Her adversary doubles over, and Astread's mouth drops open, an accusatory expression mounting her face.

I shrug. "Just trying to help. Shall I finish him, or would you like the honors?"

"I will. Thanks." Her tone is clipped, but I know she's not mad at me, not really. She goes for the warrior's neck.

He catches the air with a mighty beat of his wings, lunging to the side, but I spot silver gushing from his neck before he clutches it. She must have nicked a major vein. Like the others, he vanishes before she can do more damage.

I pause long enough to realize the other squadrons have the few remaining Fallen weenies well in hand, and I jet for Kessien.

"Kessien, permission to help the humans." It tumbles out in a rush.

Sorry, not sorry.

Before he can reply, through our telepathic link, Esme's voice quakes, "We need help, stat. So far we've found fifteen cars buried with multiple humans still inside each. There may be more. Oh, and if they're alive, there are demons."

Chapter Three

My wings twitch. Every human has a demon attached to them? What darkness, what evil were these people courting? And why?

I shake my head. Now's not the time to wonder. Those humans will run out of air if we aren't quick about it.

Kessien alerts Tubiel and Adellum, the other two squadron leaders, of our plan.

Issra and Aliyah each dispense with another Fallen warrior then swoop to a stop and hover beside me, wiping their brows and panting.

The telltale flashing lights of three red rescue trucks and another three patrol cars screech to a stop on the road near the avalanche, and their personnel barrel out, along with several dogs on leads that immediately start barking.

I'm glad humans have arrived, but they'll never make it in time with their brethren buried deep.

Jael's been surveying things beside Kessien, finger tapping his lips. I can't read him. He's always as calm as a tranquil sea. Drives me crazy sometimes, but I digress.

Astread is nowhere near as antsy as I am, but her wrinkled brow and the fact that she's biting a lip—so unusual for her—tell me she's equally concerned as she floats beside me.

A pair of helicopters arrive and hover above the scene. They keep their distance, probably so they don't stir up more dust, but their light helps illuminate the area.

"We've got this," Tubiel wheezes through our telepathic link, then exhales sharply as another Fallen warrior disappears not far away.

"Go, help with the rescue," Adellum grunts a second later. I spot her taking on a pair of Fallen a ways away. Thankfully, her partner has her back, because they're surrounded.

I extinguish Phantom's flame and sheath it as Kessien nods at Jael who holds up a calloused hand. We all respond, joining with a hand of our own, then through our connection shout, "Let's do this!" It's our squad's custom once Kessien gives out assignments. So many traditions, what can I say? We're as bad as humans in that regard.

The instant we finish, I take off like a lightning bolt, not willing to wait for the rest of the squad when humans are dying. "You good handling the demons while I check the humans?" I ask when Astread catches up; my mind's a whirl, figuring out how to save each one.

I glance over a wing. The others have caught up, too, and fly four abreast behind us. Kessien's directly behind me, and when our gazes connect, my heart skips a beat.

What is wrong with me? Kessien and I have worked together for millennia. Now, with just his nearness, my body suddenly betrays me?

My hand trembles when I run it down my leathers, trying to rein in my mutinous body. This has *got* to stop.

Astread gives me a hard look. "How about we make sure each of the human's time is not yet fulfilled, first?"

I give my wings a strong downbeat and race forward as I huff under my breath. I love her, but I want to scream. She knows how I feel about rules like this. Forget the *stupid* regulations for once. We can save lives.

"Glad, stop." She catches up and extends a gloved hand. "We've no idea how saving one whose life is complete could change the entire course of human history."

"Isn't the Almighty powerful enough to compensate?" I've never dared voice my objection, but I'm frustrated. Some regulations are just plain stupid.

The helicopter blades beating the night air grow more deafening as we near. Combined with the flashing red lights from more rescue vehicles arriving, it's sensory overload.

"You're cranky tonight, Glad. You argued about intervening with that human driver, now this." She pauses for effect, smiling. "What's got your panties in a twist?"

We've spent considerable time with humans and adopted a good many of their sayings, but this one has always conjured the funniest image to me, and Astread knows it. Leave it to her to try and lighten my mood. I can only roll my eyes.

But it doesn't change the fact that I'm sick of crap regs like this.

Kessien and the others continue flying behind us, but his deep voice still breaks through our telepathic link, cutting off my reply. Probably for the best.

"Esme and her squad are deep in the landslide on the left side. Zerell and his warriors are on the right. Jael, Aliyah, and Issra, go help Esme. Astread, Glad, come with me. We'll help Zerell. Exercise extreme caution because they tell me the soil is very unstable."

I furrow my brow, then look back to see Issra rub his chin. Aliyah tilts her head beside him. Everyone's gaze bounces between our fearless leader and me. He always pairs up with Issra and Aliyah when our squad splits in two. His partner, Jael, always comes with Astread and me. Why is he swapping with his partner?

I make eye contact with Aliyah behind us and wish I hadn't because her confusion gives way to a corner of her mouth hitching.

I shrug, playing it cool, but my stomach quivers. Astread doesn't help when she nudges my wing and winks.

I can only frown and shake my head. Jael and Issra are focused on the emergency and oblivious to the goings on—such amazing teammates… and typical males.

I choose to ignore more scrutiny and turn my attention to the scene we've nearly reached.

Seven dump trucks and an equal number of earth movers aboard flatbed trucks pull to a stop. A dozen pairs of yellow-suited rescuers are braving the shifting soil, along with their dogs, and look like yellow ants fanned out across the span of the landslide searching for any signs of life.

The others head out, and Astread and I have just finished our ritual, pounding each other's fist, when Kessien stops beside me.

Focus, Glad! I berate myself when my gaze lingers on his big, beautiful wings when he beats them down, hovering.

"Zerell said they're working from the top of the cliff, down, so we'll start at the bottom and work our way up." Kessien points to our destination on the right side of the slide, just above the pounding waves.

Seconds later, my feet sink in the loose soil and I furl my wings.

"Fan out and keep in constant contact. When you find a buried vehicle, let's work it together." Kessien extends his arms toward the wall of dirt.

"Here we go," Astread says, vanishing her wings and stepping into and then through the dirt of the landslide. Kessien and I mimic, blending with the debris.

As celestial beings, an act of will gives us the choice of blending with physical objects or accepting their resistance. I would be completely frustrated if I had a physical body like humans right now, but I digress.

Permeating a solid mass always feels like walking through quicksand, and this time is no different. Silence engulfs me as I take careful, labored steps, heading straight back, into the heart of the beast. Tuned in to my companions' telepathic frequencies, their breathing is the only sound, and it comforts me.

Cars buried down here would have been the first pushed over the cliff at the tip of the avalanche and will have experienced the worst damage based on how far they fell. I swallow hard. These people will be well and truly beaten up.

"Finding anything yet?" I ask to silence the disquieting thoughts.

"Not yet," my BFF replies.

"No. Times like this I wish we could see through dirt." I hear determination in Kessien's steady voice.

"Hear! Hear!" Astread chimes in.

I strain as I push my way through a huge basalt boulder in my path. It's definitely denser than the surrounding rock but no way will it stop me.

It's been several minutes, and we've called out to one another several times before neon blue metal comes into view in my celestial brightness.

"I've... I've got one." Excitement fills me as my heart picks up pace.

"Be right there," Astread assures.

"Good job, Glad. I'm coming." Relief flavors Kessien's voice.

I trace the outline of the car with my hands. The metal is denser than the recently sifted rock surrounding it and makes it easy to pick out.

"It's pointed downward," I relay to my companions. "Its nose is rumpled like an accordion."

"What else?" Astread asks.

"I'm heading for where the driver's door should be." My breathing labors as I feel my way in that direction. "This car is in bad shape."

"There you are." Kessien reaches me first, having homed in on my telepathic signal, the way we always locate one another. He brushes my arm with a gloved hand, and lightness fills my chest.

Stupid, traitorous body. I've got no bandwidth for this crap.

I lift my arm, effectively removing Kessien's hand as I feign searching for the door. Because it's what I *should* be doing, rather than fawning over him.

"Nearly there," Astread says.

Not soon enough.

Chapter Four

"I feel the door handle." I use the debris as a step and raise up, finding the window to my left. "The glass is shattered but in place." My jaw tenses. "Kessien, you said there's probably a demon still in there?"

"Esme said that's what they've encountered with every human they've found alive so far. No idea why."

So a blessing with a curse, like so many things.

A second later, my partner emerges beside me, placing a hand on my shoulder.

"Took you long enough." I reserve my comment only for her through our connection.

She just snickers. *Little minx.*

I unsheathe my celestial dagger; the space is way too cramped for Phantom. "I'll take care of the demon, but I need you both to get the glass out of the way so I can puncture the airbag, then go after it."

"On it." Astread moves around me until her elbow skims my shoulder.

Kessien brushes my thigh with a shoulder as he moves into position below me. Of course my treacherous body can't help but respond, sending a shiver through me despite the serious situation.

Get. A. Life.

"Ready," my BFF indicates a minute later.

"Astread, on three," Kessien says. "We'll grab the glass and pull it forward, out of the way. Keep it as close to the car as possible."

"Sounds good." I can tell from her tone that my BFF is back in the zone.

"One."

I grip my blade tightly.

"Two."

I bring it back because this sucker's gonna pay if it's still feeding on this human.

"Three."

In the light of our brilliance, one hand from each of them moves through the glass, which shatters fully as they force it out, then down.

"All yours, Glad," Astread says.

Despite all our racket, I've no doubt that if there's a demon in there, it hasn't given up its human prize and bugged out voluntarily. It's not what they do.

I swallow hard and pray this human is still alive.

"Here goes." I tighten my grip on my blade, then thrust forward, puncturing the airbag near the top and drawing a long line down.

I bat at the material, trying to get it out of the way as my partners pull it down. A second later, I spot the hideous creature and cheer inwardly.

The human male's black seat belt holds him firmly against his seat, his face cradled in the detonated airbag. But a terrier-size demon rests on the man's left shoulder, back toward me. It's just removing its boney fingers from the back of the man's head where it's been feeding, no doubt planting thoughts of crippling fear.

No more, sucker.

I give the menace no time to react, plunging my blade into its sinewy neck and pulling down hard. Excitement must give me extra strength because the thing's head flops to one side, still attached by a thread, and silver blood sprays.

I turn my head, taking it on the cheek. The spray dies down seconds later, but the demon doesn't wink out of sight like always.

How? This never—

A loud screech sounds from the passenger seat, distracting me, and another demon barrels toward me.

Two humans survived.

Yeeesss. My pulse speeds.

A burst of energy hits me as the second demon sticks its hideous face in mine, mouth open. I raise an arm to block, and my blade strikes its leathery chest. If I can hit its neck….

I must succeed because no sooner have I thought it, than the thing screeches again and vanishes. I scan the back seat for more surprises and exhale when I find none—no more demons or humans.

But as I take in the hideous, nearly beheaded demon slumped over the back of the unconscious man still leaching silver blood, my heart practically beats out of my chest. I killed it. An immortal demon. It didn't wink away to regenerate.

As if an echo, surprise flavors Kessien's voice as he says, "You killed the thing, Glad. It's been eons since an angel killed a demon." He moves up beside me to get a better look, then pokes it.

"How?" I sheath my dagger with a trembling hand, trying to wrap my head around this.

"Partner." Wonder tints my BFF's words. "You really did kill it. Its head is partly attached." Astread peers over my shoulder.

My stomach clenches for a wholly different reason because they're right. It has been ages. The last time it happened, demons took revenge on the angel who did it in a gang-style retaliation the day after.

Astread pats my shoulder. "Hey, you'll be fine, Glad. We're not going to let anything happen to you."

"She's right, they can't hurt you with us around." Kessien bobs his head.

I can only nod at their attempts to encourage me.

"Let me get that thing off him," Kessien says.

I retreat a step toward Astread, out of the way but still close enough to see, giving him room to get his muscular shoulders through the narrow window and push the demon's body up and into the empty back seat. Silver blood gushes the whole time and coats Kessien's leathers by the time he's done. It's thoroughly disgusting.

He pulls back and straightens, wiping his hands on his leathers. It does absolutely nothing to clean him up because he's covered in dirt and demon blood. We all are.

I pinch the slimy skin at my throat, worry eating me alive. They mean well, but they can't be around me all the time. What am I going to do?

Brow furrowed, Astread mercifully changes the subject. "These people need rescuing."

"Yes. Yes, they do." I move back in beside Kessien, our sides brushing, but I clamp down on the fluttering stomach crap because we've got to save these people.

Kessien reaches for the driver's earlobe and runs a finger underneath. "One zero nine, two five four."

I rub the back of my neck. He's checking for the man's expiration date. "The guy's alive. Let's just save him, shall we?" My words hold bite.

Kessien turns toward me and, with a soft tone that's rich with understanding, says, "At times, I wish we didn't have these regulations either, Glad, but we do."

Not one for sentimentality, Astread interjects from behind us, "That number's too long. That's the number of hairs on his head, not his remaining lifespan. Try lower."

Kessien meets my gaze, and a pained expression mounts his face. He pauses from assessing the man and puts a large but gentle hand on my arm. "I know you're worried about demonic retribution but don't. Everything will be okay, Glad. I'll make sure of it."

I want to look away, the intimacy is too much, but I can't because I know he's sincere. He deeply believes it.

He holds my gaze for longer than is comfortable, before finally lifting his hand and turning back, again reaching for the driver's ear. "Okay, how about two, zero, one, one, five?"

"Quick math, he's got another fifty-five odd years left," my BFF says.

I press a hand to my stomach, relief flooding me. We can save at least one.

"I'll check the passenger," I say, not giving them time to deny me. Thankfully they don't object.

I move around Kessien and Astread and force my way through the dirt, around the crumpled car, and make quick work of the other shattered window and airbag when I reach the other side.

I bite my lip. The woman's in bad shape despite the airbag detonating from the dash and her seat belt holding her firmly against the seat. Her auburn hair falls limply over her black T-shirt. Blood trickles from a nasty gash in her head just above a small rose tattoo on her cheek. The airbag bears red streaks that lead to a pool of blood directly below where she's slumped, and my heart constricts.

Still be alive, please.

Ducking in, I find the woman's ear, then feel for the distinctive bumps. "One, zero, zero, eight, four, and…. Oh, no, that's the hairs on her head."

My heart speeds as I feel for the other number. "Ah, there it is. Um, zero, zero, zero"—I swallow—"zero…." My stomach goes hard as I find the final digit.

"What is it, Glad? What's it say?" My BFF means well. She needs certainty and closure. I understand that.

I fist my free hand. I'm a warrior. I should be tough, hardened to human death, but it always hits me. I don't know which is worse, being too late or reaching a human right before they pass and not being able to stop it.

A second later, movement draws my attention. A silvery glow rises from the woman's slumped form and floats up toward the headrest, then up and through the back seat before disappearing. Small solace, it's headed upward, rather than down.

In my sadness, I scrounge for something, anything positive, and come up with only the fact that at least she'll look like her old self once they give her a celestial body up top. It's not much, but I'll take even the tiniest nugget of good news in all this destruction.

"Let's save this guy." Astread's admonition draws me back, and my gaze locks with hers across the car's dark interior.

Yes, rather than mourning, I need to celebrate the life we can save. I've told myself that too many times, but there's nothing else to be done. I take a deep breath, breathing out my heartache and breathing in renewed determination to save this man.

"What do you suggest?" I throw the question out.

"Can't we just push the car forward until it's visible to the human rescuers?" Astread looks to Kessien beside her.

"We'll have to make it look like the dirt is shifting in order to reveal it without raising suspicions to our presence."

"Easy enough. Let's do it." I don't want to debate the virtues of the best way to save the man; I just want to do it.

Kessien catches my gaze across the interior and returns a steady look that does nothing to calm me, because my stupid body sends a flutter through my gut, and I look away.

Give me a fricking break, body.

"Let me notify Zerell, Esme, and the others to expect a shift in the landslide so no rescuers are endangered." Kessien's gaze moves to the top of the car's interior while he telepathically connects with our forces.

My BFF gives me a warm smile and thumbs-up. "This'll work, Glad."

Several minutes later, I'm panting, sitting between Kessien and Astread in the loose dirt beside the car, elbows on my thighs, hair completely mussed. We're filthy from demon blood and the dirt that rained down on us the whole time as we used brute force to wrangle the wreck toward freedom.

The car's blue paint is just visible through the shifting landslide, and thanks to one of the helicopter's lights, humans on a rescue boat in the water below point up at it.

I breathe a sigh of relief. They see it. We saved a human. The man will be okay.

"Pretty freaky, huh? That demon. How do you suppose you killed it?" Astread shakes her head.

Kessien leans forward and gives her a long look.

Yes, thanks for reminding me.

"Let's see how many more humans we can save," he suggests as he rises.

Chapter Five

It's been a week since I killed that demon, and so far there haven't been any retaliation attempts, but I'm not naïve to believe there won't be, not with the second demon escaping that car. I've no question it told all its disgusting pals.

The modern, natural wood décor in our squadron's break room is usually just the ticket to get my mind off worries. I'm nice and comfy in my skinny jeans and red blouse, having stretched my legs out, ankles crossed, on the soft, white leather sofa that is heavenly comfortable. But I've read the same paragraph five times, and I still don't know what it says. As if to underscore the point, my foot keeps up a steady jiggling—I can't help it.

Humans have a saying: waiting for the other shoe drop. I've no idea of its origin, but, yes, when will the other shoe drop?

Astread gives me a pitying look across the room from where she and Aliyah are sitting at the round table. Pieces of the bazillion-piece jigsaw puzzle they've been working on for I can't remember how long are mounded in a host of piles that only they understand.

"Ah, found it. Finally." Aliyah frowns as she stares down the offending piece before adding it to the puzzle.

I turn my book over, propping it open on my leg so I don't damage the spine, and grab my coffee from behind me on the end table. Small mercy, I can't help but sigh as the nutty aroma fills my nose as I take a swig of the hot brew.

A twinkle in his eye, Issra comes in and plops down in the poofy, white leather chair next to mine in the grouping that's set off from the warm oak floor by a tan rug. His white shirtsleeves are rolled up to his elbows, and he stretches out, propping his red-stocking feet on the coffee table and placing a drink, no doubt an energy booster, on the table beside me—ever since he discovered human energy drinks, he's become somewhat of a junkie.

"You're working on a crossword puzzle?" I can't keep the surprise from my tone.

He raises a pen. "Is there something wrong with that?"

"No, I've just never seen you do a crossword before." Like ever, but I don't say it. I can only chuckle to myself.

"I've decided to increase my word power." He nods sharply.

Astread and Aliyah smile but keep adding pieces to the puzzle.

"Thank you for your support. You all are amazing, and I appreciate it, but you don't need to babysit me. I'll be fine."

Since that demon incident, this has become the new norm, and it's getting old, but I can't tell them that and seem ungrateful. I just hope their hyperprotectiveness eases soon, because it just underscores the peril they think I'm in.

Issra raises the virgin crossword book and furrows his brow as he reads the first clue.

Yeah, we'll see how long his quest for improved word power lasts.

I take another sip as Jael walks in the door holding up a board game. The dimple on his chin highlights his grin. Kessien follows on his heels.

"A game of Angels and Demons anyone?" Jael asks, heading over to the kitchenette's rectangular wooden table, then pulling out a chair.

"We figured Glad could utterly trounce the rogues," Kessien adds, giving me a wink.

Doggoned if my stupid stomach doesn't respond. I refuse to look at Astread as I set aside my book and beverage.

Issra holds up a finger. "Before we play, I need a ten-letter word for a quick board meeting."

The guys smirk.

"He's decided to increase his word power," I offer as I rise. "By the way, the answer is speed chess."

Everyone looks at me, and I shrug. "What? I read."

Aliyah snorts. "And, as a result, you bless us with all sorts of useless trivia too. Love you, Glad."

I fake offense, dropping my jaw, but she's there a second later, giving me a squeeze.

"Squadron 132. Squadron 132. We've got a code 665 on the Boardwalk in Ocean City, New Jersey," the heavenly dispatcher interrupts telepathically. *"Demonic activity suspected. Bearded male holding a female hostage at knifepoint near the fortune-teller booth. The request came in via a desperate human prayer, so nothing else is known. Proceed with urgency but caution."*

"A fortune-teller's booth." Jael shakes his head and sets down the board game before joining us.

I frown and tighten my ponytail in the leather band.

"Why must humans persist in knowing their fortunes?" Frustration colors Kessien's tone as he runs a hand through his blond locks. "They've no clue the dark forces they're playing with."

"Enough what might have been," Astread interrupts, joining our circle. "That woman needs help."

We all imagine ourselves in our black leathers, boots, and gloves, and the transformation is complete a second later.

I finger Phantom's hilt, then high-five Astread, completing our ritual. Kessien and Jael bump athletic shoulders. Issra and Aliyah have a more complex ritual that involves bumping elbows, then wrists, then slapping hands, which they complete, but I'm good with simplicity.

Jael holds up a hand, to which we all respond by joining with our own, then parroting, "Let's do this!" before bringing them down in the center of our circle.

Rituals complete, we grab the hand of the warrior on either side and prepare to transport since it's a long way from the third heaven to New Jersey; flying takes way too long in an emergency. Holding hands ensures we all end up in the same place at the same time.

"On my count," Kessien says, all business.

Astread squeezes my hand.

"One."

I squeeze back.

"Two."

I close my eyes, waiting to feel the disorientation that comes with traveling so quickly across the cosmos.

"Three."

Like always, my head feels dizzy with the speed and my stomach flips, struggling to catch up.

We stop as quickly as we start, then push off one another as we begin to fall to give room for our wings, which we unfurl seconds later.

Thankfully, there's not a demon reception waiting for us.

I exhale, relief washing over me as I take in the carnival scene that is the Ocean City Boardwalk as we hover in formation. Shadows have blended with their environs in the early evening dusk. The lights on the overlarge Ferris wheel wink on.

The sound of the rhythmic ocean waves can barely be heard over screams that sound from the giant swings with the red-and-white-striped top. High-pitched shrieks from the white, wooden roller coaster add yet more noise to drown out the idyllic waves.

Between the multitude of lights, multiplied by the number of rides and food stands, it's difficult to spot the fortune-teller's booth we're scanning for. Not surprisingly, scattered throughout the crowds are demons feeding on human hosts—cursed menaces, they introduce anxiety, fear, guilt, depression, and worse in human minds.

I huff, my impatience at not yet spotting the woman showing. It's like playing Where's Waldo?

"There." Issra points at a modest, black canvas tent dotted with star decorations that stands on the outskirts of the property. Right in front, the offending male holds a long, brown-haired female in a headlock, a knife to her throat.

I blow out a breath. Small blessing, the back of the carnival isn't a destination and not many humans are about. That said, I spot several uniformed personnel rushing in that direction, but they're still a ways off.

I don't yet see the demon that has to be inciting this, but I'm guessing it's attached itself to this man's back.

Anger ignites in my gut, and I clench my fists. How. I. Hate. Demons.

A male standing several feet away from the hostage situation, his back to us, waves his arms. He looks like he's trying to reason with the thug.

I bite my lip. It could well be his wife at risk, and both their lives may be irreparably changed depending upon the outcome.

"Jael, Aliyah, Issra, form a perimeter," Kessien barks, focused on the situation.

That means he, Astread, and I will go fight the bad guys. Teamed up again.

I tamp down on my body's fickleness.

Aliyah smiles and wags her brows, catching my gaze as she takes off with the others. I roll my eyes.

"Let's do it," Kessien says, looking between Astread and me.

We pull our wings in tight and dive until we're within two yards of the villain and land.

The pleading male waves his arms more frantically and cries, "Please, she hasn't done anything to you."

"She is an infidel! She deserves to die. So do you."

"I'll shield," I yell as they vanish their wings.

Kessien and Astread unsheathe their blades and descend on the guy, more specifically on the demon.

I leap and grab hold of the woman around the shoulders, my wings fully enveloping her body. The attacker's blade can't hurt me, and this will ensure he can't harm her either.

"Crap, there are five of them," Astread exclaims, making me suck in a breath.

"Five? No wonder this male is crazy." I can't keep disbelief from my voice.

"Two apiece. Fastest gets the last," Kessien jests.

"What do I get when I win?" my BFF bandies back.

I smile. They're both so competitive.

My smile plummets, and I swallow hard as I look over my shoulder to see the poor man fall to his knees on the pavement, hands clutched and raised as if in prayer.

"Please, I beg of you." His tone is growing more desperate.

My chest goes tight. It's tearing me apart to hear him. How I wish we could let him know his loved one will be fine. But seeing us would freak him out more.

A demon's screech fills my ears, then another, and another in short order as Kessien and Astread get to work.

"*Code 666! Code 666!*" It's Jael from wherever they're forming that perimeter. My stomach twists. Mister Calm and Steady sounds panicked.

Never have I heard him like this.

Ever.

Chapter Six

"Glad, keep this woman safe," Kessien bellows. "Astread, go defend. I've got these last two demons."

A shriek draws all our attention.

I suck in a breath as I twist around, my wings still enfolding the female. "Ambush." Over Bad Dude's shoulder, one, two… five, six… ten demons flood out from the fortune-teller's booth.

Thankfully, Astread's still here but I can't leave the woman until the demon is eliminated and the guy drops his blade.

"A little help!" Aliyah yells telepathically from wherever they set up the perimeter. *"There's a good hundred of them up here."*

"We're a little busy too," I reply back.

Astread engages two of the newcomers while Kessien dispatches the remaining hangers-on.

The terrorist's head jerks back, surprise filling his eyes the instant the demon parasites are gone and no longer controlling his mind.

"Please, let her go," the man pleads again.

The sound of footsteps has me swiveling back around as two of the uniformed boardwalk officials appear, slowing from a run to a walk, palms raised as they approach.

A female officer says, "You don't want to hurt her. Drop the knife."

No doubt their comrades have fanned out and are surrounding the area.

In seconds, the rogue demons have us surrounded, and Kessien joins Astread swinging. Despite their efforts, two demons head straight for me.

"What happened?" The bad guy's tone comes out hushed.

Still shielding the woman with one arm, I unsheathe Phantom. I pray this guy doesn't get any more ideas about knifing the woman still in his grip, because I can't hold her as tightly and manage my blade at the same time.

"That's right, drop the knife," the female officer says, palms extended as she and her partner take several more steps toward us.

"Crap, there's more." Astread's exclamation becomes background noise as I swing at the first wolf-size demon who reaches me.

The assailant drops the knife, and the male officer kicks it away while saying, "That's a smart decision. Now let her go."

I exhale, then whirl around, striking the closest demon in the neck. It winks out of sight and is replaced by its cohort.

I quickly dispatch the second demon, then scan the area that's thick with wings and hissing and make out Kessien destroying another couple of foe, but I've lost track of Astread.

The man releases the woman, who scrambles into the arms of the guy who has been begging the thug not to hurt her, and the officials converge around Bad Guy an instant later.

I refocus as a trio of Great-Dane-size demons descend on me, doing their best to get their fangs into me.

"It's her. Kill her," one hisses.

My legs feel weak all of a sudden. Seems it may be payback time for the demon I killed. Rather than wait for the worst to befall me, I plant my feet in the dusty ground and bring Phantom across my attacker's throat.

As expected, silver demon blood spurts just before it winks out of sight. But its two buddies are on me a second later, brandishing their fangs, and I go down. I strain on the dusty ground, pushing them back with my arms before they can bite me.

Crap, these things weigh a ton.

I manage to get a leg under one and thrust, sending it flying backward, which only infuriates it more, but I don't care because it gives me time to grab a dagger and rip it across the neck.

"Killer will pay." It slurs the words before disappearing.

Not if I have anything to say about it.

"Glad, Kessien." Astread's telepathic scream chills my blood, but the third overlarge demon is on me, whipping its fangs about this way and that, and I've no way to respond to my partner.

"Astread," Kessien bellows through my mind, alarm lacing his words. *"What's wrong? Where are you?"*

My attacker slices the arm I'm holding it back with, a fang slicing through my leathers, and while it's agonizing, it ticks me off more. I'm better than this.

This sucker's gonna pay.

Despite its continued thrashing, I thrust my dagger right through one of its eyes.

A second later, it disappears, to which I growl, "Good riddance."

I shake my arm, which does nothing to dull the pain as I stow my dagger and stand, grabbing Phantom.

"Astread," I call, panting. *"Where are you?"* All I get is silence, and my throat constricts.

"Glad, pair up," Kessien yells as he dispatches another menace feet away, then stops in front of me. A fierceness overwhelms his features as he pants, "When you beheaded that demon, I promised I wouldn't let anything happen to you. I mean to keep that promise."

He's never looked at me this way before. It's more than just a leader to his troop. We've fought way too many battles together, and I know him too well. My mouth goes dry, and it's suddenly hard to speak, so I do the only thing I can, I nod.

His gaze darts upward, then he grabs my bicep and thrusts me behind him before slicing another menace from the sky.

I take a ready position at his back, Phantom raised, ignoring my bleeding arm and fluttery stomach. We've paired up more than a time or two as events dictated, but I'm hyperaware of his toned, muscular body at my back this time.

Another menace barrels straight for me out of the sky, but I'm so distracted by Kessien's presence that I only connect with its wing. Thankfully, the hit alters its flight and my blade finds purchase through its neck as it adjusts course.

"Astread," I call through our connection before slicing at another demon. Again, only silence answers, and my gut goes hard. Where is she? I open my connection to the whole squad. *"Has anyone seen or heard from Astread?"*

Issra responds first, vocalizing the effort he's using to dispatch another enemy. *"The skies are thick with demons. I've been a little busy."*

"No." Aliyah's reply comes as a single word. She's never short, so she's busy too.

"I called for reinforcements," Jael pants. *"I hope they get here soon."*

I swing my blade at another three enemies, ignoring the throbbing in my arm. Reinforcements can't come soon enough.

Kessien knocks into my shoulder with his back as he bends back to slay another menace.

I have not forgotten he's behind me. At. All.

Screeches and hissing give way to what almost sounds like laughter, if these hideous menaces can do that. The suddenness of it draws my attention, and, blade up, I scan the area. Kessien stills behind me, no doubt also searching the skies that are still thick with enemy.

I brace as a line of four wolf-size demons sweep overhead but don't attack. One with overlarge, white eyes missing their pupils squawks, "Consider this a down payment, killer." He waves a celestial sword that's dripping silver to underscore his point.

He's so hideous. I swear I'll remember him forever.

No sooner has he finished his threat than something thuds to the ground as they sweep past just feet from me. A second later, four silver-streaked wings meet the ground, and I inhale sharply.

"Astread!"

No. No. No. No.

With their "delivery," I watch for only a second as they call their fellows to follow them. Then I sheathe Phantom, rushing to my partner and landing at her side.

"Astread, say something." My voice quakes as I pick up her hand because she's not moving. "What did they do to you?"

She's a mess. Bruises are already forming on a cheek and on her jaw, and her leathers are beaten and banged up. One arm lies at an odd angle, and the hair on one side of her head is singed.

"Oh, Astread," Aliyah says, soon after. I've no idea when she arrived, but there's a pained expression on her face as she falls to her knees beside me and reaches for my BFF's neck to check her pulse. Aliyah has healed all of us more than a time or two, but none of us has ever been in this bad of a shape.

I glance up to find the night air is clear, the moon is out, and the swarm of demons has vanished. The rest of the squad has found us. I've no idea where the humans went, but the fact that they aren't here has to be a good thing.

But I'm more concerned about my partner.

"Help me turn her over." Aliyah looks like she's holding her breath just like me as I put down Astread's hand that I've been holding.

"Watch her broken arm." Movement out of the corner of my eye draws my attention as Issra runs his hands over his face. Jael's athletic shoulders slump as Kessien kneels across from us.

"Kessien, I need you to ease her arm out of the way, then help us turn her toward you," Aliyah instructs.

Alarm lights his eyes, but he looks back down and does as bid, ever so slowly moving Astread's broken arm to where it won't take her weight when we turn her.

Wake up, Astread. Please.

"On three." Aliyah counts down, and I help lift my partner.

My breath hitches, and I forget to breathe the instant I take in Astread's back. It's a mess of silver blood around four stumps that still ooze.

No. No. No. No. I can't swallow.

Aliyah's jaw tenses, and moisture lines the corner of her eyes as she shakes her head. "I can't fix this. No one can."

"But her wings are—" Emotion chokes Issra's voice as he makes to retrieve them.

Jael stops him with a firm hand on his shoulder, then draws him into a hug while Kessien bows his head over Astread.

"I need to at least get the bleeding stopped." Aliyah swipes a hand over her eyes, then sets to work.

Astread moans. She's alive. She's alive. Tears well up behind my eyelids, but I swallow them down. I put what I hope is a comforting hand on her side as Aliyah finishes her ministrations.

I want to pummel the demon who did this to her. I grind my teeth. Cleave *its* wings off.

That demon said to "consider this a down payment." I'll down payment it alright. They picked the wrong cherub to mess with. They want revenge, I'll show them what revenge *really* looks like.

Chapter Seven

The mood is somber in the break room where, still in our soiled leathers, we're all slumped on one of the sofas or a chair, silent, lost in our thoughts. Mine go back to several minutes before.

"Please, help her." My words come out strangled as the five of us race into the healers' suites skidding to a stop at the front desk behind which Healer Saranda and another healer I don't recognize sit.

Kessien halts beside me, expression tense as he holds Astread in his arms. She's only moaned twice the whole way back and I'm just barely keeping it together.

Jael strides toward a gurney that's parked against a nearby wall and pushes it over.

Healer Saranda and the other healer look up.

"Demons attacked her and…" I can't bring myself to say it. It should have been me.

Issra spares me the pain when he steps forward holding Astread's wings out to them. "We have her wings. You have to save them. Please." Bless him, he refused to leave them despite what Aliyah said.

"I did my best, but…" Aliyah's voice cracks and she draws a fist over her mouth. Silver lines the corners of her eyes.

The pair of healers race around the desk, eyes wide, as Kessien lays Astread down on her side, on the gurney. She doesn't so much as moan and my stomach goes hard.

Come on BFF. You have to make it.

Two more healers stride through a pair of double doors that lead to treatment rooms. "We've got her from here," one of them says. The other grabs Astread's four wings from Issra and rush her inside.

Jael is always calm and collected, hard to read, but it's not hard to know what he's feeling as he squeezes his eyes shut and runs a hand through his golden locks.

There's only two chairs, an end table between them, in the abbreviated waiting area but Kessien directs us toward them.

"I'm sorry," Healer Saranda says, scanning the five of us "but you're going to have to wait elsewhere while we work on your squadron mate." Her voice is gentle, but her look is stern and I know we're not going to convince her to let us stay. "We'll call and update you as soon as we finish our work."

Kessien's shoulders sag and it's clear his heart isn't in it as he clears his throat. "We understand healer." Then turning to us, he says, "Let's wait back in the break room."

I shift beside Issra on the white leather sofa. What's taking so long? Aliyah did her best, but she's not trained for more than fieldwork. Spiritual bodies are far more complex than physical bodies and take more skill to effect full healing, but still. This wait is killing me, killing all of us from the looks of things.

The telepathic alarm sounds in my head just before I hear, "Squadron 132. Squadron 132." The dispatcher pauses. *"Your presence is requested before the Almighty's throne—"* Her voice takes on a hushed, almost apologetic tone as she finishes. *"—immediately."*

My stomach clenches. "Is Astread okay?" I blurt as she finishes.

"I was told to relay that this is not about your squadron mate. They're apparently still working on her."

"Then what?"

"I'm afraid that's all I know. I'm sorry. Blessings upon you."

"Thank you." I exhale, then join the others in exchanging wide-eyed looks.

Before the Almighty's throne? Can this day get any worse? Rarely is anyone summoned to appear before his throne. He's big and powerful, and I've no desire to endure all that stress with everything else.

"Perhaps he wishes to relay his sympathies," Issra, ever the optimist, suggests. But he runs a hand through his curly, golden locks like he's questioning his own words.

How about he just fixes Astread's wings and we call it even? I just pray we're not about to be reprimanded by the Almighty himself for allowing this to happen to one of our squadron mates.

The thought makes my stomach twist. Has he passed right over the chain of command? Is he about to discipline us himself?

I bite my lip, not wanting to think about it more. How I pray Issra's right that that's all this is, but if so, couldn't he have just sent a seraphim to express his condolences?

No one else hazards a guess.

"Well, we have our orders." Kessien rises from the chair. "We need to change. We can't very well go in there looking like this. Let's clean up and wear our dress uniforms."

Hearts still heavy, no one jumps up, but minutes later the five of us are standing in a circle, neatly attired as specified. Thank goodness just a thought can do the work of cleaning me up and shifting my clothes, because I honestly don't think I have the energy for more. I don't know what I'd do if I had to go through everything humans must to accomplish this result.

Astread's presence is noticeably absent with the space Aliyah leaves between us, and I swallow hard.

I need to keep going or I may break down, so I toss my long, golden ponytail over a padded shoulder of my white tunic. Phantom hangs at my side, the white leather belt of the dress holster giving definition to my waist. Two bands of silver accent the tunic's cuffs and hem that hangs at the knees of my white slacks.

Issra turns to Aliyah, his partner, beside him and bumps her elbow, the beginning of their pre-mission ritual. She halts him before he can bump her wrist, a sad expression on her face as she glances at me.

Issra follows her gaze and bows his head. "I'm sorry. I wasn't thinking."

My chin trembles, and I bite a lip. Words fail me. Astread may never be back, and we all know it. If the healers can't fix her wings, she'll never fly again and won't be fit to be a warrior.

Kessien, who always looks particularly handsome in his dress whites with his blond locks combed and in impeccable order, sends me a pained expression from across the circle, then clears his throat and nods to Jael who holds up a hand. We all respond by joining with our own, saying, "Let's do this," then bring them down in the center, but the sentiment lacks its usual enthusiasm.

The throne room is just a short flight away, so we follow Kessien out the warm acacia wood door to the right. Only the sound of our boots on wood rises as we pass one after another of the beautiful murals carved in more of the same wood that covers the walls of the hall.

We stride past a host of other squadron break rooms. Some doors yawn open to reveal their members hanging out; a burst of laughter reaches us from a couple. Other doors are closed, their residents working or training at this hour.

We pass through the soaring lobby where a white-marble, life-size sculpture of the Archangel Michael, wings spread, slaying demons nipping at his feet, stands directly below the two-story peak.

We clear the double doors at the front and head down the two steps. Spreading out on the immaculately manicured lawn in formation, we each unfurl our wings, then spread them as we take flight.

I squint in the bright light as Kessien and Jael beat their wings, gathering altitude and speed, taking the lead while the rest of us assume our positions in formation behind them—minus Astread at my side.

My limbs feel heavy. How I miss my partner.

Aliyah sends a sympathetic look from beside me as we pass over the busy training yard. I appreciate her sensitivity, but nothing is going to fix this if Astread's wings can't be healed. My grief seems to have blunted the anger that ignited at the boardwalk, but if I can't have my partner back on the job, make no mistake, I *will* avenge her loss.

My caustic thoughts continue swirling, making my stomach tense as Kessien and Jael dip low as we approach the children's court.

Jael glances over his shoulder and catches my gaze with his steel-blue eyes, and it's all I need to know. Kessien knows this is one of my favorite places to spend free time. It's a sweet gesture and so like him. He's a tough warrior, but he's got a gentle side too. It's what makes him such a good leader.

I spot the spirit of a goldendoodle dog barking as it romps in the meadow with a little girl dressed in a red jumper, brown pigtails bouncing. A little boy, face alight, rides on the back of a Shetland pony. A group of children play with a colorful parachute, bouncing a ball in the middle. A warren of rabbits hops about the field, unafraid of the goings on.

They're freer than they've ever been, and their unadulterated joy normally makes me laugh, but not today, so I paste on a plastic smile.

Kessien glances over his broad shoulder.

"Thank you," I tell him through our link, because Astread's situation is not his fault. If it's anyone's fault, it's mine, but I refuse to go there. I killed that demon, but I didn't cause those menaces to attack her. They should have attacked me, but they're cowards.

Kessien smiles his beautiful smile. "It was on the way."

Issra's expression turns pained when he sees my smile fall as soon as Kessien looks away.

We regain altitude, and it's not long before the crystal palace, from which the Almighty reigns, rises on the horizon.

Tingling erupts in my fingers and toes at the sight, and I clench my hands. Despite my years, I've never been inside the palace. I've been curious for sure, haven't we all? But this is not how I envisioned seeing it. If this is because of Astread, as Issra suspects, I would have taken a hard pass.

I scrunch my eyes against the brightness of the Almighty that illuminates the whole city—his reflection on the gold streets makes things even brighter.

We're soon flying over a huge district of monstrous, white-stucco mansions, and my heart speeds because we're nearly there. My stomach feels like I swallowed a rock.

The sounds of construction—hammers pounding, saws whining, the works—meet us. It seems like they've been building these homes forever, one right after another. It's where future citizens will live, but I question how many more they can possibly need.

Seven workmen, wings straining, faces twisted with exertion, lift into place a white plaque with gold lettering that reads SOLOMON'S LIBRARY. A pang of jealousy strikes as I take it in. It will be the grand house for human literary works, works that angels aren't permitted to read. I've never understood why—something about human wisdom tainting angelic sensibilities. The bookworm in me chaffs.

"That's new." Issra points at a mammoth yet artfully crafted marble fountain spewing water high into the air in the middle of a square. The mist creates rainbows everywhere. It reminds me of the Trevi fountain in Rome, a place the Almighty blessed with a plethora of gifted craftsmen a few years back that ignited a whole renaissance in art and beauty.

The fountain's gone up since the last time we were here, and if I was in a better mood, it would take my breath away with the three intricately carved, life-size statues of seraphim, their six-wings together, blowing long trumpets, in the middle, along with a host of other heavenly beings crowded around.

One day this will be one of the busy community centers for citizens, but like the rest of the area, it's currently empty except for craftsmen in coveralls and their tools.

Aliyah's expression mirrors mine when I glance over. She looks like she's having trouble swallowing as we approach the sprawling lawn that surrounds the majestic crystal palace.

Kessien directs us to land on the patio near the front doors, avoiding the spirits spread out across the lush grass. Laughter rises from several groups who are chatting or playing lawn darts or badminton or some other outdoor game as they enjoy eternity.

I scan the grand front steps as I vanish my wings beside Jael who does the same. Ornately carved, emerald handrails scale the sides of the mountain of translucent steps that bear emerald highlights of their own.

I stop beside Issra when we reach two fellow cherubim clad in white leathers, flaming swords holstered, who greet us.

"What is your business?" the taller one on the right asks.

Kessien salutes. "We were summoned to appear before the Almighty."

Aliyah shifts on my other side, definitely as uneasy as I am, beside Jael who surveys the spirits at play.

The stockier greeter on the right puts a white gloved hand up to his ear, no doubt telepathically communicating with whoever inside is in the know. A minute later, he nods.

The taller of the two soldiers opens the right door, and the stockier says, "If you'll follow me, please."

I'm nervous enough already, and the grandeur of the palace makes my mouth go dry. Our boots on the translucent stone floor echo in the cavernous space as we pass one of several towering, ornately carved, crystal pillars.

Grand buttresses rise from the sides of the space, stretching to meet at the pinnacle of the four-story atrium. With the translucent nature of the materials, it radiates the brilliance of the Almighty, which only adds to the magnificence. And heightens my angst.

What will he do to us?

Chapter Eight

It's not long before our guide stops before another set of double doors, this one clouded but no less luminous.

"They are here at the Almighty's summons." That's all he says before he salutes the soldiers posted on either side of the hulking doors and turns.

This is it. This has to be the throne room. On the other side of these doors, we'll see the Almighty and meet our fate.

Kessien salutes the pair of cherubim soldiers, but his hand trembles as he brings it down, and my heart crawls into my throat.

Aliyah's eyes go wide. Issra starts clenching and unclenching a fist, and Jael, who is always silent and steady, clears his throat, his Adam's apple bobbing.

That's all it takes for nausea to wrack my stomach.

The pair of sentries each grab a handle of the towering doors and heave them open.

The instant the doors crack open, the sound of singing escapes, and not just any singing. It's choral music by what must be a huge choir, and their pitch is perfect.

Oh great, we're about to interrupt some grand performance or something. Somehow it doesn't seem like a good idea. I swallow hard, doing my best to keep the contents of my stomach where they belong.

Yet the Almighty summoned us… with instructions to come immediately. If he gets upset….

Um… nope, ain't no way I'm setting him straight.

I squint as the doors open further and wait for my eyes to adjust to the added brightness. The Almighty illuminates the whole of heaven, so of course this is the brightest place.

The singing stops, along with my heart, as we follow one of the two sentries several steps until he halts.

Well crap. Now what?

I feel thousands of eyes look me over, and I barely tamp down on a whimper.

I'm a warrior. I'm better than this. But I feel like prey, and no matter what I tell myself, it's hard to breathe.

I jump as a peal of thunder echoes from the mammoth throne that's ringed by an emerald rainbow ahead. Brilliant lightning flashes follow an instant later, and I swear I'm going to pee my pants. My squadron mates look no better.

Another earsplitting peal of thunder sounds, and still everyone just stares at us, not so much as twitching.

Our guide takes a knee and bows low. "Majesty."

We follow an instant later. I can't get low enough, and my brow practically brushes the crystal floor.

More lightning flashes reflect on the shiny floor, along with more booming thunder every few seconds.

We're in deep doo-doo.

"Rise and approach." The Almighty's voice is always full and booming, and this time is no different. Surprisingly, I don't detect pissiness.

Or maybe it's just me hoping.

We all ease to standing, and our guide continues forward. I try to block out all the eyes I still feel on every inch of me and focus on the twenty-four smaller thrones encircling the Almighty's. Their white-outfitted, angelic occupants have golden crowns on their heads. But they're also watching our every step.

The longer I focus on them, the more wigged out I feel with their staring, so I tear my gaze from them and focus instead on the four humanlike creatures we approach. And quickly wish I hadn't because they've got eyes all over their bodies, all of which also follow us. I force myself to ignore that and take in each's six wings and four faces: a human in front, a lion on the right, a bull on the left, and I think I spot an eagle in back when two of them turn as the Almighty raises a hand.

It must be the signal to stop, because that's what our guide does fifteen or so feet from the three steps that lead up the dais. It's way too close for comfort, and my breathing labors as I take in the Almighty in his usual, tailored, white suit and tie that coordinates with his white, impeccably trimmed beard, sitting up straight on his throne. Aliyah and Issra look like they might faint.

More lightning flashes, but the thunder dies and the throne room is deathly silent for several seconds before the Almighty says, "Gladriel, approach."

I inhale sharply. Me? My legs start to tremble.

Kessien and Jael, who have led us behind the sentry, turn and step aside so I can pass between them.

But my feet don't want to move. I lock gazes with Kessien. He looks as worried as I feel with the pained expression he wears. He forces a smile that doesn't reach his beautiful azure eyes, and I know he's rooting for me, my whole squad is, but I can't help feeling alone.

Why in heaven's name did the Almighty call just me?

Aliyah reaches over and squeezes my hand, and I give her a half smile before I force a foot forward. It feels like lead fills my boots.

I swallow hard and will my feet to comply with another step. Jael gives me a nod that I'm sure he means to reassure but fails. My heart feels like it may beat out of my chest as I pass the sentry and stop perhaps eight feet from the bottom of the dais. I can't force myself to go closer.

I clasp my trembling hands behind my back and plant my feet, at attention.

The Almighty knows everything, so there's no point in even trying to pretend I'm anything but terrified of what's about to happen.

His ash-gray eyes are intense as he leans forward. "What have you to say for yourself?" His tone is even and his face neutral. I can't read him, so my mind goes where it naturally does, to worst case.

Astread's injured because some cowardly demon attacked her to get revenge on me... and he's holding me responsible.

My breathing labors, and my chest constricts. I swear it may be my first ever panic attack. I need to calm down.

I take several deep breaths. I shouldn't assume. I shouldn't. I should ask for clarification. How I pray he doesn't mind.

I barely resist scrunching my face. "Majesty, can you say more? I'm not sure I understand what you're asking."

One of my squad, I can't tell who, takes a quick breath behind me.

Not helpful. At all.

"You are not responsible for the result of a demon's decision." The Almighty says it through the telepathic link between us. It's nearly impossible to remain at attention when he's speaking directly into my head, and the words barely register. I clutch my trembling hands more tightly behind my back as my fingers start to tingle.

Everything but him fades away, and I replay what I think he just said. I'm not responsible for what happened to Astread.

"Real-really?" I squeak my response back through our link.

"Unless you would like to be held responsible." His voice is rich and deep, and I sense a hint of humor in it.

"N-No, that's okay."

"I thought as much." He clasps his hands beneath his bearded chin, elbows on the arms of the throne, staring intently at me with those ash-gray eyes.

It does nothing to slow my hyperactive heart.

"Gladriel, I am as upset as you about what happened to your partner." His tone is even, and it makes me question whether he could possibly be as upset as I am. Perhaps in response to my doubt,

his tone turns soft and gentle, nearly like a babbling brook. *"But what concerns me more is that a seed of vengeance has taken root in you as a result. It is why I summoned you."*

"It… It is?" I can't keep the disbelief from my tone. I mean, I've no reason to doubt him, but still… it seems like… I don't know.

His tone remains gentle. *"Gladriel, do not feed this seed. For if you do, it will utterly consume you."* He's still holding my gaze as he drops his arms. I take a shallow breath, then hear gasps behind me as the Almighty's eyes start to blaze like they're on fire, and his voice turns cold. *"Vengeance is mine. I will repay this evil."*

I'd no idea what he would say, but it certainly isn't this. I mean, I've no doubt he's more than capable, but… really? I guess he really means it.

"Do you trust me?" His eyes return to their intense ash-gray color, and he leans back.

That's a loaded question if I ever heard one. He's my supreme commander and the most powerful being ever. *"Of course."*

A corner of his mouth hitches. *"Then leave things to me."*

I bob my head, because what else am I going to do?

But then a thought occurs to me, and I have just enough boldness to ask. *"Could you heal Astread's wings? Please?"*

He gives me a kindly smile and hope rises in me.

"Gladriel, have you considered that I have plans for Astread beyond that of a warrior?"

My eyes go wide. But… but… she's my partner, my BFF. I want to protest, to say all this and more, but I bite my tongue.

"Have you considered that I am able to create something beautiful out of what was intended for harm?"

But I just want my partner back. *"Maybe you could find someone else to do whatever you have in mind?"* The thought slips out, into our connection without thinking, and I gasp in horror.

He smiles, and my shoulders droop.

"What are you going to do with her?" I'd like to at least know what I'm losing her to.

He continues smiling, and it's clear he's not going to say. He's not mocking me but rather asking me to trust him; I can see it in the warmth of his expression.

My whole body feels heavy. Can I trust him? Do I have a choice?

Then again, he didn't have to tell me anything. The very fact that he told me all he has is amazing, and I should feel honored. I should.

But my heart's too heavy for that, and tears threaten. I take a shuttering breath, trying to suppress them.

He catches the eye of someone behind me, and I can tell this conversation is over.

"Gladriel, remember what I said. Do not allow revenge to take root in you."

I close my eyes and bob my head as a firm hand comes to rest on my shoulder. A tear leaks from the corner of an eye before I can swipe it away.

Chapter Nine

I feel lost.

Nothing registers as we make our way out of the palace.

The instant the doors thud behind us, Aliyah, then Kessien and the rest of my squad mates, envelop me in a hug, and I lose it.

I sob. I can't help it. It's too much.

After several minutes, I pull myself together. My mates are quiet as we make our way back to our quarters, but they keep sending me worried looks. They've no doubt figured out from my reaction that we're losing Astread.

The moment we reach our break room, the questions begin.

Kessien sits down on the sofa beside me, worry creasing his brow. If things weren't so dark, my stomach would quiver, but they are and even it seems to understand that now is not the time for frivolity.

"What all did he say to you?" His tone is gentle, like he's afraid I might break down again. I hate feeling pity, but I've brought this on myself.

Aliyah sits down on my other side as Issra leans in from the puffy, leather chair on the other side of the end table.

I summarize the conversation between the Almighty and me, leaving out what he said about not giving vengeance room to take root. That part feels too close, too personal, no matter how close I am to my mates.

"No offense, but why did he speak only to you?" Jael questions from the sofa across from us.

"Because Astread's her partner," Issra says, a little huffy.

"But why did he call all of us if he planned only to talk with you?" Jael persists, blowing out his cheeks. "It makes no sense. We've all lost Astread."

I understand his annoyance. We're all protective of each other, but his frown makes my chest tighten, and I wonder if he suspects the Almighty said more, but no way am I going there.

Kessien clears his throat. "I can only assume he summoned all of us because he wanted us there to support Gladriel."

I can't tell if he, like Jael, might suspect more was said, but he takes everyone's attention off me, for which I'm grateful.

But deep down inside, I know life will never, ever be the same, and I'm not sure what to do about it.

———

I clench my jaw as I finger the hilt of my celestial blade.

Hideous, overlarge, white eyes missing their pupils. It's what I've been dreaming of seeing again for more than a month—along with that demon's three pals.

I barely squelch a growl as I spot my destination. Tel Aviv just after sunset near the waterfront is aglow with streetlights, swaying palm trees, and crowds hunting for dinner. Fluffy clouds drift by as I scan the crescent-moon illuminated skies for any sign of my enemies, but I spot none.

The Almighty promised to exact vengeance on the demons who maimed Astread. He promised. Yet he hasn't bothered to so much as lift a pinky in her defense in over thirty days.

I'm sick of it.

He must subscribe to the notion that vengeance is a dish best served cold, but count me out. I like my vengeance fast and hot.

Astread moderated my hotter side, but without her, I'm giving it a bit of latitude in her honor, because I can't stand feeling this way any longer.

And it's not just me.

A mood of fatigue and exhaustion besets the whole squad.

Other squadrons see us in the halls, in the training yard, or in group meetings and go quiet. It's gotten very wearing.

It's not blame I sense, but rather a realization that the same could happen to one of them, and they've no idea how to work through it. I mean we're nearly indestructible. It's what I've always believed. I'm sure they've thought the same. Bullets and knives go through or bounce harmlessly off our bodies, and we're immune to all nonsupernatural weapons, bombs, and objects. So to have this happen to one of us....

I shake my head. We're reminders to them of their weakness.

A car horn blares not far away as I set down behind a huge, concrete flowerpot with red flowers whose blooms have closed for the day and vanish my wings. The trellis they cling to adorns the edge of an outdoor food court. A decorated half wall runs several feet to my right as part of a landscape feature to beautify the area.

I inhale and smile as a mixture of grease and a spice blend with fresh herbs from the falafel eateries lining the area hits my nose and makes my mouth water as I peer through the vines.

It's early yet, and a handful of smaller demons have congregated on the far side of the area, rubbing their hands together and drooling as they gaze at several tables of humans eating dinner, waiting for demons already feeding on them to finish and give them a shot at the unsuspecting humans.

Makes. Me. Sick. But I can't worry about them tonight. I have bigger fish to fry. Or demons to hunt, as the case may be.

If my intelligence proves correct, one hideous, overlarge demon with white eyes missing their pupils will be here, looking for an innocent human to latch on to, along with its three buddies.

A family with a cute, gibberish-speaking little girl finishes eating, and after pushing in their plastic chairs and disposing of their trash, the man pushes the stroller out of the food court while holding the woman's hand.

I can't help but smile at how at ease they are.

How much we take for granted. I clear my throat.

The squad doesn't know I'm here, and it's just the way I want it. After making a big enough nuisance of myself with a cranky mood this afternoon, Kessien sent me for an attitude adjustment, namely he suggested I find some books at the library—he knows me too well—and to take as much time as I need.

That said, he didn't order me to go to the library. He just said I had to improve my mood. I just decided to do so in a slightly different way than he suggested, a way that necessitated taking a *slight* detour... all the way to Earth. If I succeed, this will definitely lift my spirits, far more than even a great read. And that's saying a lot considering how much I love books.

The junior demons are practically yelling as they strategize which of the humans they plan to latch on to when they get their turn, gesticulating all manner of vulgar obscenities.

I crack up, quietly of course, when the humans at one of the tables bow their heads and say a quick prayer before digging in. It startles and quiets the schemers for several seconds. Demons have no power over a human of faith, and they know it.

The comic relief is welcome because I'm a bit high-strung right this minute with hope that my plan will come together. I know I'm going against what the Almighty... suggested... yes, it was a suggestion, right?

I've been tracking this menace for the last three weeks, and while I'm not some expert investigator or in covert ops, I'm highly motivated, and I think I found that son-of-Satan. In fact, tracking this menace down is the only thing that's kept me sane.

Jael nearly discovered my research at one point, but thankfully Issra, unbeknownst to him, diverted his attention.

My thumb caresses Phantom's hilt. How will I feel when I avenge Astread's loss tonight? My thoughts go back to that fateful evening, and I swallow down emotion. We were all a mess when we met Astread at the infirmary after the healers summoned us back.

I take a deep breath and let it out slowly.

She cried for her loss. We cried for hers and ours.

She told us she'd been reassigned as a process engineer, leveraging her considerable discipline as a warrior to improve efficiency in a host of areas. Apparently they need to handle a whole lot more citizens soon, and they're trying to gear up for it. I've no idea why, but whatever.

I flex my gloved fingers. The Almighty said he had something better in mind for her, that he could use even what seems bad, for good. I don't doubt that… but I lost my BFF at my back.

Like a good soldier, she's making the best of it. I can't tell if she really enjoys it or if she's just not saying because she's afraid I'll feel even worse for her if she doesn't like it.

All I know is life will never be the same. It's not just that we had to change our usual pairings during training and combat to accommodate one less. Pfft, that part was easy, all things considered. I now pair with Kessien and Jael, which definitely isn't all bad. Kessien still makes my stomach flutter even though I'll never act on it. Truth be told, I miss Astread kidding me about him, not that I'll ever tell her.

I sigh. How I miss always having her near….

Even though Astread's disciplined nature sometimes frustrated me, she kept my head screwed on straight during missions.

I blow out a breath, then snort to myself because I hear her voice in my head reprimanding me for being too loud while blowing out a breath because it could potentially draw attention and compromise my mission.

The adjustments, while many, are not the root of my problem. No, the heart of my problem is that I trust only her completely. Period. We've protected each other's back for eons, and that creates a bond no one and nothing can replace.

She's like an arm or a leg… or a wing. She's my BFF. We shared everything. And now that we don't get to see each other as much, there's an Astread-size hole in my heart that nothing else can fill.

I brace as four wolf-size demons sweep in and land on the half wall to my right, shutting the junior demons up in an instant. The demons feeding tremble, and their eyes grow wide.

"Scram, you little nuisances," one of the new arrivals bellows as it tucks its wings.

I don't usually agree with demons, but in this moment, I'll make an exception.

Two yips sound, and all the junior demons rise en masse and beat a hasty and raucous retreat.

I ease a leaf over as things quiet, remaining hidden behind my foliage shield as the four thug demons start scanning the humans.

Come on, look this way. Look this way.

Was my intelligence correct? Are these the foe I seek?

Chapter Ten

One of the demons glances at a man who stops at the edge of the seating area, looking for an empty table. The thing's got black eyes with a yellow stripe down the middle. Not it.

Demons two and three have black eyes too. But one has a yellow stripe and the other an orange stripe down the middle.

Come on. Come on.

I lean forward, practically smashing my nose against the trellis as I try to get a look at the last one.

Come on, big boy, look this way.

It takes forever, but it finally follows demon number two's nod at a woman who sits down in the middle of the seating area, and I cheer inwardly.

Overlarge, white eyes missing their pupils. My heart accelerates. Yes. This is my foe and its three buddies.

I rub a thumb on the hilt of my blade.

Should you do this? My obstinate little voice just won't quit.

I shake my head.

I have to.

But the Almighty....

No, I have to avenge Astread.

Time to roll. These demons need to go.

My primary target is just two long strides from me. Its side to me, its fat butt sags over the half wall. It's the closest to me of the four.

My skin tingles. It's a sign. I'm meant to succeed.

I draw my blade, and my heart accelerates.

Make it count.

I rub my thumb on the hilt.

Avenge Astread's loss. She deserves this. She did nothing wrong except being in the wrong place at the wrong time.

Another thought strikes me: am I the tool the Almighty is using to mete out justice? Was he waiting on me to act? The setting wouldn't be so perfect if he didn't intend that, right?

With that encouragement, I refocus on my task. Experience has taught me not to think but to let instinct guide me during battle, so I make my blade flame white, it's hottest, and focus on the primary menace's neck.

I step out from behind my hiding place and close the distance.

For Astread!

I bring Phantom down with more force than I need to, but I'm not holding back. Not after what it and its buddies did to my BFF.

The demon doesn't have time to react before I separate its head from its shoulders.

Silver sprays on me, on its pals, on everything nearby, as its head goes flying.

I lop the head off the next demon on the return swing. I'm so fast that the other two menaces only now react. Their expressions turn feral, and they snarl as they scramble up from sitting and turn my way.

I'm glad humans can't see or sense us, or they'd be freaking out and no doubt stampeding to get away. As it is, they continue eating, oblivious to the reality around them.

Together, my targets pounce, and I become prey.

Crap. Crap. Crap.

I can't get my blade up before the weight of the first bowls me over behind the wall.

Uff. I will myself to merge with the concrete so the wind isn't knocked out of me, but Mr. Fatso's still on top of me.

I might have miscalculated my opposition a tiny bit.

He's the size of a wolf and no less heavy.

Even though Phantom's too long for such close quarters, it's all I've got to defend with, so I bring it up, but before I make contact with this guy's back, its companion smacks the back of the hand I'm holding it with and it goes flying.

I reach for a celestial dagger hidden in my leathers, but the brute's in the way and its buddy bites my shoulder. I yelp, wishing I could blend with it like I can with material objects, but no.

Searing pain races down my arm, and my breathing speeds.

I really didn't think through the taking them down part. I was too excited to find these bastards. I'm a warrior. I *always* have backup. Seems I've taken it for granted. Now I'm in a world of hurt because I've got nothing.

An idea strikes, but I *really* hate to consider it.

Mr. Fatso shifts, grinding his bony butt into my ribs. Between that and his companion who still has its fangs in my shoulder, I've got no options. I'm at the mercy of these thugs.

I close my eyes. *"Help! Warrior down!"* I yell through my telepathic connection to the widest range possible.

Please be close. Someone. Anyone.

My sword is out of reach, and the demon sinks its needle-sharp teeth in farther, making the pain intensify. Mr. Fatso stands, and I suck in a breath, but Needle-Mouth clamps down harder and starts shaking me like a rag doll, sending pain racing through my body. It's all I can do to keep blending with the concrete every time my head should hit it. That's all I'd need.

Keep calm, everything will be okay.

Who am I kidding? Panic makes my breathing labor.

It's hard to focus with all the shaking, but I reach for a dagger anyway. But every time I've nearly got it, my hand flies away.

"Warrior down!" I try again as the reality of my predicament sets in and my chest tightens.

I punch Needle-Mouth in the eye, but it doesn't even stun it.

And then Mr. Fatso sinks its teeth into my leg.

Spots cloud my vision. *Calm down, Glad.*

I kick the demon with my free foot. My boot connects with an eye, making it growl, but it doesn't loosen its hold.

You've really done it this time, Glad, I chastise myself, barely avoiding hitting the cement again. What am I going to do?

"Please, anyone. I need help! Warrior down!" My tone turns pleading, but there's no way I'm getting free of these two brutes by myself.

Seconds later, the shaking stops and Needle-Mouth goes still before winking out of sight. A white-blazing celestial blade slices through Fatso's back, and the tension on my leg releases as it follows its companion into the ether.

I exhale loudly and rest my head against the pavement, panting.

"Gladriel, are you okay?" Worry mars Esme's face as she comes into view above me, sheathing her blade beside Tabbris, her svelte second-in-command.

I close my eyes and try to still my trembling hands. "Thank you for saving me." It comes out a croak with my breathing not yet calm.

Never in my wildest imaginings did I envision that avenging Astread would turn out this way. I just wanted a horrible wrong righted.

"What happened?" Surprise flavors Esme's tone. It's no wonder as she takes in the two foes I decapitated.

"Where's your squad?" Tabbris quizzes, hands on his hips, surveying the eatery along with Esme.

I throw my good arm over my face. I knew my squad would be pissed when they found out I went on my own, but it would have been worth it. Astread's loss would have been vindicated, and hopefully every warrior would feel avenged. Life would have moved on. But now?

Esme kneels. "You're bleeding." She looks at another of her warriors who has crowded around me. "Lailah...."

The fit female tosses her dirty blonde ponytail over a shoulder and kneels beside me.

"Thank you. My shoulder and my leg."

Tabbris and three other warriors haul the beheaded White Eyes and its buddy away while Lailah works on my injuries.

Once she's done, Esme and my healer help me stand up in the circle they've formed around us.

I rotate my arm, testing my shoulder until the quietness and questioning looks on five of my rescuers' faces register and I stop. Their gazes keep bouncing between me and their leader who frowns.

"While Lailah healed you, I spoke with Kessien," Esme says.

Ah crap.

"As you might expect, he and your squad were more than a little concerned"—she draws out that last word—"when you blasted a distress cry across the entire system. We were in Jerusalem and the closest, so we came as fast as we could." Esme rubs an eyebrow, no doubt gathering her thoughts. Seems I've vexed her to her limits. The tightness in her expression tells me she'd love to let me have it, but she's more disciplined than that.

"Thank you." I force myself to meet her gaze. My execution may have been off, but I'm not sad I did what I did. I avenged my BFF, and I will not apologize for that.

None of the others so much as peep, but their continued ping-ponging gazes speak volumes.

Esme's lips part, readying to say more, but Tabbris interrupts, "I think we should get back."

The pair exchange looks, but Esme finally presses a hand to her stomach and nods.

Tabbris crosses the circle and hands Phantom to me.

"Thanks." I sheathe my trusty weapon, then hold hands with Esme and Lailah as we wink out of sight.

How much trouble am I in?

Chapter Eleven

The mood in the break room is deadly silent when I stride in. No one rises to meet me.

I want to shout, "Let's celebrate. I avenged Astread." I want to.

Aliyah scrunches up her face, a pained expression where she sits on the white leather sofa against the wall where I usually do.

Seated beside Aliyah, Jael's expression is neutral, like it always is. Stable and steady, he's never easy to read.

But when Issra looks up from the poofy chair where he's working on his crossword puzzle and doesn't so much as smile, I swallow hard.

Oh boy. If optimistic Issra isn't smiling, this isn't going to go well.

A feeling of doom descends on me. How much trouble am I really in?

I stop shy of where Kessien pauses from pacing, halfway between the seating arrangement and the puzzle table, and our gazes meet. There's no playfulness, much less warmth in his beautiful azure eyes. They look icy at the moment, and my stomach twists.

He runs a hand through his unusually disorderly blond locks—it's clear he's done it a few times—and blows out a breath.

Perhaps things will go better if I start, so I move further into the room and stop behind the back of the sofa across from Aliyah and Jael, taking care not to use it to steady me. No, I need to stand on my own two feet. I turn so I can take in everyone and their reactions. "Kessien, I'm sorry I broke the chain of command"—I pause briefly—"but I avenged Astread's loss." I add as much optimism to my tone as I can muster.

Aliyah's eyes go wide, and she draws a hand to her chest. Issra's mouth falls open, and he sets his crossword on the end table.

Kessien stills, then stares at me. No doubt his thoughts are reeling, but at least he doesn't yell.

Jael just shakes his head.

I need to make them understand. The words flow quickly as I look between them. "We've all been miserable the last month. I couldn't take it anymore. The Almighty didn't do anything to avenge her loss—"

"So you decided to take things into your own hands." Kessien scowls.

Jael glowers. Aliyah looks down at the book in her lap.

"You're *sorry* you broke the chain of command." Kessien's tone rises. "Glad, you didn't just break the chain of command, you annihilated it. No warrior ever goes off on their own, you know that." His hands go wide to exaggerate his point.

I force my quivering legs to remain still. I need to let him vent.

"Do you have *any* idea how surprised we were, then afraid for you, when we heard your distress call?" He grabs the back of his neck. "You were supposed to be at the library."

I grimace.

"Do you realize the position you've put your squad in?" He motions around the seating area.

I put my hands on my hips and furrow my brow. "What do you mean?"

"As the leader of this squad, I'm responsible to ensure the safety of my troops. What do you think Michael will have to say about my performance?"

I swallow hard. The Archangel won't be happy.

Kessien wags a finger. "You also put in question this squad's unity and commitment to one another."

My jaw drops, and my temper rises along with my arms. "How can you say that? I avenged Astread's loss *because* I'm committed to her."

"Yes, to one member. But what of the rest of us? Everyone who hears about this will know you acted on your own with no regard for the squad."

I lower my arms, some of the wind sucked from my sails.

Kessien takes a step toward me and gets in my face. "Do you understand what you've started?"

My heart accelerates, and it's not from pining. "Started?"

"Do you honestly think the demons won't retaliate in a bigger way? You've single-handedly made every warrior's job harder. What's more, the attacks on humans will probably come more frequently and be fiercer as added retribution." He brings his head down sharply.

I don't think I've ever seen him this angry. A lump forms in my throat. I hadn't thought about those consequences.

"Why did you do it by yourself? Didn't you think we'd want to avenge Astread's loss too?" Issra's nostrils flare.

Aliyah bites a lip.

My shoulders slump. "I didn't want to get you in trouble."

"Why would we have gotten in trouble?" Jael asks in an even tone, gaze locked with mine.

"The Almighty said more to you than what you told us, didn't he?" Hurt laces Aliyah's voice, and my heart breaks.

I scuff a boot on the wood. "I'm sorry. I never meant to hurt you. I didn't think everything through, you're right. I was just so pissed that no one was avenging Astread."

"You didn't answer her question." Kessien's tone is hard and insistent. "What *didn't* you tell us?"

My mouth goes dry. "The Almighty said...." My gaze travels around the four. "He said to not let... to not let vengeance take root. That he would repay the demons for her loss."

Jael sits up straight, and his eyes go wide. "And you disregarded his explicit instruction?"

Aliyah rubs an eyebrow, face scrunched.

Kessien drops his hands and blows out a breath. "That takes guts, Glad. It's the height of stupidity, but it's gutsy." He shakes his head and steps away.

My body feels heavy. I've disappointed the whole squad, and I don't know how to fix it.

"I'm sorry." I grab the back of the sofa for support. I have no other words, and even these feel completely inadequate.

No one looks at me, and it only makes it worse, but I guess I deserve it.

"*Squadron 132. Squadron 132.*" Everyone freezes as the heavenly dispatcher announces, "*Your presence is requested before the Almighty's throne…*" Her voice takes on a hushed tone as she finishes, "*…immediately.*"

And the arrows just keep on flying.

I bite a lip. Sure I'm in trouble with the squad, but chain of command violations are brought before our commanders over whom Archangel Michael presides, not the Almighty. I blow out a breath. It's wishful thinking, I know.

I'm in deeper doo-doo than ever before.

The Almighty's breaking the chain of command too, I realize. If the situation weren't so serious, I'd laugh.

No one says a word as we shift into our white dress uniforms. The hall is eerily quiet, and every break room door is closed as we head out after doing a very rote team cheer that lacks all enthusiasm. I pull at the silver trim lining my tunic sleeves. I've never heard the hall completely quiet. Ever. Where has everyone gone? And why weren't we told to go too?

I try to push worry back as we step out the front door and launch. The squad is never quiet when we fly, so when no one says a word telepathically, I flex my hands, trying and failing to manage my angst.

We approach the crystal palace before I've fully prepared myself to give account before the Almighty.

I rub my hands the instant I spot, not a lawn full of spirits engaged in fun activities, but a field of soldiers in white uniforms. Every warrior is arrayed in formation, ready for the Almighty's review. It explains why the halls were silent.

"Why weren't we summoned for review?" I can't help but ask my silent mates.

"I believe we were," Kessien replies from ahead. His voice hitches, sending a chill down my back.

We fly over the gathered assembly and land on the patio near the front doors and vanish our wings. The two cherubim in white leathers don't so much as ask who we are. They don't call anyone inside to check our identities, nothing like last time. Rather they simply pull wide the pair of doors.

Aliyah's eyes go wide beside me, and I clasp my hands together. Seems we're the only ones they were waiting for.

"We know the way," Kessien assures them when one of the guards makes to lead.

Issra's gaze ping-pongs between the guards and our fearless leader.

One of the guards nod, and our boots soon echo on the translucent stone floor as we make our way to the throne room… and questioning. Somehow the brilliance that the Almighty radiates through the crystal doesn't comfort, much less calm. If anything, it feels like I'm about to be interrogated and everything will be laid bare in the light.

We near the hulking, clouded set of double doors of the throne room, and just like outside, the pair of soldiers don't so much as salute but heave them open, and I squint as my eyes adjust to the Almighty's brightness.

Kessien and Jael salute anyway, but my stomach twists when I immediately notice there's no choral singing emanating from the room like there was the first time.

We're not interrupting anything.

My heart races. They're waiting for us.

Chapter Twelve

I question whether Aliyah and Issra are breathing beside me as we follow Kessien and Jael, stepping into the throne room. Except for our footsteps, it's so silent you could probably hear a falling feather sigh against the floor.

The hall isn't filled to capacity like last time, so I'm spared the feel of millions of eyes crawling over me, scrutinizing me. No, the hulking room is empty save for the Almighty who sits atop his throne. Well, him and four soldiers dressed in white leathers who stand off to one side of the dais.

The twenty-four smaller thrones that circle the larger one sit empty, and the four, six-winged, multi-animal-headed beings with eyes all over their bodies are noticeably absent. The echoing emptiness leaves me with a sinking feeling.

Kessien stops abruptly and drops, forehead to the crystal floor. We all mimic because we're not stupid.

"Rise and approach." The Almighty's voice is full and booming like usual and reverberates in the cavernous emptiness.

He doesn't sound upset. At least I tell myself that. I'll take any positive at this point, even if I have to make it up.

We scramble up and continue forward toward the mammoth throne with that emerald rainbow that rings it. We all jump as lightning flashes, followed by a peal of thunder.

My stomach crawls into my throat. My squadron mates look equally distressed.

As we near the throne, the detail of the Almighty's bright face comes into clearer focus—he wears a downturned expression and his eyes are dull.

Well crap.

His impeccable, white suit is crisp as usual, but it just serves to accent his slumped shoulders. He brushes his free-flowing, white hair over a shoulder. Then he stands.

I suck in a breath.

I've never seen the Almighty stand. Ever. Not that he can't, he just never does.

I swear Kessien jumps, his nerves betraying him, before he freezes a dozen steps from the dais, at attention. Jael is a statue beside him.

Aliyah and Issra's eyes are wide.

I've heard only one story of the Almighty standing—apparently one time a human he was particularly fond of was being stoned to death and he stood to welcome him. But never has he stood for angels. Not that I know of.

My stomach goes hard, and I focus on something, anything else.

I've never considered the Almighty's physique, but he's tall and toned like most warriors. I'm not surprised. Imagine a short, dumpy almighty. He wouldn't exactly fit that all-powerful bill.

Another peel of thunder sounds, accompanied by more lightning flashes as the Almighty runs a hand down his ample, white beard. My heart may beat out of my chest. He looks as if he's contemplating something.

The Almighty glances at the four soldiers standing at attention by the dais, then returns his focus to us.

I've no idea what he's thinking, but the tension he creates by his silence is freaking me out.

After what feels like an eternity, he rests his gaze on me.

Crap!

Aliyah whimpers, sneaking a glance at me.

My breathing labors as he strides forward. Only the sound of his white leather shoes echoes about the space as he descends the three steps.

I want to look away, but his eyes mesmerize me and I can't.

Kessien and Jael step back quickly as he reaches them, and he takes a moment to look both in the eye and squeeze a shoulder before returning his focus to me.

My legs beg to twitch, but I tense them as he stops before me, hands at his sides.

Aliyah and Issra take a step away to the side.

Thanks, guys! Way to support me. But I don't blame them.

I tighten the grip on my hands behind my back, no doubt making my knuckles turn white.

"At ease. Please." His ash-gray eyes hold warmth.

I exhale, relax my stance, and bring my hands forward despite my racing heart and clasp them in front of me.

"Gladriel"—his voice is filled with sorrow—"how I wished to show you the better way, but I would never take away your choice."

I swallow hard because I clearly didn't follow his better way.

"Do you know what that better path was?" He tilts his head, and I swear I see silver lining the corner of an eye.

I inhale a ragged breath. "You didn't want me to avenge Astread's loss."

He nods. "Do you know why?"

"You said… revenge would consume me." I need to explain. I bring my hands up. "You said you'd get revenge for her"—I'll probably regret saying this, but I can't stomach not saying it—"but you weren't doing anything."

Kessien chokes and starts coughing.

Issra's mouth falls open.

"Gladriel, you know that time has no meaning to me. A day is as a thousand years and a thousand years as a day. *When* I acted was not your concern. I asked only that you trust me to avenge her loss. But you didn't."

My mouth goes dry.

"You decided you had a better way." He sighs. "This is what vengeance does when it blossoms. It blinds you to reason."

I shift, my body tingling as I clasp my hands more tightly.

"By taking matters into your own hands when I expressly told you not to, you usurped my authority."

I drop my hands and slump my shoulders.

His voice wavers. "It brings me no joy to execute judgment on you for your wrongdoing, Gladriel, but I cannot overlook your transgression." He grips my shoulders with firm hands, looking me squarely in the eye. A tear runs down his cheek as he says, "I am expelling you from Heaven, away from my presence."

My legs go weak, but he keeps me standing. I shake my head. He didn't just say….

"No." Kessien's voice breaks.

My stomach twists as I gaze into the Almighty's ash-gray eyes, looking for I don't know what, that I misheard him, that he's joking, anything. But all I see is pain.

I look away. I just wanted justice for Astread.

He drops his hands, steps back, then turns. "Kessien."

My heart races. "No, you can't punish him. It was me. He didn't know." I step forward. He *has* to understand. "Please."

Kessien looks white. He swipes at his eyes as the Almighty approaches him, ignoring me.

"I will give you all a few minutes."

Kessien bobs his head, then turns and locks his gaze with me.

My knees threaten to buckle with relief that he's not punishing Kessien.

Before my thoughts venture further, Aliyah and Issra barrel into me, enveloping me in firm hugs. Neither of them speaks, but Aliyah's shaking back and Issra's trembling hands wrapped around my neck tell me enough.

Tears well up, and I can't hold them back as I join them in grief.

The Almighty is sending me away.

I won't see them again. The thought is nearly impossible to comprehend.

My tears flow unabated for I've no idea how long, but Issra and Aliyah have pulled back by the time I control them, and I swipe a hand over my face.

I look between them. "I'm going to miss you." Tears threaten to well up again, and I croak, "Take care of the squad."

Aliyah bobs her head, holding a hand over her mouth as tears continue streaming down her cheeks. Issra's barely holding it together judging by his quivering lips. He runs a hand over his eyes, but it does no good.

I turn slowly to find Jael with an arm around Kessien's back, holding his shoulder. Jael drops his arm and steps toward me. A second later, he throws his arms around me and pulls me close. "Your heart was in the right place, Glad. You always were one to try to make things right, so I understand why you did what you did. Just know that I don't hold anything against you." He pulls back and, with a small smile, looks my face over. "Take care of yourself, Glad."

"I'll miss you, Jael." It comes out quivering. "You're strong and steady. They'll need you now more than ever."

I step out of his embrace when he reaches up to wipe his eyes.

Kessien hasn't moved. He's just standing there watching my goodbyes.

My shoulders sag, and I look down, having absolutely no idea what to say to him. He was beyond pissed at me. Is he still? Do I tell him how I feel about him down deep? Do I leave him with something that heavy? I'll never have a chance to tell him if I don't.

I feel his embrace before my thoughts get farther.

"Glad." His voice cracks. "I should never have waited to tell you...." He pulls back enough to look into my eyes, but he doesn't drop his arms. "Glad... I love you."

My mouth drops open, but all that escapes is a whimper.

A tear trickles from his eye, but he doesn't swipe at it. "I don't know when I started loving you, but I can't remember a time before then."

"Oh, Kessien." Regret fills my voice as I bring my hands up to cup his face. "But you're angry with me."

He shakes his head. "Forget about that. It doesn't matter. What matters is right now."

"I love you too." The words come naturally. "I should have told you ages ago."

"I know." He reciprocates, cradling my face in his large hands.

My eyes go wide. "You do?"

His lips turn up. "I'd have to be blind not to. And if I was too stupid to see, Astread certainly made it abundantly clear. But I didn't want to pressure you. I wanted you to feel comfortable with the notion no matter how it went."

"Oh, Kessien."

His lips crash down on mine. *"I've wanted to do this for a very long time,"* he says telepathically.

I return the kiss with equal fervor, throwing my arms around his neck.

"I shouldn't have waited." His kiss deepens like he can't get enough of me.

His lips are so soft. *"Don't blame yourself. No regrets."*

It's a long while before he pulls back, but when he does, I open my eyes to take in his azure blues, refusing to acknowledge the silver lining them. "I've always loved your eyes."

He runs a hand through my golden locks before his expression turns serious. Telepathically he says, *"I give you my word that I will find a way to reverse this."*

"Oh, Kessien, no. Don't—" I don't want him to suffer my fate.

His lips find mine again. *"Glad, I love you. I'll be careful."*

Jael clears his throat as the four soldiers who had been standing to the side of the dais stop beside us.

Chapter Thirteen

Aliyah gives me a watery smile in Jael's embrace; he has an arm around Issra's shoulders and another around hers. Issra holds himself, seemingly not knowing what to do with his arms that he keeps shifting.

I never wanted to hurt them. Ever.

Kessien puts an arm around my back, his hand settling on my waist, and turns us both around to take in the Almighty who retreated back to his throne.

The Almighty drops his steepled hands, then nods to the soldiers, and they surround Kessien and me.

The particularly broad-shouldered soldier steps forward and says to me, "Relinquish your weapons."

My eyebrows rise as his words register. They want Phantom as well as my celestial dagger. A lump forms in my throat.

Kessien's hand tenses on my waist as my hand moves reflexively to Phantom's hilt and my thumb rubs the top like has become second nature.

Kessien's Adam's apple bobs as he drops his hand so I can comply, but he doesn't step away.

My throat turns gummy as I look down, then reach for the buckle of my white belt, already feeling the loss of my faithful companion. It takes but a minute to unfasten it, and I wrap up the fine leather around the blade's hilt.

The soldier takes it when I hand it over and passes it to his comrade. I do the same with my dagger, lifting my tunic and undoing the belt from around my thigh. I'll never again have them among my repertoire of apparel to shift into.

Kessien returns his arm around me a second later and gives me a squeeze. I appreciate the gesture, even if it doesn't reassure me.

I put my hand on his at my side to give it a place to belong without my sword as the soldier steps back and looks up at the Almighty.

"As you know, as a reminder of your transgression, I cleave the lower wings of cherubs I cast from my presence."

My back starts to tingle, and it's not from Kessien tightening his grip.

"No." Aliyah's voice is pained before a sob escapes.

"You'll need to let her go," the vocal soldier says.

The muscles in Kessien's jaw bulge. "She may have to lose two wings, but I won't let her go," he grinds out.

We all look to the Almighty. "Let him comfort her."

The soldier bobs his head, then says to Kessien, "Very well. Just be sure you're out of the way."

Jael and my other two squad mates join us, bringing a frown to the soldier's face. Their presence is clearly not within protocol. Tough. Aliyah takes one of my hands and squeezes it gently.

The soldier huffs. "Kneel and extend your wings."

Another of the soldiers draws his blade.

My pulse races as I do as bid, taking to all fours. My tunic sags without a belt, and my knees get twisted in the fabric. Pulling it up, I focus on the crystal floor as I unfurl my wings. They quiver. I can't keep them steady with my nerves as they are.

It's going to hurt. I can't even imagine how much.

Aliyah puts a hand on my shoulder, then sits on her haunches beside me. Issra does the same on my other side.

"Thank you." My voice quakes.

I'm terrified. My breathing speeds, but just as I might hyperventilate, Jael's boots come into view as he steps close, beside Issra. He pulls my upper wings up and out of the way.

His kindness makes me whimper because I doubt I could have held them up through this.

My whole body starts to shake, but Kessien appears. He throws himself on his back and scoots right up under my face, beside Aliyah.

"Thought you might appreciate a distraction," he says as he reaches for my blonde ponytail, pushing it up and back, over my shoulder. His hand caresses my cheek as his beautiful, azure eyes drink me in.

He cups my face, pulling my head toward him, then kisses me deeply, and I swear I'd no idea he could be so passionate. Why did I resist him? Why?

As he intends, I lose myself in the kiss until the blade comes down. I can't hold in a scream as the weight of my lower wings vanishes. Searing pain that I've never known anything close to replaces them. Then I feel something wet.

Tears well up in his eyes that match mine. "How I wish I could take your pain."

I moan in agony and fall on my side. This is what a celestial blade feels like. I've nicked myself upon occasion, and it's smarted, but nothing close to this.

Hands touch the wound, and I shriek. My back feels like it's on fire.

"Sorry. Sorry, Glad. I'm stopping the bleeding." Aliyah's doing her best, I know she is, but knowing doesn't ease the anguish.

Kessien moves around in front of me where I pant, lying on my side, and takes my hand. His beautiful face is scrunched up as if feeling the agony right along with me. I suppose he is in a way. It's always hard to watch someone in pain.

After several minutes and several yips, the pain eases and I can finally exhale, although doing so sends a zing through me.

The pain continues to lessen until Aliyah pats my side. "I think that should do it. It won't get infected."

"Thank you," I croak. I feel exhausted.

I push up and tense my back. She's right. It feels much better, although way too light.

A wholly different pain besets me, the pain of loss. It's no less agonizing, and I suck in a breath. But now is not the time to indulge my loss, so I try to swallow my angst. It doesn't want to go down, so I blow out a breath instead.

Kessien's gaze is sympathetic, and I again chide myself for resisting him.

Kneeling on her haunches beside me, Aliyah bites her lip. The number of times she's healed me…. I try to take a deep breath, but that doesn't work well either. This is the last time she'll ever do that for me.

My lips quiver and tears well up. I just wanted to avenge my BFF.

I won't even get to say goodbye to Astread. The realization is the last straw, and my heart breaks. Utterly and completely. I cover my face with my hands as moisture breaches the dam and trickles down my cheeks.

Kessien rubs my shoulder. If only it could ease the ache.

"Rise," the verbal soldier commands.

I choke back more tears as Kessien takes my arm and helps me up to standing. The blood rushes back to my head, and I wobble, but he's there, steadying me in an instant.

"I'm okay."

He raises an eyebrow but remains silent.

Jael has an arm around Issra's shoulders, who is again holding himself.

"It's time," the same soldier declares.

Two of the four warriors hold my severed wings, and another has my relinquished weapons as the vocal one motions me forward with a hand.

This is it.

I move to vanish my remaining wings.

"Stop." He shakes his head. "You will keep them visible."

So this is to be a public shaming. My chest tightens.

I gaze up at the Almighty, but his expression is neutral, no hint of the emotion I saw earlier.

"No, you will not accompany her." The vocal soldier holds up a hand when my squad mates move to follow.

I survey my friends. "I've got this. I'll be okay." Amazingly, I keep my voice even despite their pained expressions.

Kessien catches my gaze and says into my mind, *"I love you, Glad. Never forget my promise. I'll—"*

His words cut off midsentence, and my eyes go wide as the soldiers surround me.

"Your telepathic connection has been severed," the verbal one informs.

I frown. But of course they'd cut that off. No fallen angel has access to heaven's communications.

The notion wallops me over the head. I've *fallen*… I've become my enemy… exactly what I and all heavenly beings despise.

I'm not like them.

There's way too much to unpack to that sentiment, so I push the thought back and find Kessien between my escorts' broad shoulders. "I won't forget."

I won't either. The squad and I share love, but Kessien's love is different. He *loves* me. They've taken every vestige of heavenly warrior from me, but they can't take his love. It's the one thing I have to buoy me through whatever storms lay ahead. He loves me. My heart pangs. I'll hold on to that no matter what.

Inhale, exhale, inhale, exhale. I just need to keep breathing.

I turn, not allowing myself to look back as we step toward, then through, the throne room's towering, frosted doors, the last remnants of my life here, carried by my escorts.

Being so close to my relinquished weapons and bloodied, severed wings adds an extra measure of pain, and I can't help but feel their absence on my back and at my side. I tense my back muscles. It no longer hurts physically; the same can't be said for emotionally.

I summon my courage as we walk for the next several minutes, readying myself, because the moment we emerge from the crystal palace, I'll confront the host of cherubim of all of heaven arrayed in formation.

I'm to be an object lesson.

Chapter Fourteen

I ruffle my two wings as we stop before the palace's hulking doors and they swing open. I'm a mess in my loose tunic that's filthy with dried blood everywhere, but I lift my chin, pull my shoulders back, and take a deep breath.

One of the soldiers carrying my severed wings looks like he might be sick. The other wrinkles his nose, his gaze bouncing between my appendage and me. An ugly twist besets his mouth, and it's not hard to imagine what he's thinking.

I best get used to it. He won't be alone.

The soldiers spread out as we make our way across the balcony, then stop before heading down the grand stairs with the emerald banisters.

"Turn around," the verbal one commands.

"Excuse me?"

"Turn. Around." He gives me a hard look.

And so it begins.

My hands tremble as I do what I'm told. No doubt he's telepathically telling all the troops to learn from my example because there's a decided stirring among the massive formation the longer I hold my wings aloft for their scrutiny. I feel like I'm standing here naked, but I refuse to hold myself. A girl's gotta have some dignity.

Let them look.

"Proceed." The command comes several minutes later, and relief washes over me as I turn around and head down the steps.

I train my focus ahead, at the end of the path. It feels like I'm walking a gauntlet as we head down the long row that divides the host. Out of the corner of my eye, I can't help seeing a mix of curled lips, shaking heads, pinched eyebrows, and more that range between disgust, disapproval, and downright hostility.

"Let me pass!" a higher-pitched shout sounds from the left as we approach the end of the troops, and my heart soars.

"You can't—" a lower voice objects.

My feet move faster as I outpace my escorts. The vocal one tells me to slow, but I ignore him as Astread sprints around a soldier at the end of a row, in formation.

She swats at her pursuer, then maneuvers around another soldier who tries to block her. She's still as quick as ever despite wearing heels and a dress.

We run into each other's arms.

"Forgive me, Captain." The soldiers' conversation blends into the background as we hug.

"Oh, Astread. You came." I'm sobbing.

"Kessien notified me. They'd have to have tied me down." She's sobbing too.

At length, she pulls back, eyes watery, and says, "I knew I shouldn't have left you to your own recognizance. The rest of the squad was not equipped to keep you in check."

I snort a soggy snort. "You got that right."

Her look turns serious. "Thank you for avenging my loss, even if the Almighty took offense."

I hadn't realized it until this moment, but all I really wanted was to have her appreciate what I did. I can't keep more tears from spilling down my cheeks.

I take a deep breath and clear my throat, trying to keep my voice even. "You're welcome."

"I'm going to miss you, BFF." She pushes my ponytail over my shoulder.

"And I you." I take in her face, sealing it in my memory. Whether we're together or not, she'll always be my best friend forever.

"Time's up. Let's go." It's the vocal soldier again.

"Astread, thank you for coming." I step back, and my four escorts close around me as I dry my face on a sleeve.

"Take care of yourself." She forces a smile.

We move forward, nearing the end of the grass of the palace's sprawling lawn and the beginning of the golden streets that surround it. I realize the three soldiers who bore my severed wings and celestial weapons handed them off while I said goodbye because their hands are empty.

The vocal soldier stops. "We'll transport from here. You may vanish your wings."

I do as bid. I don't ask permission as I also take the opportunity to shift from my baggy dress whites into black leathers. I instantly miss Phantom's weight at my hip.

Wherever they're taking me, might as well make a good first impression.

Second heaven lies between the edge of Earth's atmosphere and the third heaven. With the Almighty's brightness, rarely, if ever, do demons and fallen angels come into the third heaven; they stay in first and second heaven.

Conversely, warrior angels—myself principle among them—don't spend time in second heaven, so I'm not sure what to expect when we rematerialize.

My escorts' expressions change from the neutral ones they've held thus far and are replaced with narrowed eyes, clenching hands, and stiff postures. My stomach twists. Unlike me, I can only assume they know what we'll face.

Ready or not, here we come.

I take hold of a hand of the soldiers on either side of me, and things go dark.

Chapter Fifteen

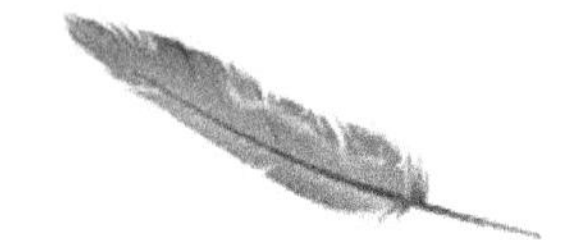

A dry, barren wasteland of rocky outcroppings interspersed with raw, pitted craters lays to my right when things come back into focus. A line of six soldiers clad in black leathers stands maybe twenty or so feet before us, guarding a towering pair of wrought iron gates with an ornate, emerald dragon design in each.

I drop my escorts' hands and grab for Phantom.

My escorts grab their celestial swords. I look down and realize my mistake. Of all the changes I'm about to endure, this may well be the hardest. I swallow down angst.

My party has assumed ready positions, eyes intense, as they hold up their flaming blades when I look up.

I'd never realized second heaven was so desolate. I hope it's just the outskirts. Between that and the rotten egg smell—is that sulfur from burning brimstone? I push the thought away—the only redeeming features seem to be the top of an enormous pink and blue planet on the horizon and, further away, a yellowish-orange one against the star-studded blackness.

One of the black-leathered soldiers chuckles as he, along with two others, stride forward. "Thadeus, you're always so uptight. You really think we're going to attack you? Right, and what, take you prisoner? Like we want to spend more time than we have to with an uptight cherub like you."

My vocal escort has a name, Thadeus. Not that I'll ever need it again. But they know each other, that much is clear.

Thadeus lowers his blade, but my other three escorts hold their positions. "Spoken like the forked-tongued serpent you follow."

Forked-tongued serpent. I give him a side glance.

The soldier rolls his eyes as he stops before Thadeus, then crosses his arms and leans back, a grin on his face. His other two cronies bookend him, one on either side, but they're nowhere near as relaxed.

"As much as you enjoy bloviating, Sorath, we've business to attend to." Thadeus leans forward, toward his nemesis, and sniffs the air, then wrinkles his nose.

With them exchanging "pleasantries" like they are, I'm clear it's not the sulfur stench he's making as if he's objecting to.

I roll my eyes. *A pissing contest. Oh joy.*

Thadeus looks over at me. "As it happens, we're here to deliver her to you."

Sorath shifts his attention to me and, still wearing that stupid grin, his dark eyes fill with hunger as they roam over every inch of me.

I squint, returning a piercing glare. I cross my arms and lean back, mirroring him for good measure. Two can play this game. I may technically be Fallen, but never in my life have I allowed a fallen angel to disrespect me, and I'm not about to start.

Sorath bursts out laughing. "Bit of an attitude, I see. We'll soon fix that." His two companions chuckle as he takes two steps, getting in my face. His joviality dies. "Get over yourself, little cherub. You've fallen. You're no better than anyone else." Turning to Thadeus, he asks, "What are her charges?"

My heart picks up speed. If they know I killed….

No. No. No.

Thadeus opens his mouth to reply, but I cut him off. "What difference does it make what I did? I'm joining your happy little family." I give him my best toothy smile.

Sorath frowns, clearly not amused. Tough.

A corner of Thadeus's mouth hitches. I think he enjoyed my rejoinder.

Please don't say. Please don't say.

At length he clears his throat. "She's right. Her charges matter not."

Bless you.

It's a parting gift for which I will forever be indebted to him, and I'm really good with that.

Sorath retreats a step and puts his hands on his slender hips. "I can only assume you discovered a fuller understanding of the Enemy. In addition to all his positive attributes, he also has a not-so-seemly side to him—judgmental, unsympathetic, insensitive, inflexible." He raises a condescending eyebrow like he's giving me insight into the Almighty. "I congratulate you for waking to this reality." He smiles broadly, then giving my escorts a long, dramatic look, he says, "Most inhabitants of heaven never get to this point. Clearly they're not as smart as you."

I furrow my brow. Unseemly side?

"You're a bit slow, girlie, but better late than never." He laughs, and his companions lend an obligatory snicker.

Thadeus shakes his head.

Sorath motions me forward with an outstretched hand. "I think you'll find your new home illuminating as well as liberating."

I take the two steps, then turn and stand beside him.

My escorts join hands and, a second later, vanish.

My stomach tenses. For the first time in my life, I'm completely alone in the second heaven.

I feel like prey as the six enemy… no not enemy… Fallen… like me—that's going to take *a lot* of getting used to—soldiers give me a thorough looking over, their eyes alight with I don't know what, but whatever it is, it makes me uncomfortable.

One of the pair of Sorath's bookends asks, "Sergeant, shall we begin her attitude adjustment?" He wags his brows, making my skin crawl.

Crass troglodyte.

I've been here all of maybe two whole minutes and the guy's baser nature rears its ugly head. Then again, I probably should have expected vulgar. It's the way these brutes operate.

I may technically be Fallen, but ain't no way I'm adopting these kinds of behaviors.

Sorath considers, drawing a hand to his chin, to which I roll my eyes. *Seriously?*

One of the soldiers back by the gates loudly clears a throat. "Vistran, knock it off. Don't be a Philistine." The voice is feminine, and my heart accelerates.

Hope grows as a female steps forward, hands on her hips, frowning.

Sorath turns and returns a scowl. "Major Adoel, you spoiled the suspense I was carefully crafting. She's too big for her britches and needs to be brought down a few notches."

Adoel tosses her golden ponytail over the shoulder of her black leathers and smiles as she reaches me. "Hi, I'm Major Adoel. Ignore these idiots. What's your name?"

"Gl…." I stop myself. They may know who killed those demons. "Uh, Dree. Call me Dree."

"Well, Uh Dree"—she smiles—"if you're newly fallen, you have an appointment at Morningstar Academy."

I furrow my brow.

"Founded by the most beautiful angel ever created, who left the third heaven." I note the positive spin she puts on her description of Lucifer, the despicable leader of the Fallen, and how she says he "left" the third heaven. He didn't "leave." He was tossed out on his ear, far worse than what happened to me. The chaos he created upset the third heaven for weeks, what with him taking half of the cherubs with him.

She continues, "Morningstar Academy is where you'll receive an introduction to life here and where you will be assigned an occupation."

While her words sound sweet, my chest tightens. I'm not sure I should trust her. Or anyone here, for that matter.

I push worry aside, because what choice do I have, and force a smile.

"Sorath, I'll escort Dree to the school." She glances about. "And the next time I come and review your post, I expect to see your soldiers better prepared." She looks him squarely in the eyes. "Are we clear?"

Sorath shifts, and his fingers caress the hilt of his blade. "Perfectly, Major."

They exchange salutes before she turns her attention back to me. "Shall we?"

My stomach twists. What will this school be like?

Chapter Sixteen

Major Adoel unfurls her wings. Two just like mine.

Hating the feel of the lightness with my absent lower wings, I resist peeking to check their color, but there's no avoiding the truth, and my stomach sinks as I take in my wing's new charcoal coloration. They lack even a muted celestial brilliance.

I try to distract myself from the mental pain. The school must not be far if we're flying.

Major Adoel launches. I bobble as I follow, lacking my usual grace. My heart squeezes. This is going to take some getting used to.

The air is clear way up here—small mercy—as I fly to the major's left as we soar over the barren landscape, some mountainous, most of it flat. Striking is the overall dim of this heaven. I'm used to the Almighty's brightness illuminating the whole of the third heaven nearly to blindness, so its absence is glaring.

Earth has the sun to bring light, but this heaven is devoid of even that, save for a small shred of that brilliant ball's light. It's as if the blackness of the space devours the very hint of illumination. The dingy gloom leaves me feeling homesick.

No, this is my new home. I sigh.

A giant streak of light whizzes past, startling me, and my eyes grow wide.

My escort looks over, grinning. "That was a meteor, also known as a shooting star."

My heart speeds. "Is it dangerous?"

She laughs. "Only if you're in the way. They're normal. They're actually kind of fun to watch when there's a shower of them."

I give her a long look, not believing her.

She points at a monstrous but stunning haze of red, pink, orange, and blue. "See that? It's the Orion Nebula. There are many other nebulas just as pretty. They're the birthplace of stars."

"Seriously? Can humans see them?"

"I'm told they can. Humans just can't see our home, no different than where you left."

I shake my head. "That's amazing."

She motions in the other direction. "If you look hard, you can see what looks like a long, thin band of stars with a bulge in the center. See it?"

I squint and scan the blackness for what she describes. "I see something that looks like a milky haze. Is that what you mean?"

There a gleam in her eye. "Yes, exactly. That's a galaxy. Specifically, that's the Milky Way galaxy. It's a huge collection of stars. There are lots of galaxies here in the second heaven."

I shake my head. "That's incredible. You know a lot about...." I wave my hand, indicating the blackness.

She grins. "Call it a hobby of mine."

Maybe the second heaven has some redeeming qualities after all.

As we continue, I train my focus on a ball with blue, white, and green hues mixed randomly that's suspended a ways off. "What's that?"

The major laughs. "That's Earth, of course."

I suck in a breath. "Earth? No way."

My reaction sets her to guffawing. When she finally stops laughing, she says, "You miss all this when transporting between Earth and the third heaven. Have you never been here, to the second heaven?" There's a hint of disbelief in her tone.

I can only shake my head.

"Typical."

I'm not sure how to take that, and I glance over, but her expression is neutral.

"How were you never curious?" I sense arrogance in her tone, and my scalp prickles.

"I… uh…." I can't very well tell her the truth.

She frowns. "Spit it out, girl."

I huff. Fine. She wants to know, I'll tell her. "I had no desire to venture to the home of my… enemy." I wince as that last word comes out.

She juts her chin out, then smirks. "Funny how things work out." She gives me a dismissive nod, then looks ahead again.

She's ticking me off. I'm not like everyone here. The Almighty set me up. I'm not a bad cherub. I'm not. My aims were honorable. Astread even appreciated it.

I should, but I can't let her jab stand. I add a bit of snark as I reply, "If you're judging me for never visiting, what about you? Did you ever come here before you fell?" Time for her to turn that mirror on herself.

Her whole demeanor shifts, becoming fierce. Then she growls, "Never, ever, talk about… the before."

I jerk my head back. What? What'd I say?

"As a matter of principle, we do not acknowledge nor refer to anything before here. You'll do *well* to remember that." She gives me a stern look that we hold, her piercing green eyes unwilling to back down.

I don't want to be the first to look away, but it's clear she means to set me straight. After glaring for what feels like forever, I can't stand it anymore and finally surrender, glancing away.

"There is no before. The sooner you understand that, the easier your life will be."

I furrow my brow and only barely keep my jaw from dropping. What is she talking about? There most certainly is a before. If there wasn't, I wouldn't be here. Maybe she doesn't have friends. Maybe she's that pathetic, but I'm certainly not. I have friends, darn good ones too. And Kessien. My heart constricts. I should have told him how I feel about him sooner. He loves me. And I love him.

The next time I look over at her, a smile has again mounted her face. "Shall I continue narrating your little tour of your new home?"

I'm at a complete loss for words with her verbal whiplash—Dr. Jekyll and Mister Hyde?—so I do the only thing I can; I nod.

Psycho much?

She points out satellites and weather balloons floating below, along with what she calls an aurora. I've no idea. What I do know is that said aurora is very pretty with green and purple and blue light waving in a curtain of light.

"Here we are." She points to a sprawling complex of buildings we approach, around which a massive wall rises.

Why bother with a wall if we can fly right over?

As if reading my mind, she says, "You don't see them, but if anyone thinks to land inside these walls, their guards will shoot them down."

"Good to know. The front door sounds great."

A minute later, the stench of sulfur from burning brimstone again assaults my senses as we land. This stink is going to take a *very* long time to get used to. It's all I can do not to fan it away—not that it would do any good. My escort vanishes her wings, and I mimic.

Rising before us is a pair of hulking, wooden doors with a circular dragon in emerald color emblazoned on each, along with Morningstar Academy spanning the pair.

I'm detecting a theme with dragons. I suppose I shouldn't be surprised, what with Lucifer's obsession with the creatures. He's such a fanatic about them that the Almighty even refers to him as one these days.

One of the doors creaks open, and a long-haired, leather-clad male guard emerges. "Ah, Major Adoel, good to see you."

"Hello, Ophiel." The major bobs her head as we stop before the muscled male.

Adoel glances at me. "I have a newly fallen for you."

"Very good. Zephon's on duty, let me fetch him. Won't be but a minute, Major." With that, the gate shuts and we're left alone again.

True to his word, the guard's back not long after, accompanied by another, this one a leaner and slightly taller guy dressed in a black tunic and pants. I can only assume it's Zephon.

"Hello, Major. Ophiel filled me in. Any preliminary assessment?" He steps outside the creaking door.

Preliminary assessment?

The major looks at me and sniffs. "She'll require *intensive* adjustment based upon what I learned from her on our way here."

I turn my head and furrow my brow. Was that flight a test? Was she using our conversation to understand what I think about second heaven? It sure sounds that way, and I fell right into the trap.

I shake my head. How could I be so stupid?

"Understood, Major, and thank you. As always, we appreciate your input."

The major swats away his praise. "Happy to help."

I'd wondered if I could trust her, or anyone here. Seems I have my answer.

My stomach twists. I just wonder what she means by "intensive adjustment."

Chapter Seventeen

Kessien

My chest is tight and my stomach hard. I don't care that the Almighty is watching from his throne several feet behind us. He knows everything, so he has to know how heartrending this is for me, for all of us.

I run my hands down my face, wishing the events of the last hour have only been my imagination. That when I open my eyes, Glad will be standing here, smiling like she always is, a ready quip on those beautiful lips of hers.

"I've got this. I'll be okay." That's what she said just before they led her away. She put on a brave face for all of us, like the selfless, frustrating, at times reckless, warrior she is despite there being no way she wasn't scared out of her mind. I certainly would have been.

I swallow hard. I love her so much it hurts. Does she realize just how much?

The pain goes beyond bodily. No, this is a whole other type of anguish, one I've never felt before. At times Glad was infuriating. She'd follow her heart no matter what rule got in the way.

But it's one of so many things I love about her.

Jael shifts back and forth on his feet, a pained expression clouding his face. "We should go."

I'm thankful for my partner in this moment because I'm in no condition to lead.

We head toward Aliyah and Issra, who hold each other not far away. I spread my arms across their shoulders when we reach them, and we link up in a line before heading toward the throne room's towering, frosted doors.

Only the feel of their bodies bumping mine grounds me. Seems I'm not the only one, because our holds tighten on one another. Emotionally, we're all barely hanging on.

The flight home is a blur, but as we land on the grass out front of our quarters, Jael rubs a wrist as he turns to me. "Talk to me, brother."

Aliyah and Issra pause beside us.

I shake my head. "There's nothing to talk about." I can't keep a waver from my voice.

I can't begin to put into words my swirling thoughts, let alone writhing emotions.

"What happened is not nothing," Jael insists, his features tightening.

I bury my head in my arms.

"We should train. It'll help us all work through it," Issra says.

Training is the last thing I want to do, but when I drop my arms, I see pain etched across his face. He needs it, something physical to pummel with his anguish.

Aliyah chimes in, "I agree. It'll be good for everyone."

Looks like I'm outnumbered.

Jael fists his hands. "I'll lead."

I sigh. "Fine."

It's not long before, shifted into our black leathers, the curls of fresh sawdust partially obscure our boots where we stand under the Almighty's brilliant light in one of the thirty wooden-bench-ringed sparring circles of the outdoor training yard. I usually love the smell of wood shavings, but not today. Thankfully, Jael picked a circle away from several others in use, because the last thing any of us need is attention.

"Kessien and Aliyah against Issra and me," Jael says, rubbing the back of his neck.

A shout, followed by cheering, erupts from the far side of the training yard. Glad someone's having fun.

Aliyah, Issra, and Jael get into ready positions, the blades of their practice swords up.

Hands limp at my sides, I don't move.

Jael slumps his shoulders and sighs. "Kessien, I—we all love Glad"—he holds up a hand—"clearly not the same way you do, but she's one of us and… my heart aches too."

"Mine too," Aliyah says, lowering her blade.

Issra nods. "What would she want us to do? Sit around and mope or do something?"

He's right, I know he is, but it doesn't make it any easier. I shuffle into position, my feet feeling like lead, and stop beside Aliyah. For her part, she bites her lip as I join her, across from Issra.

"And ready," Jael says, lifting his sword again.

We all follow his lead.

"Go."

Gloom makes me slow, and Jael's in my face a second later, swinging his blade. Only reflex allows me to block in time. He's all wound up, and it's clear he's not going to go easy on me, because he follows up with another slice a second later. This one finds my side. But rather than stop and celebrate his point, he brings his blade up and charges me.

I furrow my brow. He's more than just wound up; I've never seen him like this.

Out of the corner of my eye, I spot Aliyah execute a roundhouse kick, connecting with the back of Issra's knee. He goes down with a grunt. She may be smaller than him, but she's no less fierce.

Jael's blade connects with mine, and my arms tense as he pushes. I'm forced to retreat a step, then another as he keeps pushing. His steel-blue eyes are intense, and I yield another step, but still he presses.

Enough already.

Suddenly, Jael pulls back and kicks my groin, hard.

I groan and nearly double over. An expletive races through my mind, but the pain is too intense to voice it.

What the heck?

I haven't even straightened when he's on me again, walloping the top of my head with the flat of his blade.

"Again," Jael yells. There's no playfulness in his eyes.

What is his problem?

I manage to straighten, my groin still throbbing as we face off again. Like before, Jael's on me in an instant, charging me and bringing his blade down from above, aiming for my head. I thrust my arm up and block, our blades singing.

This is more than releasing anguish. He's ticking me off.

I'm sick of being his punching bag. I step forward, coming under our locked blades, and drive the bottom of my hilt into his chin. It sends him back several steps.

Surprisingly, he comes right back at me, swinging.

Oh really?

Our blades again connect, but this time he slides his edge down mine, then steps forward and whacks me on the side of the head with the sharp edge of the practice blade.

I grimace and clench my jaw. Okay, he's moved me from annoyed to angry.

But he's not done. Of course not, because he's on me again an instant later. I throw my arms up, crossing them, and connect with the hand that holds his sword.

It does nothing to deter him because he keeps pushing, bending me backward. He releases one hand from his hilt and wraps his free arm around my neck. Stepping forward, he hauls me down.

For the love of all that's holy.

I'm utterly vulnerable, and he takes a cheap shot, punching me in the nose.

Pain zips through my head.

That's it. I'm sick of this.

I swipe at the blood flowing from my nose. My head feels like something exploded inside, but I'm not letting him get away with this. I drop my blade, roll on my side, and grab his leg, taking him down.

It's an all-out brawl after that. Issra and Aliyah flee the ring, and wood shavings fly as we trade messy punches. Jael doesn't hold back and neither do I as I land one to his gut. He grunts, then answers with another kick, this one to my thigh, which just infuriates me further.

I've had it. I don't care that he's in pain. So am I, but I'm not beating on him. Enough is enough. I land a blow to his chest.

"You love Glad," Jael growls between punches. "How long have we been partners?" He pants as he takes another swing at me.

I block, just barely.

"Yet you didn't…" He connects a fist with my middle. I'm not fast enough to cover and I grunt. "… tell me how you felt about her."

Aliyah stops beside us, fists on her hips. "It was pretty obvious, Jael. I'm not at all surprised. Now stop, both of you."

Jael gives her a long look.

I exhale.

Issra's standing beside Aliyah, and his gaze bounces between her and Jael. He looks like he'll take Jael on if he so much as hints at moving toward his partner.

"What difference does it make, Jael?" Issra's words come out sharp.

"I know you, Kessien." My partner gulps in air. "You're not going to just sit idly by and take it. You're going to do something."

I swipe at the blood flowing from my nose as I sit up, looking away. I meant every word of my promise to Glad. I will find a way to get her back, but I'm not about to put my squad in danger. If I fall in the process, it's on me. At least she and I will be together. No, I'll do it alone.

"Kessien, answer his question." Issra pinches the skin at his throat. "What are you going to do?"

Aliyah bites her lip.

Jael sits up, wood shavings hanging from his blond hair, and points a finger at me. "Don't you dare do something stupid on your own."

My silence communicates more than I intend, and I drag a hand through my hair.

"Kessien." Jael's voice wavers. "First we lost Astread, then Glad. I can't lose you too." For the first time in our history, tears fall from my partner's eyes.

My breathing labors. Never have I seen my even-keeled partner cry.

All three of them stare at me.

I open and close my mouth like a fish. How do I even begin to explain?

"We love her too. You don't have a corner on that." Issra runs his hands through his curls. "Don't say we don't love her enough to help."

Aliyah nods. "Our love for her may not be the same as yours, but we're no less committed to her. And for that matter, I'm sure Astread would like to help in any way she can."

I throw my hands up. "We could all fall. I don't want to be responsible for that."

Jael stands, nostrils flaring. "No one's asking you to. You're not responsible for our decisions."

Issra and Aliyah both nod sharply.

I roll my eyes as I shake my head. "Alright, fine. Fine."

Issra extends a hand, and I take it and stand.

"So what are you planning to do?" Aliyah asks.

Chapter Eighteen

"Trainee, follow me," Zephon, aka Mister Black Tunic and Pants, says after looking me up and down with his steely, cobalt eyes.

Trainee? I do have a name, you know. I barely bite my tongue. It probably wouldn't be the best thing to say to start off my time here.

He pivots and retreats inside the gate, not indicating whether I am to follow or not, but what else am I to assume?

Seconds later, the heavy, wood gate thuds shut behind us, thanks to the help of a pair of other guards who don't so much as glance at me. It's as if I don't exist.

My chest tightens as I take in the long, yellow path before me. The streets of third heaven are paved with gold, but this isn't that. They don't sparkle for one thing, but I sniff and the unmistakable stench of rotten eggs is so strong it overwhelms my senses, and I wrinkle my nose. This is the yellow of brimstone.

The path leads to a fountain that crowns a circle where two other paths converge before a well-worn, hulking, five-story, stone building that gives me the creeps in the dim. The skeletons of dead ivy cling to its facade.

Horror show anyone? Some humans love them. Me? Nope, nope, nope.

I yip when a flame shoots a good six feet out of a hole in the ground just a couple yards to my right, accompanied by a popping sound. My eyes grow wide, but Zephon doesn't so much as acknowledge it.

I hurry my steps, only to have the scene repeat itself to my left seconds later. The fields on both sides of the path are littered with holes from which fire keeps spouting.

Note to self: stay on the path.

As we near the circular fountain, I spot the first beings I've seen other than my guide and those guards—three pairs and a single Fallen. They stride to some destination unknown to me, intent in conversation.

But the fountain distracts me, and I do a double take because standing in the middle, amidst an inferno of flame, is a red caricature statue of the image some humans hold of Lucifer, the leader of second heaven, aka the devil, with horns and a pitchfork. The angry flames lick up to his waist, while the statue grins.

Is he poking fun at what humans believe him to be? He's anything but that.

One pair of students pauses and gives me a thorough looking over. I've no idea the pecking order here, but it probably won't be long before it's drilled into me.

I hurry after as Zephon follows the quarter circle path to the right, and we continue on toward another old and spooky building. That blasted fire field continues belching to my right and unnerves me. Who would have something so dangerous where beings could get hurt? It's sadist—

I stop myself. Of course it is. That's what this whole place is. My stomach twists. What have I gotten myself into?

I swallow hard, then refocus. There's no going back. I'll need to make the best of this. I blow out a breath, quietly so as not to give my guide any hint concerning how this place is already affecting me.

I make out the name "LIBRARY" carved into a plaque across the lintel of the building we approach, and I clutch at my chest, a shred of hope rising in me. Perhaps this place has one redeeming destination. Although, what reading material might it house?

I banish worry. I'll have plenty of time to investigate, but for now I will assume the best because not everything here can be evil or warped, right?

I hurry after my guide as he turns right, at the library. There's only one building between here and the wall that surrounds the school, so it seems that's our destination.

My mouth goes dry. What will my first taste of "intensive adjustment" entail?

We approach another old and creepy building, this one a two-story that I can picture something jumping out of the unkempt bushes that line the front. Between the dim, the sulfur stench, and the macabre vibes radiating from it, a chill climbs my back.

My guide mounts a single step and hauls open an old door whose hinges protest, and we head down the long hall that stretches before us. To the left, we pass a door, above which hangs a sign that reads "BOOKSTORE." I only have time for a quick glance, but it seems to be substantial, with a couple of floors filled with everything a student would need.

Several Fallen chat. No one pays me any mind, and I'm good with that.

With my gawking into the bookstore, I don't notice Zephon stop and open a door to the right, and I run into him.

"Sorry, sorry, sorry." I jump back like I've been burned, because his gaze might as well be flames.

He scowls, then in a gruff voice says, "Pay attention, trainee."

There's nothing I can say to fix this, so I bob my head and hunch my shoulders.

Still holding the door, he nods for me to go inside.

We enter a smallish lobby, in which a waist-high counter takes up most of the space.

"Anak, I have a newly fallen for you," Zephon says to the round, balding male behind the counter. "Major Adoel brought her and recommended an intensive adjustment based upon what she learned from her on their way here."

Anak's gray brows rise. "But she's female. This is highly unusual."

My stomach clenches. What are they going to do to me?

"It is." That's all Zephon says. His expression is hard, and my breathing labors. It's all I can do not to indulge my fear.

Anak fingers the pages of a spiral-bound book laid open on the counter. "Fine." I can't miss the huff he adds, and my pulse speeds.

He sends me a pitying look as he turns and directs me through the archway and into a spacious room with a good dozen swivel chairs spaced maybe ten or so feet apart.

As soon as I spot a mirror in front of each chair, along with a small table with an assortment of combs, razors, and shears, swallowing becomes difficult.

They mean to cut my hair.

This can't be good. It can't.

I bite my lip as Anak motions me with an open palm to the second chair in on the right side.

Zephon stops behind Anak and crosses his arms over his chest. Seems he plans to make sure my haircut is to his satisfaction.

I don't miss the barber's reflection in the mirror as his gaze flits to my guide, then darts away before it comes to rest on me. He forces a smile as he reaches for a black cape.

"Now then…." Whatever he was about to say I'll never know because his sentence trails off as Zephon locks eyes with him.

Anak clears his throat, then secures the cape behind my neck and reaches for shears. He blows out a breath, then gathers my long ponytail in a meaty hand.

I'm holding my breath as he glances up and catches my gaze in the mirror. I think I read an apology in his eyes just before he looks back down at my hair and brings his shears across it.

I suck in a breath, then fist my hands under the cape.

He drops the length on the floor, then removes the band I'd held it together with and hands it to me over my shoulder, giving Zephon a quick glance as he does.

I bat the cape aside and grab it, then bring it back under.

The barber grabs another bunch of my hair, and I raise my brows.

No, he can't mean to....

The shears again sing, and my heart races.

They can't mean to....

Again and again and again, the man chops large chunks of my golden hair.

An intensive adjustment.

I swallow hard as I try to slow my breathing.

This is all that major's fault.

Anger ignites as more of my hair falls to the floor.

Why would just one being get to determine how I integrate here?

Anak won't look at me anymore despite me locking my gaze with his downcast eyes in the mirror.

That female has earned a special gift from me if I ever see her again. Oh, yeah. Making out to be all friendly and then stabbing me in the back like this.

After hacking my hair to bits with those abominable shears, Anak reaches for the razor.

I can only close my eyes as he continues working, but my hands are balled tight.

They mean to break me down.

Zephon's stance and hard expression never change despite the barber continuing to glance at him.

Anak brings the razor to my head, and I feel the cold metal against my scalp as he makes a first pass right down the center of my head. He's going to shave me, I know he is.

I'll admit this smarts, more than a little. I clutch my hair band in one hand but open the other under the cape and breathe in and out, slowly, until I swallow down the threatening tears.

I can't let them get to me. I won't let them break me.

Chapter Nineteen

I shift on the hard oak bench beside the door bearing—surprise, surprise—a dragon emblem. The bench might as well be a torture device as a seat.

I stop myself. They no doubt have ideas for if I don't conform. I swallow. Let's not go there.

The sound of keys tapping fills the dim, smallish area outside the headmaster's office as the long-haired, blonde female across the way ignores me. She turned up her hawkish nose the instant I arrived, giving my bare head an imperious look and shaking hers.

It's been an eternity since Zephon dropped me here after Anak finished and we backtracked to that hulking, five-story, creepy building just behind the flaming, caricature-of-Satan fountain. A shiver mounts my back remembering the feel of Zephon's cold hands fingering my bare scalp. He made the barber keep working until my head was completely clean without so much as a trace of blonde fuzz.

It'll grow back. It'll grow back. I keep reminding myself.

Ms. Assistant shifts in her padded chair, exposing more of her abundant, barely concealed cleavage as she continues typing.

I run a hand across the chest of my leathers. The scantily clad admin leaves me feeling uncomfortable. Is she supposed to be a seductress? If so, she nailed the look, what with her tight shirt, barely there, black leather mini skirt, and fishnet stockings.

I attempted to shift into something more in line with what some of the other students I spotted are wearing, but it seems my entire wardrobe has been blocked from access along with my telepathic abilities. Who knows when I'll get access to something else to wear. No doubt this is yet another part of making me feel like an outsider, to break me.

I scan the countless bookshelves lining the walls for the thousandth time, the toe of my boot tapping the well-worn, wood floor. The books seem to range from topics concerning the administration of an institution of learning, which I expected, but others include investigative techniques, celestial warriors, weapons production, temptation, and more. It's these that pique my curiosity.

Unfortunately, when I went to investigate, Ms. Admin sent me a fierce look and told me to remain seated, that I hadn't earned the privilege of pissing much less reading treasured tomes such as these.

A trim male with a man bun enters the office, and Ms. Admin lights up. "Jacob, thank you so much for dropping these off for me."

I'm behind him, and he doesn't see me as she swivels her chair around and scoops up a stack of thick binders from the credenza, then stands and hauls the armload back around her desk.

"It's not like I had a choice." His reply is hushed, and Ms. Admin misses it.

Jacob takes the binders and turns, spotting me. He gives me a quick once-over, then lifts his head and sniffs.

"Fine, I don't like you either." I can't hold back a retort. Sorry, not sorry. They shaved my head, and it's made me a bit defensive.

His blue eyes turn icy, and despite the binders filling his arms, when he raises an eyebrow, my stomach clenches. "You, trainee, will not address your betters unless spoken to." He stares daggers at me for several seconds before adding, "Is that clear?"

I refuse to look away, and we remain locked in challenge until he laughs. "Oh, you're going to be a fun one to break."

I lift my chin in defiance, to which he laughs again. "Yes, a lot of fun." He shakes his head and rolls his eyes before leaving.

"That was stupid. You know that, don't you?" Ms. Admin says, adjusting her skirt and taking her seat again.

I swallow a pithy reply. It'll just be lost on the likes of her.

How I miss my friends. My heart aches. *Stop wallowing, it'll make you weak. That's the last thing you can be right now.* I pep talk myself, but seconds later, my thoughts wander to Kessien. He loves me. And I love him.

Tears well up. Will I ever see him or any of them again?

I can't help sniffing, and Ms. Admin looks up in an instant, a toothy grin mounting her face. She pushes the locks of her beehive bouffant, which she's left down, over a shoulder as she continues staring at me.

Two big, fat, traitorous tears roll down my cheeks, but I refuse to swipe at them, not when she opens her mouth, her smile bursting.

"Do my eyes deceive me? Do I see tears?" She throws an open palm across her abundant chest and stands, then slinks around her desk.

Her mocking is all it takes for my anger to ignite, and I mimic, shooting up. I suppose I should thank her because it dries my stupid tears in an instant. I'll have to remember that trick. No doubt I'll need it.

She points a stubby, well-manicured finger at me as her expression goes hard in an instant. "Sit yourself back down, trainee. I didn't tell you to stand." It comes out as a growl.

We're pretty much the same height, and she gets in my face.

Her seductive, barely there outfit undermines any respect I have for her, and I'm not about to let her get under my skin.

"Fine," I growl back at her.

"Trainee, I am your better. You are scum. You are nothing. You will address me with the utmost of respect. Now try your response again."

I furrow my brow. Scum? Nothing? Is she kidding? I was going to sit. Is she trying to provoke me?

Her piercing eyes tell me she's serious. Or might she be putting on a good act? Which is it?

Humor strikes, and I can't hold back a snort. "That's good. You almost had me. Fine, I'll sit down." I hold up a hand and take a seat.

She bends over and brings her nose to within an inch of mine. In a quiet and deadly serious calm, she says, "Trainee Scum, did I give you permission to sit?"

I pull back, disbelieving.

"Did I?" she asks, in my face again.

I feel like telling her, "Yes, that's exactly what you told me to do to begin with," but I refrain. "No."

"Then stand back up and try your response again, Trainee Scum."

I furrow my brow as she backs up a half step, only far enough for me to stand, so she'll be in my face again.

I ease up, resisting the urge to flinch as I draw to within an inch of her nose.

"Now what would you like to ask, Trainee Scum?" Her eyes hold no humor.

"Permission to sit?" It comes out quieter than I intend.

"Permission to sit what?" she shouts back at me.

I jerk back, the backs of my knees hitting the bench. I barely avoid sitting but lock my knees and manage to stay up.

"Permission to sit what?" she again yells in my face.

What is she asking?

"Trainee Scum, you will respond 'permission to sit, ma'am or sir.' Do. You. Understand?"

I bob my head.

"Do you understand, Trainee Scum?" Her voice grows more insistent, if that's even possible.

"I understand, ma'am," I shout back at her.

"Now ask permission. Again. Trainee Scum," she barks.

I hold my gaze locked with hers and bark, "Permission to sit, ma'am."

"Granted." She pulls back but holds up that stupid finger, and in a more civilized tone says, "Before you sit, tell me your name."

I resist shaking my head. She actually wants to know my name? I may get whiplash at this rate.

"My name is Dree, ma'am."

She's back in my face in an instant, her expression fierce once more. "Your name is Trainee Scum. Say it."

She can't be serious. But she is. Her scowl tells me as much. Ah, what the hay.

"My name is Trainee Scum, ma'am." I bark it out.

"Again."

"My name is Trainee Scum, ma'am."

"Again."

I repeat my "new name" in her face a good twenty times before she finally tells me to sit.

I do, but she's in my face again in an instant. "You will use this name with everyone you meet, until you earn more. Am I clear?" She raises an eyebrow.

Earn more? I have to earn my name? Seriously? And if I don't?

I tamp down on an objection and, holding her gaze, bark, "I understand, ma'am."

Our gazes stay locked as she eases back. No doubt she'll yell if I drop it.

Amazingly, she retreats back to her desk.

It's a relief to have her out of my face. Geez. Intimidation much? And from a female like her? Is that how this place works?

I roll my shoulders. If so…. My chest tightens.

What have I gotten myself into?

It's another eternity, during which I sit more quietly and patiently than before. I refuse to think that I'm conforming, I'm not. Not to a place like this. I'm better than that. I'm just not stupid.

It's what I tell myself.

"Umbrelle, send in Trainee Scum." It's a low male hiss.

My gaze jets to a black box on Ms. Admin's desk, and I swallow. The headmaster is calling me Trainee Scum too. He overheard the whole exchange with her. Then again, who wouldn't have in the other room?

The female snorts and sneaks a glance at me before punching a button. "I'll send her in, Headmaster Arioch." She turns to me. "He will see you now, Trainee Scum."

Should I say something to acknowledge her statement? I'll probably get yelled at if I don't.

"Thank you, ma'am. Permission to stand, ma'am," I bark for good measure.

She grins. "You're learning, Trainee Scum. Permission granted."

Her saccharine words grate on my nerves, but I reply, "Thank you, ma'am."

Chapter Twenty

I'm wound up from my confrontation with Umbrelle, so when I reach the headmaster's door, the top half of which is frosted glass with his name spelled out in large letters, I'm unsure what to do.

Should I knock? Should I just go in?

I'm better than this and hate my indecision, but what am I to do?

I catch Ms. Admin grinning out of the corner of my eye but ignore her.

Raising a hand, I ready to rap softly, but I'm saved when the male bellows, "Enter, Trainee Scum."

I take a deep breath as I reach for the doorknob, praying this encounter goes better than the one I just had.

A blond, bearded, burly male sits at a hulking, ebony desk before a large window that overlooks the odiferous, pale yellow walk out front. The male's steel-gray eyes take me in with a neutral expression as I shut the door and take four steps into the large space before stopping, hands at my sides.

He remains silent for over a minute, and it's everything I can do to not twitch. No doubt he's taking my measure. Then again, I should probably fidget and do all manner of idiot things, he'd think poorly of me and lower any expectations he might have.

But I won't. A girl's got to have some dignity.

He continues staring, and I pull my shoulders back, making a corner of his mouth hitch.

"Seems reports are correct." He pulls an open file toward him but doesn't drop his gaze. "Approach, Trainee Scum."

I've no idea how to respond, so I go with what was just drilled into me, barking, "Thank you, sir." I stop behind one of a pair of upholstered, ebony side chairs. "Permission to sit, sir."

A frown clouds his expression, and my stomach twists. What'd I do wrong now?

"Denied, Trainee Scum. You have not yet earned that privilege. And at the rate you're going, it will be a very long time before you do."

I bite back a quick retort. Of course these creeps haven't deigned to let me sit. Because that's such an honor. "Of course, sir."

My eyes flit to a mammoth, gray stone fireplace with a significant mantle to the right, before which lies a dark rug with an emerald dragon emblem in the center—what else could it possibly be? Warm flames dance in the grate that's probably my height, if I had to guess.

"Focus, Trainee Scum." His roar startles me, and I flinch. "You've not earned the privilege of looking about my office." He slams his fist on the desk.

I redirect my gaze and meet his fierce, icy eyes.

"Morningstar Academy exists to initiate every newly fallen to our expectations and ensure your allegiance is to our cause and not that of the Enemy."

My stomach quivers.

"We have three primary objectives." He lifts his chin and leans forward. "Learn them and learn them well, Trainee Scum."

I swallow. Intimidation much?

"Number one, you will exercise power and control over humans at every opportunity."

My eyes go wide. But the Almighty gave them free will.

"Number two, you will exploit every opportunity to make humans betray what they care about."

I barely bite my tongue. Oh, no, no, no.

"Number three, while we are not permitted to kill them, we can make human lives a living hell, introducing all manner of mayhem to their lives." He rubs his hands together and chuckles.

This is what I'm supposed to learn to do? I can't. I won't. "Permission to speak, sir."

He closes his mouth and raises a bushy brow. Clearly I haven't earned the privilege of asking a question, but I don't care.

He leans back in his cushy, high-back chair and brings his fingertips together, a smile playing on his lips. "I'll allow a question, just once, Trainee Scum." He nods.

"Why do you hate humans so?"

He chuckles. "Of course, you wouldn't understand. Well, allow me to begin your education." He rubs a black ring on one of his fingers. "We do not hate humans."

I furrow my brow.

"The Enemy created humans and sees himself as a father figure of sorts. As such, he will do whatever he must to protect and nurture them." He grins. "They are his greatest weakness, and we have found ways to exploit that to our advantage."

The Almighty created us too, but I won't confuse reality with facts. My stomach twists.

A rapping on the door interrupts. "Enter."

"I'm sorry for interrupting, Headmaster Arioch," Umbrelle says behind me.

I don't dare turn. No doubt I haven't earned the privilege.

The male bobs his head, and I hear Ms. Admin's shoes scuff on the wood floor, and she appears beside me.

"It's her schedule, sir." She hands him a single sheet of paper.

Out of the corner of my eye, I spot her preening, running a hand through several of the long locks that have breached her shoulder and rest on her bosom.

I barely resist fidgeting when his gaze lingers on her cleavage for way too long, but at length, he clears his throat and smiles. "Thank you, Umbrelle."

"It was my pleasure, sir." With that she turns.

I may be sick. My skin crawls just thinking about what may well go on between these two behind closed doors.

Arioch moves the folder toward him absently, like he's trying to remember where he left off with me, as the door snits shut. He glances down and studies the top page. At length he frowns and looks back up. "You've killed a total of five demons over two occasions, Trainee Scum. What's your story?"

I inhale sharply. How did he know? More importantly, how much should I reveal? Everything I've said here so far has been used against me. I raise a hand, wanting to brush my bare scalp, but I think better of it and lower it again.

I open and close my mouth like a fish out of water as I organize my thoughts. Finally, I decide on, "Technically, I only killed three, sir."

His frown morphs into a scowl. "As if that makes it any better. So you admit you killed several."

I bite my lip and in a hush say, "Yes, sir."

He motions with a hand for me to continue.

"The first, I killed while on a mission for the Almighty to save humans buried in a rockslide." Surely they can't hold that against me. I was a warrior.

I was…. My heart pangs, but a blaring alarm cuts my thoughts short. I plug my ears, my gaze bouncing about the space.

Headmaster Arioch looks to the ceiling and huffs, not that I can hear him over the alarm. He fumbles under his desk, and the alarm quiets.

I look around, despite probably not having earned the privilege, just as the door to the office bursts open. I pivot in time to see Umbrelle along with two beefy males thunder in.

"I've got it under control. You may go." Arioch waves them off.

The trio scans me up and down as if I'm the cause before turning around.

I'm hardly the culprit. Find another scapegoat.

I turn back around as the headmaster growls, "The Enemy's name is never to be uttered here or anywhere else in the second heaven. Is that clear?"

My mouth drops open. "I caused that?" I realize only after the words are out that not only did I not ask permission to speak, but I also forgot to add the honorific part. So, yell at me some more.

"What do you think?" He straightens the papers before him.

"Yes?" It comes out higher pitched than I like, and I scrunch my face. I guess I am the culprit. How was I to know?

"Do I make myself clear, Trainee Scum?" he repeats the imperative, eyes glaring at me.

I cough. "Perfectly, sir."

Guess it's a good thing I never came to second heaven before, even though that major made a big stink about it. Our squad surely would have been found out.

My heart pangs at the thought of my friends, but there's no time to pine because Arioch says, "Finish your story."

I quickly recount the barest of details of my exploits in decapitating those mongrels. I'm still not sorry.

He exhales loudly once I finish. "While we and demons don't see eye to eye all the time"—I tilt my head. That's interesting. I always thought demons and Fallen were in league with one another—"Demons want to indwell a host to control it." He draws a hand to his broad chest. "We find indwelling a human needlessly time consuming. We have far more… creative and interesting ways to accomplish our desires." His gray eyes dance.

My chest tightens.

"Nevertheless, we are aligned in our objectives, and they are helpful to our cause."

Oh, boy.

"Word will no doubt get out…." A corner of his mouth hitches.

Yeah, and I bet I know someone who will happily help that along.

"No one here cares, but don't expect any help if you find yourself at the mercy of a demon. We believe in education through natural consequence when possible." He snorts.

My stomach goes hard.

He runs a finger along the edge of the folder.

"Permission to ask another question, sir."

His eyebrows become a unibrow as he frowns.

Before he can decline, I barrel headlong. "How long will I be enrolled here?"

He leans back in his chair. "As long as it takes for us to determine that you will be an asset to the cause, of course."

"Who is 'us'?" It slips out, but I'm on a roll.

His eyes dance, but he gives no reply. Rather, he says, "Do not fail, Trainee Scum. Those who do not measure up are sent to be grunts with demons. And it seems you have more reason than most to avoid that."

My eyes go wide.

Knocking draws his attention to the door. "Come in."

I pivot to see a toned male in a black, thigh-length tunic with matching pants enter. Begrudgingly, I acknowledge his beauty, because it's true despite his overlong hair, though he's got nothing on Kessien's good looks. Call me biased, I don't care.

"Headmaster Arioch." The male nods, acknowledging his superior as he shifts the couple of books he's carrying.

Arioch motions him forward with a hand. "Dante, meet our newest arrival. I'm sure Umbrelle filled you in. I felt that you have excelled in your studies, and I want to reward you by making you her mentor."

The male's pinched expression, along with hands that briefly clench, doesn't tell me he appreciates the headmaster's praise. Nevertheless, he says, "Thank you, Headmaster. I'm not worthy of the honor."

I narrow my eyebrows. *Brownnoser.*

Arioch chuckles. "Dante, as always, you're too modest. I know you'll ensure she successfully completes her education here."

"I'll do my best, sir." He forces a smile that doesn't reach his eyes.

"That's all I ask." The headmaster smiles warmly at Dante, and I may just barf. "Refer to her as Trainee Scum until she earns more."

A corner of Dante's mouth hitches. How I wish his first positive reaction to being assigned to me was from something other than my ludicrous moniker.

He brushes his long bangs back with a hand, making me a little jealous. With narrowed amethyst eyes, he looks me up and down, holding his gaze on my bare scalp for several uncomfortable seconds, during which I force myself not to twitch. I exhale when he finally looks back to the headmaster.

"I understand, sir."

I'm sure he does. Especially my name.

Arioch hands him my schedule, which he scans.

Turning to me, he says, "Looks like we're in the same class. Temptation. A good place to start your initiation."

Temptation? Initiation? I barely bite back a comment.

"With your permission, Headmaster."

Arioch raises a finger. "A moment, Dante, in private. Trainee Scum, please wait outside."

I've no idea what that's about, but I make my way out the door and close it behind me. While curiosity has me wanting to linger, Umbrelle's presence makes it impossible, so I stand out of the way with my hands clasped in front of me, not saying a word to the admin who ignores me.

Just as well. No good thing could come from her acknowledging me.

Thankfully it's not long before Dante emerges. He turns to me and, with a sneer, says, "Come, Trainee Scum." He accents that last word.

Chapter Twenty-One

Kessien

"So what's your plan?" Jael asks, leaning in.

I draw a hand to the back of my neck where I sit propped against one of the wooden benches that surround the sawdust-covered floor of the training ring. I'm still breathing hard from Jael pummeling me, as I scan my three squad mates. I may rank higher than them, but rank hardly matters right now. They're my closest friends, and I'm actually pleased that they want to help.

I blow out a breath. "I don't actually have one, but I gave Glad my word that I'd find a way to reverse her banishment. After humans screwed up, the Almighty found it in his heart to forgive them, so there has to be a way to accomplish the same for her. We just have to figure out how."

"We need to find her first," Aliyah interjects.

"Yes, there is that." I crack a smile, to which Issra looks skyward, shaking his head, but he's chuckling, clearly relieved I relented and am letting them help.

Jael exhales loudly. "Astread could probably help us with that."

I furrow my brow. "How so?"

Aliyah perks up. "Yes, that's brilliant. With her new role, she has access to the Tree of Insight." Her expression turns serious. "And assisting might help her heal from losing Glad too."

Issra runs a hand through his curly locks. "I think this might help us all heal." He tilts his head. "On the bright side, there's nothing like having third heaven's most secret information at your fingertips."

Jael bobs his head. "She can probably figure out who Glad's escorts to second heaven were and where they took her. It's at least a place to start." He holds up a hand. "But we don't want to cause her any problems."

"Completely agree. Let's see what she can do." I blow out a breath. It's a start. I draw a hand to my chest. "You all are amazing. I don't deserve you."

"Darn right, you don't." Aliyah's voice is joking, but there's sadness there too as she extends a hand to help me up.

Gratefulness fills my chest. I'd no idea how I would accomplish my promise, but I'm desperate to.

Issra unfurls his wings. "Well, what are we waiting for?"

"Nothing, absolutely nothing." I stretch out my wings.

"Um…" Aliyah grimaces. "No offense, but I think we should change."

I chuckle. "Probably a good idea."

We all shift into something more appropriate than our sweaty leathers, namely dressy casual; we males sport button-downs and slacks while Aliyah dons a feminine peach dress.

"Let me let Astread know to expect her favorite fan club." I reach out to her telepathically as we launch. Fingers crossed she's not too busy.

It's not long before we land in the tree-lined, grassy courtyard in front of the Central Insight Agency, a heptagonal, two-story, translucent office building that's sandwiched between the crystal palace on the left and the Celestial Guard's headquarters on the right. The verdant Tree of Insight stands in the building's center courtyard, towering a good story taller than the building itself.

Astread bursts out of the building's front doors and jogs toward us despite her heels. "What a nice surprise."

She's frequented our break room over the last month and we've paid her none too few visits since she was reassigned, but this is the first time we've paid her a visit during work hours.

She envelops Aliyah in a hug, then moves on to the rest of us.

When she gets to me, she places a hand on my cheek. "I knew you loved her. I didn't know the full extent. I'm sorry."

I try to take a deep breath as I choke back grief. "I should have told her."

Earlier, while we were on our way back to the squadron from the palace, she filled us in on her final moments with Glad. She fought emotion the whole time and brought me to tears, that's for sure. So much so that Aliyah had to be the one to tell her of our experience before the Almighty's throne. Yes, we males couldn't handle it.

Stepping back, she says, "Thanks for coming." Her voice breaks, and judging by her trembling chin, she looks to be in the same spot as me. I'm glad we came. We need each other.

Astread swallows hard, reigning in her emotions.

"I was wondering…" I push the grass with the toe of my shoe. "We don't want to presume, but…"

Astread pulls at her dress's collar as she furrows her brow. "What is it?"

"We don't want to get you in trouble, but…," Issra adds, his shoulders drooping.

She looks him up and down and takes to rubbing an eyebrow.

"We were wondering if you have access to records that might help us locate Glad." I draw my arms across my chest.

Her eyes go wide. "You want to go after her?"

She looks like she's holding her breath.

I nod. "We do."

The others mimic.

Her mouth drops open, then she wraps her arms about herself as tears spill down her cheeks. "I haven't cried this much in ages." She sniffs, then wipes her eyes.

Jael clears his throat. "Like we said, we don't want to get you in trouble."

Astread shakes her head. "I'll be careful. Count me in."

We collapse into one large group hug. It's a long minute before I step back, regaining my composure.

"Come on in. You can finally meet my co-workers." Astread extends an open palm toward the front doors of her office building.

It takes no convincing, and we all traipse after her.

"Soldin, these are my friends. I want them to meet my co-workers," she says to a guard I've never seen before just inside the doors.

Like usual, that's all it takes to move past security, although I guarantee it'd be a different story if she wasn't here.

We turn right out of the entry and I run a hand over the walls that are covered in a gnarled, interwoven texture. The whole building is one big mass of tree roots to the Tree of Insight and they glow. It's how the Tree of Insight connects all of its users, at least that's what Astread told us. Apparently, wall art is strictly forbidden.

I again feel like what I imagine an ant experiences navigating its home with rounded root tunnel hallways that branch off every so often. The halls are brisk with angelic traffic as we pass the Office of Public Affairs, the Facilities and Logistics Services Office, the Applications and Data Office, and many more as we make our way to and then up the ramp that leads to the second floor where we head into the Resource Planning Office.

"Guys, I want you to meet my squadron." Astread's eyes sparkle as co-workers pop their heads out of the cozy cocoon workspaces formed by the roots. "This is Nanaelle, Conah, and Rhamiel."

Nanaelle, a particularly chic dresser with a stylish red dress and matching heels, extends a hand. "I'm so pleased to finally get to meet you. Astread's told us so much about you. She's been a great addition to our team. We're thankful to have her."

Conah and Rhamiel extend similar greetings, and I judge them to be decent enough males for our Astread. I chuckle to myself.

"We best let you get back to work. There's so much to do and not much time." Astread extends an open palm, directing us. "Let's go to a conference room where we can talk."

I glance in Astread's workspace as we pass and notice she's added a picture of the squad since the last time we visited.

A couple minutes later, Astread closes the door to a small room, and we take seats around a long table.

"We should have privacy here."

"Your co-workers seem nice." I run a hand over the smooth wood top.

Astread smiles as she sits at the head. "They are. We're working on finding hosts for several children that are expected soon. But you didn't come here to talk about that." She leans in, her expression turning hopeful. "You mentioned going after Glad. What did you have in mind?"

Issra reclines back in the comfortable, black leather chair and starts jiggling a leg beside me.

I catch Jael's eye across from me, then look back at Astread. "Do you have access to any information about maybe who escorted her to second heaven and where they took her, at least as a place to start?"

Aliyah raises a hand. "Without getting yourself in trouble."

Astread taps a finger against her lips, her gaze on the ceiling. "Honestly, I've never tried accessing anything not directly related to this child hosting project, but…."

Issra's eyes go wide when she pushes back the section of the table directly in front of her to reveal what looks like a bunch of roots with nodules.

Her fingers hover over the round knots as, to herself, she asks, "How to phrase a query so as not to raise questions?"

Aliyah rolls her chair closer to Jael to get a better look.

Astread starts touching various bumps. "Do the Almighty's attendants ever venture beyond the throne room in service?"

Issra furrows his brow. "We know they do. They escorted Glad."

Astread holds up a hand.

A hum breaks the silence and she tears off the paper that appears from a slot in the table, then reads, "In what capacity are you interested?"

Astread wags her brows, then types, "In helping to organize arriving children."

Jael grabs the paper when it appears. "They can assist in such a capacity if called upon."

"One more question." She chuckles, then starts brushing the nodules. "To ensure they are safe to attend children, have any of them been anywhere"—she glances around the table—"concerning"—she smiles as she continues stroking the bumps—"in the past week? Because that will disqualify them. We can never be too careful when it comes to the spirits of children."

I shake my head, then grab the response when it appears. I snort. "It's a list of four."

Astread grins and holds up a finger. "To clarify, please provide location-tracking for each of them."

Jael grabs the response. "They were in contact with second heaven earlier today. Their coordinates are listed here."

Issra high-fives me.

"You're brilliant, Astread." I lean across the table and snatch the paper from Jael, then wave it. "Let's go find her."

Chapter Twenty-Two

The door to the headmaster's office hasn't even shut, and Dante practically throws my schedule at me. "I see you've pissed off the wrong people already, Trainee Scum. Brilliant, just brilliant." Under his breath he adds. "He hates me."

The plain, white, institutional walls and worn linoleum of the hallway come into view as he strides right.

"Why do you say that?" I grab the paper out of the air.

Dante practically runs into another student in his haste, drawing a scowl. He doesn't apologize, much less excuse himself.

"Sorry," I mouth, scurrying after. I'm rewarded with an obscene gesture.

Jerk.

I shake my head and hurry to keep up as Dante continues taking long steps to wherever we're going—temptation class I'd wager— ignoring my question.

He pauses for half a second. "Were you the cause of that alarm?"

I scrunch up my face.

He rolls his eyes. "Of course you were." He resumes striding past what I'm guessing are more offices on both sides of the hall.

"How was I supposed to know what would happen if I said—"

He whirls around, his bangs swishing, covering half of his face, but the look he shoots me with the amethyst eye I can still see cuts me off.

"What? I wasn't going to say… that name," I grind out, waving my schedule. I feel like slapping him, but that would probably land me in more trouble.

We reach a stairway at the end of the hall and head up. Emerald-color paint has chipped off the metal of the handrail as well as the decorative metal balusters. I grab the ball top of a post and propel myself up after my gazelle-of-a-mentor as he takes two stairs at a time.

A bell clangs as we head up the second flight, and the sounds of doors opening and voices mixed with laughter greet us, but he doesn't stop, nor look back, just grips his books as he continues up.

A pair of students snicker at my lack of hair as they pass, heading down.

I feel like mimicking the gesture that the jerk downstairs gave me, but I resist.

Another student bumps me as he passes me, heading upstairs, and I roll my eyes.

Seriously?

Other students, arms stacked with books or shouldering backpacks, pass us, heading up or down as we near the third landing. Several give my bare head and leathers long looks. Some titter, others laugh outright. I shrug it off, or at least try to.

My breathing labors, but Dante bounds up another flight before stopping on the fourth landing and turning. Shock of all shocks, he's waiting for me.

His breathing is a bit labored, and I cheer inwardly. "You're not as out of shape as I figured." It comes out a snip.

I'm still breathing hard, and my mouth drops open. "I was a warrior—" The words taste like ash on my tongue.

Frowning, he holds up his free hand. "You have no past, only the present and the future. Clear?" It comes out a growl.

It's not the first time I've heard that, that traitorous major nearly melted down on our way here trying to instill that notion in me. My response now is what it was then, like hell I don't. They can't just erase my friends. They can't erase Kessien. I refuse.

I grunt, and he rolls his eyes, shaking his head and turning.

Students duck into rooms, the hall emptying, as another bell clangs, and it's just us left.

Beside me, he says, "You're going to have to be open to changing or you're going to have a very difficult transition."

I frown, looking ahead.

Without warning, Dante brings his forearm up and connects with my collarbone. He pushes me across the width of the hall. So sudden is his move that I don't think about blending and my head slams against the institutional white wall halfway between two doors. Forearm still up, he presses, pinning me as he gets in my face.

"You have a huge chip on your shoulder. Let's get this straight, *you fell*, Trainee Scum. You're not a little angel anymore."

My nostrils flare.

He chuckles, his nose an inch from mine. "What? Don't like me calling you a little fallen angel?"

I grit my teeth and push against his arm, but he doesn't budge. On the contrary, his books thud to the floor and he adds his other arm, pressing me harder into the wall. "Fume all you want, Trainee Scum, but stop lying to yourself."

I re-center enough to blend with the wall, but with the pressure, Dante pushes me clear through, right into whatever class is meeting in this room and into the first desk, and I stumble back.

"Hey," the exclamation sounds and someone scrambles out of the way.

Dante grabs the collar of my leathers, righting me, but he's not letting go. At least he stops pushing. "Apologies, instructor. I have a new mentee that needs to learn her place." He raises his free hand, appealing to the female at the front.

Every eye is on us. A few students grin.

"We'll be going now." With that he yanks me back through the wall.

The instant we're back in the hall, he's pulling me close by my collar. His hair flops down in his face, again covering half, but his amethyst eye is fierce. "Get this through your thick head, Trainee

Scum. You're no better than anyone else here. Get used to it." He shoves me.

I huff. I'm not a rag doll.

But he's not done. "And if you *ever* try that stunt again, you will rue the day. Do I make myself clear?"

I want to blow his floppy hair out of my face, but I resist.

When I don't answer right away, he jerks me again. "Do I?"

"Perfectly." I scowl.

He glowers, still in my face for several more seconds, before releasing me.

I jerk to adjust my leathers, then swipe my schedule off the floor. Going with him is the last thing I want to do, but what choice do I have? No doubt he'd tackle me if I tried to flee. Even if he didn't, where would I go?

He picks up his books, then heads past two more doors, holding the next one open for me. I don't mistake his actions for chivalry, not after that altercation.

I give him a side glance as I go through, into the dim, worn institutional classroom, then stop, cutting off whatever the hunk of an attractive male at the front was about to say. He's not beautiful like Kessien, but my eyes wouldn't mind lingering on him.

The room's silence interrupts my woolgathering, and I swallow, grasping my schedule in a tight fist. Seven pairs of eyes stare at me.

Welcome to temptation class….

The male at the front is the first to move, nodding at Dante as he stops beside me.

"Sorry to be late, Forcas." Dante draws himself up to full height, like he's not sorry at all.

The instructor takes a few steps toward us, then stops. "Ambrielle mentioned you'd be late because you were called to Headmaster Arioch's office." He crosses his arms and leans back, a grin erupting on his face. "But who do we have here?"

It's all I can do not to squirm under his gaze.

Dante eyes me. "He assigned me a mentee." He flexes his fingers. "This is Trainee Scum." Several of the class snicker. "Call her that until she earns more."

The response to his verbal jab digs, but making things worse, I feel really out of place standing here in my leathers. The three females sport dresses or tops and slacks, and the four guys, including Dante, wear tunics and pants, though they're all different colors and patterns.

Only the teacher and I are dressed differently, but even he fits in with his cream turtleneck, cream slacks, and cream longcoat with upturned collar—seems he's taken his course to heart and made himself tempting eye candy, not that I have a taste for it.

Between my leathers and lack of hair, I do my best not to fidget. No doubt that's the point—it's another way to try and break me down.

Hair and clothes don't matter. They don't... much. Oh, who am I kidding?

I sigh to myself.

Dante heads to a desk in the middle of the second row, between a female in a casual black dress and a male with a man bun, and sits, leaving me to figure out my own seating.

Thanks, just thanks, ya jerk.

While I have four empty rows to choose from, I opt for the third and ease into the chair directly behind Dante, alone in the row of four desks, as everyone but Dante watches.

Forcas saunters forward and stops just before the first row. "Trainee Scum." The way he says it makes it sound like he's rolling it around on his tongue.

My stomach twists.

"A new initiate." His blue eyes sparkle as he cracks his knuckles.

Chapter Twenty-Three

"I assume by the addition of those four little letters to your name as well as the fact that you have no hair…" My heart climbs into my throat as Forcas pauses for way too long. "… that you've already demonstrated no little obstinacy to accepting your position with us."

"She's got a superiority complex," Dante interjects.

Thanks for clarifying that, mentor.

Forcas tilts his head. "Does she now? That takes courage considering you're *all alone* in a world new to you."

I shift in my chair, wishing I could just tell them to leave me alone.

"Quite impressive—not very smart—but quite impressive." He looks to the peeling ceiling as if thinking. "Honestly, I can't remember the last time a female joined us without hair." He clucks his tongue and shakes his head.

Everyone but Dante is still turned toward me, and the female in the black dress beside Dante chortles.

Arms crossed, Forcas draws a hand to his chiseled chin and starts moving a finger back and forth. "I had other plans for today, but I think with our new initiate, I'm going to change things up a bit." He wags his eyebrows.

I clutch my schedule below the desk as my breathing labors.

"Yes." He runs a hand through his short, perfectly styled locks. "Where to start for a problem like this?" It sounds like he's thinking out loud, but I'm sure it's part of the show, just for me.

Dante continues ignoring me. I wish they all would.

The instructor raises a finger. "I have it. I think we should begin her initiation with a field trip to Earth with a séance. I just happen to know of one that's about to start."

A couple of the guys snort.

Isn't that convenient? But a séance? Surely no. My feet take to bouncing.

"Come, everyone and Trainee Scum." Forcas motions the class forward with the wave of his hand.

Right, because I haven't earned the privilege of being considered "everyone" yet. I roll my eyes to myself, but a séance? Communicating with the spirits of the dead is frowned upon where I come from, and for good reason. It opens a human to demonic possession, and I am not down with that.

The thought of a demon being present sends a chill up my spine. Will there be more than one? Will it or they recognize me and attack? Also, what am I to do if Forcas forces me to participate? I can't see it going any other way.

I stuff my schedule into a pocket of my leathers and ease up from the desk, every muscle in my body resisting because this is a really, really bad idea.

I amble forward—I guess that's what you'd call my snail's pace—and join the others circling up. Dante is already holding hands with a female in white jeans and a male with a cleft in his chin on the other side by the time I get there. I end up beside Forcas.

Of course I do. Like that wasn't planned. I growl to myself.

The male on my other side frowns when I grab his hand. *Tough.*

I give him a toothy grin and squeeze.

Everything goes dark for several seconds until a dim room with five people seated around a decorative, cloth-covered, circular table comes into view, and we drop hands. The scent of cinnamon fills the air. The only illumination is from three candles, one white, one violet, and one blue.

I barely stifle a shriek when a hideous, junior-size demon nearly collides with Dante as it swoops. He barely gets an arm up in time to deflect it; then he swats at it.

The thing bounces off my mentor, screeching its upset, then beats its wings and regains altitude, joining another junior-size demon and a larger one circling the ceiling.

Crap. Crap. Triple crap.

Forcas chuckles. "Oh, we're going to have fun."

Ain't no way. I can only hope these menaces don't recognize me.

The male whose hand I squeezed nudges the female beside him, smirking.

Our teacher points. "See those candles, in those colors? Seems their leader has been led to believe they enhance psychic powers and communication." Forcas grins. "We'll show them enhanced."

Another of my classmates, a female with fancy nails, snorts. I shift from one foot to the other, praying those menaces don't spot me.

I go completely still, and my stomach twists as I make out a bony hand on one of the participants. It's clutching the back of a short-haired, brunette woman's neck part way around the table. I can't see the rest of the demon at this angle, but there's no mistaking that bony appendage.

"Is everyone ready? You all have your questions prepared?" the brunette asks.

Crud. Seems she's the leader. Figures. No doubt that creepy tagalong called its buddies and they're just waiting for an opportunity to control one of these people.

The four humans bob their heads.

"Seems we're just in time," Forcas oozes, straightening his jacket's lapels.

Barf-ola. Ooze somewhere else.

"Then let's begin." The woman closes her eyes, and the others follow.

Forcas rubs his hands together. "Yes, let's do."

The airborne demons shriek. Do they sense something? Or is that leach communicating with them?

I bite my lip. With Forcas's glee, all I can think about are the three primary objectives Arioch said the Fallen seek to accomplish when it comes to humans: exercise power and control over them—check, at least of this leader—make them betray what they care about, and, just short of killing them, make their lives a living hell.

"Everyone join hands." The leader reaches for her neighbors, and the demons sound off again.

"No doubt her demon has her thinking that joining hands keeps the 'psychic energy' in the circle." Our teacher snickers. "Humans are so gullible."

Chills mount my back. A corner of Dante's mouth hitches.

"Tonight we gather to seek guidance from the spirit world."

"And we'll be generous with it." Forcas bounces on his toes.

My chest tightens. None of these people have any clue that their leader's possessed or the danger they're flirting with.

"We welcome any spirits who are near us to join our circle. Please make your presence known."

The three demons take to swooping inside the circle before taking another lap around the ceiling.

"Watch this." Forcas nods as a junior demon brushes one of the women's hair.

The auburn woman starts, inhaling sharply. "I… I think I felt something… on my head."

I furrow my brow and, in a hushed tone, ask, "How… how did that woman feel it?"

Forcas draws a hand to his chest, a smile playing on his lips. "Oh, I might have had a little something to do with that."

I give him a disbelieving look. A couple of my classmates do too. At least I'm not alone this time.

"Very good, Gladys. Go ahead and ask your question."

Eyes still shut, the woman sits up and squares her shoulders, like she's summoning her courage. She's no idea. "Will... will I ever find love?"

"Spirit, we ask you to rap once for 'yes' or twice for 'no,'" the leader says.

Forcas raps the table once.

I'm surprised. What's so harmful about that?

The auburn-haired woman smiles.

Forcas strides behind the leader's back and grabs the cling-on by the back of the neck, making it hiss. "Demon, you will yield to me." The parasite growls but doesn't resist further. "Tell the leader her client will only find love if she nearly dies saving another."

I bring a fist up and bite the side of a finger. Is that true? How would he even know? There's no way he does. I barely suppress a huff. He's weaving lies, and she'll never know.

The leader recites what Forcas said, and the questioner's shoulders slump.

Point number three, just short of killing humans, make their lives a living hell. He'll accomplish that with this woman alright. I clench my teeth.

My classmates share mixed reactions, but none are incensed, not like me.

Were they always like this, indifferent to humans? The thought brings me up short. No, couldn't be. We all came from the third heaven. Another question piles on. Will I eventually be like them? My stomach twists. I can't let that happen. I can't.

I duck when a demon gets too close for comfort above me.

A man with curly, chocolate-brown hair goes next. His voice wavers as he asks, "My son needs a new heart. Will we find one in time?"

Forcas thumps the table twice, and I sigh.

Destroy all hope. Again, number three, make his life a living hell.

The woman across from him asks, "My husband and I are having... difficulties. Will we ever get past our differences?"

Forcas doesn't thump the table, he just tells the demon to pass on a message. "You will soon meet a seductive man who will sweep you off your feet. Allow him to."

I close my eyes. He's suggesting an extra-marital affair. And that would be a definite number two, make them betray what they care about.

My stomach goes hard. What will the last man ask? And what will Forcas do to him?

Chapter Twenty-Four

The final participant says, "I'm thinking about running for public office. Will I be elected?"

Forcas's face lights up. This can't be good.

His hand still grasps that hideous abomination attached to the leader's neck as he scans the eight of us; then he points at me. The female next to Dante chuckles.

My heart speeds.

"Come here, Trainee Scum." His tone leaves no room for argument.

The demons' squawks bounce off the ceiling as I amble over to him, dread filling me.

Forcas grabs my wrist the instant I get close enough, closing the gap with a hard yank. Worse, I'm inches from the demon that I really want to snatch off this woman.

He brings his mouth up to my ear, making my scalp prickle. He growls loud enough for my classmates to hear, "When I give you an order, you will comply *immediately*. Is that clear, Trainee Scum?"

Not missing a beat, I straighten, hitting his face with my hard leathers as I throw my shoulders back, and belt out, "Yes, sir."

He recovers with a huff. I cheer to myself because he asked for that.

A couple of my classmates stifle chuckles. The guy with the man bun even coughs.

His hand is cold as he shifts it to the back of mine and replaces his hand with mine on the demon's neck.

My stomach goes tight. I've never touched a demon before, and it's as gross as I imagined, with coarse hair and dry skin. With the force Forcas is employing, there's no way I'm moving my hand.

"Pinch its neck as hard as you can or it won't obey."

Despite my revulsion, I pinch the loose skin, making the thing squeak, to which Forcas nods.

"Repeat your question," the human leader suggests when he still hasn't gotten a reply.

"I'm thinking about running for public office. Will I be elected?"

"Tell it to have the leader ask, 'Will you allow the spirits to lead you?'"

I do as bid despite my legs twitching. I fear where this might go.

"Uh… yes, certainly. I'll allow the spirits to guide me," the man replies.

Forcas wags his brows as he says to the room, "The politicians always do."

He releases my hand and grabs the demon's neck again. "Trainee Scum, move behind the future politician. Go. Quickly."

Again I belt out, "Yes, sir."

Even Dante smirks this time despite Forcas's face being out of the line of fire. Too bad.

I stride to behind the human and stop.

Am I going to have to pinch this man's neck too? How will he even feel it? Or will Forcas do his hocus-pocus again? I despise hurting humans, but at least it'll be quick.

"The leader invited this demon into her life. In a case where a demon's presence is needed long-term, a similar invitation must be made and you, Trainee Scum, will be the one to do it for this man."

"What? No." I can't keep the horror that overwhelms me out of my tone, and I shake my head. There's no way I'm doing that to this man.

Forcas bares his white teeth. "Oh, but you will, Trainee Scum. You have no choice."

My classmates' eyes ping-pong between Forcas and me.

I cross my arms. "No, you can't make me. I won't do that to this man."

The séance leader leans forward. "I sense a disturbance, perhaps a greater message for you, Carl. Let's wait a bit longer."

I'll show them a disturbance alright.

The man nods, his mouth in a line.

"Dante. Sorath." Forcas nods to my mentor and the guy whose hand I held coming here, and the pair stride for me. Without warning, they both grab one of my hands.

"Stop, let go of me." I struggle to break free, but they're a whole lot bigger and stronger than me, and they wrap my hands around the human's neck.

One of my female classmates, the one wearing the black dress, draws a fist to her mouth—is she commiserating with me? The one with fancy nails grins.

The swooping demons shriek, clearly sensing something's up.

"You will now invite, oh, let's see…" Forcas taps his chin. "I think *two* of these demons to control this man. He'll be wildly popular."

"No. I won't." I struggle against my captors, yanking my hands, to no avail.

"Perhaps Trainee Scum needs a demonstration. Dante, since she is your mentee, please do the honors with one demon."

I yank the hand free that Dante holds when he leans back, and he gives me a frown.

"Don't do this to this man, Dante. Please." It comes out a strangled whisper that I hope only he can hear.

Dante looks to the three swooping demons. "Demons in this room, I invite one of you into this man to control him and do your will to accomplish his political aspirations."

No. No. No.

The trio dive, and Dante steps back to avoid the melee of wings.

One hand still held tight in Sorath's grasp, I duck, then shriek as their wings brush my back and neck. Sorath covers his head with his free arm.

"I said *one* of you, not all of you." Dante steps forward and grabs one of the creatures that's flailing, flapping its wings in the confined space. "You."

The other two squawk, then take flight.

I straighten but stay back, completely grossed out by Dante holding the thing around its neck, away from his body, as it continues flapping its leathery wings.

He brings the demon's head toward me, and I nearly screech, but he angles it toward the man's neck. The thing's flailing wings brush against my leathers, and I shield with my free arm as I step as far away as I can, which isn't far since Sorath still holds one of my hands against the man's neck.

The demon opens its mouth and clamps down with its spiky teeth, right beside my splayed fingers. Dante releases it and steps back as it finally furls its wings and makes a cooing sound as if it's content.

Content my eye. I want to scream, to yank the thing off the would-be politician, but Dante grabs my free hand.

The man sits up straight, and his eyes go wide. "I feel... I feel... different."

"That's wonderful, Carl. Let's wait a bit longer to see if the spirits are done."

It's not wonderful, Carl. It's anything but.

"It's your turn, Trainee Scum." Dante's expression holds no playfulness. He leans forward, and under his breath, he adds, "Don't make me look bad."

Look bad? This is a human's life we're talking about, and he's worried about looking bad? Seriously?

The remaining two demons flit about the ceiling, oblivious to my outrage.

When I don't respond, Dante nods and Sorath steps back, retreating to the circle. I jerk my hand away, but Dante tugs my arm, drawing me closer still. Bringing his lips to my ear, he growls, "If you don't comply, I will announce to Forcas, to our classmates, and especially to those demons that you killed three of their brethren."

I suck in a breath. How does he know? Arioch. Has to be. That little conference they had, just the two of them in his office. I should have known.

Dante's hair flops in front of half his face as he continues, "I can assure you they will react, and not alone."

I let my shoulders slump and stop struggling with the hand Dante holds. "You wouldn't."

Dante forces a grin that doesn't reach the eye I can see. "Try me."

Is this what happened to my classmates when they first arrived? Have they been beaten down from being exploited like this? Or do they just not understand the ramifications of demon possession on people? I have a hard time believing that.

Maybe they just don't care. Is that even possible?

I look into Dante's eye. He said I couldn't ask about "before," but his coming seems like fair game.

"Is this what happened to you when you first arrived? Did others force you to betray your convictions? Did they wear you down until you finally capitulated?" I speak quietly enough for only him to hear.

He brushes back his hair as his eyes widen. "We're not talking about me."

I keep my eyes locked with his.

It's a couple seconds, but he huffs then whispers, "You need to be more strategic in your objections. You can't refuse to comply with everything."

My eyes go wide. What's he saying?

"Hey, you two lovebirds, enough exchanging sweet nothings."

Sorath and Miss Nail Polish snort.

Dante and I both turn and frown at Forcas.

"Let's go." The instructor releases his demon's neck and claps.

"Trust me on this," Dante pleads, turning back to me. His shoulders drop.

Is he trying to manipulate me or is he serious? He grabs the back of his neck. I sense resignation, either that or he's putting on a good act, but I don't think so.

I swallow down revulsion as I study the demon already feasting on the man, no doubt implanting all manner of evil ideas in his mind. Can I let him be possessed by a second of these demons? Can I live with myself?

I've no idea how the demons flying around haven't figured out who I am, not that I'm complaining, but the thought of being attacked by a horde of demons terrifies me. Arioch said Fallen feel no compulsion to help if demons attack, so I'm on my own if I'm found out. My stomach twists. I well remember what they did to that angel, not to mention Astread.

I glance at Dante out of the corner of my eye. Can I trust him? He was nothing but horrible to me on our way to class, roughing me up against that wall.

Don't trust anyone here. That's the first lesson I've learned.

But what kind of life will I make for myself if I shut myself off from everyone, trusting no one?

Wait. Stop. How can I even consider trading demon possession of even one human with me not feeling isolated? What is wrong with me?

I scan the circle of my classmates. They act as if they're bored, what with their pinched expressions, heavy sighs, folded arms, and tapping feet.

I look more closely. Miss White Jeans smiles, but it wavers as she looks away. The guy with the man bun, his gaze keeps darting between me and Forcas. The male with the chin cleft pulls at an ear. The thin female in the black dress smooths her skirt.

They're not bored; they look conflicted.

Are we all at the mercy of Forcas? Do none of us have a choice? Do what the instructor says or… what?

I glance at Forcas, then back at Dante. He looks like he's holding his breath.

Against my better judgment, I bob my head.

Dante exhales. "That's a wise decision, Trainee Scum." While he uses that stupid name, his tone is soft. Under his breath he adds, "Let's get this over with."

Turning to the group, he announces, "Trainee Scum has made a wise decision."

"About time," a couple of my classmates mutter.

Miss Fancy Nails studies her nails.

"Well done, Dante." Forcas picks a string off his lapel and sniffs. "Please proceed."

My heart rate picks up as I look down at the man and the demon feeding on him, its disgusting, bony fingers touching him.

How can I do this? Carl's severely misguided.

"Call one of the demons to you," Dante coaches, clearly not giving me time to reconsider.

I'm going to hate myself. I already know it. I'm trading my miserable life for this man's because I'm afraid for my own hide. Is that pathetic or what?

"Trainee Scum." Dante squeezes my hand.

I swallow, hard, then look to the flying abominations swooping about the ceiling. Pulling my hand from Dante's, I say, "Smaller demon"—I'm certainly not taking a chance on the larger one— "come here if you want to—" My throat constricts, the words tasting like ash. "— control this stupid, stupid human who has idiotic political aspirations."

Bile burns the back of my throat. I may retch.

Both demons shriek, pushing me nearly over the edge. The smaller of the two swoops, and only Dante's steadying hand on my back keeps me from ducking.

"Catch it, Trainee Scum." It's an order.

My body knows what to do with orders. I lock my knees and throw my arms up, catching the demon around the neck. The thing flaps wildly just like the other one did, and I nearly let go when it brushes my bare scalp.

"Hang on to it, Trainee Scum. Bring it to the human."

I bite my lip, my arms trembling, but I manage to hold on to the disgusting, undulating thing and bring it to Carl's neck.

The thing opens its mouth to bite, and I pull it away. "No. Bad demon. You may not bite. You may only touch this human. Is that clear?"

The thing lets out a series of squawks. I've no idea what it's saying; I only hope it understands my directive.

"It's not happy, but it agreed. Let it latch on," Dante instructs.

I practically throw the thing at Carl's neck, eliciting another squawk, but it furls its wings and nestles beside its brother, extending its long, bony fingers at the base of the man's neck. It's so gross.

I shake my hands, glad to no longer be touching it, and turn to Dante. "How'd you know it agreed?"

"Just a guess. Why, did you want to keep holding it?"

"So it could have gone either way?" My voice rises.

Dante shrugs.

I roll my eyes.

I will never, ever forgive myself for unleashing a demon on that unsuspecting human. I'm a pathetic wimp.

My chest constricts. It's only my first day. If I gave in to Dante's cajoling that readily, what am I liable to do by the time they're done with me?

Chapter Twenty-Five

Kessien

"Squadron 132. Squadron 132." The alarm wheezes in my head, beside Astread in her conference room.

I throw a hand up to silence her midsentence as the heavenly dispatcher says, *"We've got a code 627 in Saint Rafael on the southern coast of France. An exorcism went wrong. Multiple humans involved. Proceed with caution. As an aside…"* The dispatcher's voice gentles. *"Archangel Michael sympathizes with your loss and feels that keeping you busy is the best way to help you cope."*

Astread's voice wobbles as she says, "Sounds like you've got work to do."

Work that she clearly misses despite feeling fulfilled in her current role.

"So it seems."

We all rise and push in our roller chairs.

"Thank you." I hold up the paper with Glad's coordinates. "You're helping in ways we don't have access to." I tuck it inside my pants pocket.

Astread nods, but it does nothing to ease the feeling of wrongness that she's not coming with us. From the looks on the others' faces, I'm not alone.

A second later, I've shifted into leathers, along with the others, and the four of us exchange quiet hugs with our missing squad mate.

"We'll let you know what we find." Aliyah draws her lips into a line as she steps back.

"The second we do," Issra adds, running a hand through his curly locks.

Astread crosses her arms and hugs herself, stepping back as we circle up and do our pre-mission rituals. She forces a smile and gives us a quick wave as we hold hands. My heart feels heavy, and it's all I can do to vanish us.

Red, clay-tile-roofed homes come into focus beside an idyllic coastal harbor with all manner of boats moored to a maze of docks. Gulls squawk, circling above, as we unfurl our wings.

I pinpoint the coordinates the dispatcher gave me and direct us to land on a wooden deck that's attached to the back of a large, two-story home overlooking the sea.

A scream from within the house pierces the calm, and we pair up, Jael joining me. I draw my celestial sword, we all do, and I motion us forward, through the tan stucco wall, silent as a whisper.

We follow the cacophony to the front room where a fuchsia-haired young woman dressed in goth apparel with multiple facial piercings sits on a wooden chair in the middle of the sparsely furnished room. She looks dazed but better than the dozen adults, both men and women, who have fallen down, surrounding her. They babble to themselves, some pull at their hair, others claw at themselves.

Every one of the Fallen has at least one demon feasting on them. Some have multiple.

The dispatcher said this is an exorcism gone wrong.

"How could this happen, God? We just wanted to free Macy from possession." A wail sounds from the far corner of the room. "Please make it stop. Save them. I beg of you."

It's another woman, hands clasp, eyes shut, tears streaming.

She's the only human not possessed.

No doubt it was her call that dispatch picked up on.

I motion Issra and Aliyah to take the far side of the room, then nod to Jael.

Together we start hacking on the demons feasting on six of the humans. They're so intent on their banquet that they never see us coming, and it's not long before the menaces have all vanished.

The dozen humans sit up and rub the back of their necks where the demons were feasting, shaking off the malaise.

The woman in the far corner rushes to them and falls on her knees, throwing her arms around a man. "I was so scared, Jason."

The man pivots and envelops the woman in strong arms. "Ashley, that was unreal. What happened?"

A man beside them shakes his head.

"I don't know. You all put a hand on Macy, and Ash commanded the demon to leave her. The next thing I know, you all collapsed and started babbling. It was like the demon came out of her and into you all. It scared me to death." She hugs Jason again.

"What happened to me?" Macy asks. "I feel different, better than in a really long time."

The humans fall into hugging and comforting each other.

Aliyah sheaths her blade. "I wish humans would instruct each other to never touch a demon-possessed person when exorcising it."

"Yeah, nothing like inviting the whole legion into a new host," Jael adds, shaking his head.

"They were lucky. There weren't that many demons in Macy," Issra says, nodding at Goth Girl. "It could have been a lot worse."

"Are we ready?" I interject, wagging my brows. I'm glad for the outcome, but I can barely contain my excitement. "These humans will be fine. I'd like to make a slight detour on our way home." I pull out the paper Astread wrote Glad's coordinates on, bringing smiles to everyone's faces. "I'll bring us close so we can get the lay of the land. Exercise dampening when unfurling your wings."

The three nod, and I vanish us.

A dry, barren wasteland riddled with rocky outcroppings amongst jagged craters appears below us where we hover when things come back into focus. A foul stench, like rotten eggs, makes me recoil.

Issra wrinkles his nose to my right.

"Oh, what died here?" Aliyah whispers, across from me.

"I'd wager it's burning sulfur," Jael offers in a hushed tone. "Brimstone."

Issra's eyes go wide.

It's dim, far darker than Earth. Seems the only light is from the sun that illuminates this part of the galaxy. The blackness of second heaven makes the stars look like twinkling diamonds and showcases the colorful planets on the horizon and beyond.

"Where's Glad?" Aliyah asks, beating her wings.

Indeed, where is she? I've never once visited second heaven, so I've no idea what to expect.

I consult the coordinates again, then point to my right. "She should be that way, not far."

My heart speeds as Jael falls in beside me while the others follow behind us as we fly toward where Glad was last known to be. I can't wait to see her again. There's so much I want to tell her.

"What are we going to do to rescue her once we find her?" Issra asks.

"I don't know. Let's see what we've got first," I call over my shoulder.

A hulking pair of wrought iron gates accented by an emerald dragon comes into view as we near. A group of six Fallen guards laze about on the smooth stone area in front of it.

If they were mine, I'd have words with them, but their lack of discipline doesn't surprise me. Excellence does not define our adversary—not that I'm complaining. It makes them easy to defeat.

Disappointment nibbles as I stop far enough away that those guards won't spot us, not with our muting. Nodding, I say, "They brought her there."

"A transfer point between second and third heaven." Jael frowns, then scans the area.

"So where'd they take her from here?" Issra blows out a breath and joins Jael's perusal of the area.

Aliyah's shoulders bow as she and I follow their lead. I'm not seeing so much as one measly structure; not a barracks, building, mansion, anything.

I don't know why I thought it would be easy to find her. I shake my head. Who am I kidding? I know why. Hope. My breath hitches. I love that female. It took losing her to make me realize just how much.

I clear my throat. "I've never considered where they actually live here."

"Maybe it's not far. Should we search a perimeter?" Jael draws a semicircle in the air.

"Sounds good to me." Jael and I take the lead again as we navigate, starting to the right of the gate, taking care to remain unseen.

"Demons." Jael points, not long after.

A pack of ten demons appears off to the right, headed our way. If we can see them, they can see us. My heart speeds. I pray they haven't. We can't be seen by those grudge-holders. They took revenge on Astread. Who knows what they'll do if they realize we're friends of an archnemesis. We've got to get out of here.

Grab on to me.

I feel hands, one on both of my feet, and another on a wingtip before I vanish us a safe distance away.

Issra's eyes are wide when we circle back up. "That was close."

Aliyah sets her jaw. "It was, but I'm not giving up that easily."

I smile. "Me either."

We turn and watch the pack return to specks before resuming our search for Glad.

It's a remote outpost, and I don't expect much activity, but we're scared into moving twice more by messengers or runners of some sort approaching the gate. Despite the jumpiness it creates in all of us, it gives me an idea.

We huddle up after completing our search of the area. "I think we should stake this place out and follow those messengers."

I furrow my brow, we all do, and start looking around.

The distinct sound of a trumpet fills the air; the notes aren't a sharp warning or quick blast like a rallying cry. They're slower, like whoever's sounding it is taking their sweet time. It lasts several seconds before it fades.

"What's—" I murmur without thought.

The six guards in front of the gate hear it too, judging by their swiveling heads.

It sounds again, and again lingers. The same lazy, unhurried tones.

Where's it coming from?

A third call sounds, just like the others.

"Squadrons 132, 698, 546, 427, 336. Report to third heaven's front gate, immediately." The telepathic message cuts off abruptly. I've never heard the dispatcher sound harried, nothing like this, and my stomach tenses.

"The front gates?" Aliyah questions.

"What's going on?" Issra searches mine and Jael's faces for answers we don't have.

Chapter Twenty-Six

Turns out I'm in Dante's espionage class too, along with three of the others from temptation class—Black Dress, Man Bun, and Cleft Chin—as I discover when Dante strikes up a conversation with Man Bun, leaving me to tag along behind him.

Black Dress and Cleft Chin move to flank me, and I've no clue what to do. I squeeze my schedule in a hand. Do I talk to them? I probably shouldn't. I couldn't have earned that privilege yet, and the last thing I need is for either of them to get in my face and yell at me.

I look straight ahead, leaving it up to them to make the first move, if they do.

"Looks like Trainee Scum is a bit stuck up," Cleft Chin says to Black Dress. "Won't even look at us. Are we that disgusting to you? Truly?"

I can't win for losing. I'm damned if I do, and I'm damned if I don't.

I scrunch my face as I look over at him. "Permission to speak, sir?"

Black Dress draws a hand to her chest. "Behold, Trainee Scum speaks. What have we done to merit such favor?"

I pivot my head toward her. "Permission to speak, ma'am?"

"Just spit it out, Trainee Scum." Black Dress rolls her eyes.

Spit it out? I raise my eyebrows.

"I got yelled at"—my stomach twists at the memory from just hours before—"for speaking out of turn. I didn't mean to come across as stuck up. I'm sorry."

Black Dress and Cleft Chin exchange nods; then she bumps my shoulder with hers. "We've been there too. They get you off-balance until you give in. By the way, I'm Ambrielle."

My chest loosens for the first time since I arrived. "Thanks for that, and it's great to meet you. I'm—"

Cleft Chin holds up a hand. "Don't tell us your name. If we slip and call you anything but Trainee Scum, we'll be the ones in trouble." He winks. "I'm Bethor."

"It's great to meet both of you." I may actually have the beginnings of two friendships. Or wait… are they just tempting me with friendship and I'm gullible enough to fall for it? Can I really trust them?

Ambrielle leans over and whispers, "Meet me after espionage, and I'll help you get some other clothes."

I inhale, then a small smile mounts my face. "Thank you so much."

She shrugs. "Hey, it's nothing. Been there. Done that."

Okay, I'm leaning toward trusting them whether I should or not.

Dante looks over his shoulder. "Wipe that smile off your face, Trainee Scum."

Bethor reaches forward and brings a folder down on his head. "Stop being a jerk."

Man Bun looks over his shoulder as Dante whirls around with an indignant look on his face.

I can't keep a snort in. Ambrielle bursts out laughing, drawing questioning looks from passing students.

My mentor shifts his books to his other hand. "You're corrupting my mentee. How am I ever going to instill discipline in her if you're being nice? I'm trying to keep us both out of trouble. If Mossad sees her smiling, I'll be in a world of hurt."

"And everything is about you, is it?" Man Bun asks Dante, raising an eyebrow.

I've no idea who Mossad is, but my mouth drops open and I cover it with a hand. Man Bun's ragging on him too?

Dante looks to the ceiling and shakes his head.

Man Bun turns to me. "I'm Nisroc, by the way."

"It's very nice to meet you." I bob my head, grinning. Yep, I'm definitely leaning toward trusting them.

"If you hadn't guessed, as a trainee you'll need to always look miserable to the teachers and big shots, or they'll make life miserable for both of you," Bethor adds, the cleft in his chin lengthening as he frowns.

From the hush that falls on all of them, he's not kidding, and I swallow. "Thanks for the heads-up."

"And on that cheery note...." Dante holds out his open palm and directs us toward the classroom we've reached.

I school my expression; we all do, as we follow Bethor into what must be espionage class.

The instant I enter, I feel eyes studying me. Instinct directs my gaze to a trim male standing at the front of the classroom, arms crossed, leaning back, wholly masculine in his black sweater with pushed-up sleeves and matching slacks. He wears a bracelet and a simple silver ring on his pinky finger that contrasts with the tattoos on his arms and neck. With his close-cropped, blond locks, close-set, obsidian eyes, and thin lips that I question whether they've ever cracked a smile, he exudes a fierce, stormy, mysterious vibe.

"Trainee Scum. There." Dante makes sure the teacher and two other students, both female, are watching as he points at a desk in the second row, behind the one he's dropped his books on.

Jerk. But what should I expect?

Nisroc and Bethor bookend him in the first row, completely ignoring me, while Ambrielle wrinkles her nose at me and takes a seat at the end of the second row, leaving an empty desk between us.

The disparity between their treatment in the hall and now would have left me questioning their sincerity if Bethor hadn't mentioned the expectation that as a noob they expect me to be miserable or Dante's not being hard enough on me.

How I pray I haven't been played for a fool.

The two other females opt for the third row after giving me cold looks as the bell rings.

Mossad steps forward. "We will be going on a field trip to Earth today."

My chest constricts. What will they make me do this time?

Straight-faced, he continues, "Since we have a new trainee, pop quiz, give me the ten rules of espionage. Nisroc, let's start with you. Give me two."

I can't help but still think of him as Man Bun as he leans forward. "Blend in as much as possible and assume nothing."

Mossad looks to the row behind me. "Give me two more, Diniel."

"Obey your gut and never look back because you're never alone."

Mossad clasps his hands behind his back and starts pacing across the front. "Ambrielle, two more."

"Vary your pattern and stay within your cover."

"Dante."

"Lull them into a sense of complacency and don't harass the opposition."

"Bethor."

"Keep your options open and, um...."

Only a couple seconds pass, but Mossad says, "Too slow, Bethor. You should know them by now. If you miss like that again, you'll be doing detention with me." Bethor's shoulders slump. "Dahlia, give me the last one."

"Trust no one."

I feel sorry for Bethor, but I guarantee I won't ever miss that one.

Mossad gives me a hard look with those obsidian eyes as he pushes up his sleeves. "Trainee Scum, you will memorize the ten rules for next class."

I straighten in my seat and belt out. "Yes, sir."

I sure hope Dante can recite all of them, or I'm in trouble because I've got nothing to write anything on. If he wants me to make him look good, I suggest he helps me out. I chuckle to myself.

Mossad turns and strides toward the whiteboard, then writes: Operation Pet Poof.

Turning back, he keeps his expression neutral but puffs out his chest. "I have had the honor of assisting his Excellency in ensuring the secrecy of this project, but since it is nearly ready to launch and cannot be stopped, he has encouraged me to share it with my students as a teaching moment."

His Excellency? *Barf-ola.*

A corner of Mossad's mouth hitches for a split second, then falls away. It makes my stomach twist.

"We have been working on this top secret project for a good two decades." Mossad starts pacing back and forth, hands behind his back. "So when I say all care and diligence have been taken to ensure its success, you will appreciate the effort that is finally coming to fruition."

Dante, Nisroc, and Bethor are still as statues in the row ahead of me. I've no idea what that might mean, so I chance a glance out of the corner of my eye. Ambrielle tightens her hands into fists below the desk, leaving me with a distinctly uneasy feeling.

Mossad stops pacing and turns toward us, his dark eyes scrutinizing. "Operation Pet Poof is none other than his Excellency's plan to eliminate the Enemy's pet, that coddled nation of Israel."

I furrow my brow. Did I hear that right?

He raises a golden eyebrow. "Your stillness betrays your surprise. Dante, tell me what you're thinking."

My mentor draws his shoulders back. "I am surprised, sir. I mean, I know the Enemy has a soft spot for his pet, but I hadn't thought about exploiting that. It's a brilliant strategic move."

He sounds like he's brownnosing again.

Mossad runs a hand along his jaw, his ring glinting. "Trainee Scum, what do you think?"

I inhale sharply and do my best to calm my racing heart. "I've never understood why... the Enemy feels that way about... his pet based upon how they've acted toward him over the years, but there's a good nine or ten million people living there. You plan to wipe them all out?" I can't keep my voice from rising.

Mossad glares at me, but I refuse to squirm. "Dante, you will see that your mentee's perspective shifts by the end of this exercise."

Or what? Nothing like a dangling threat.

"I understand, sir." My mentor raises his chin. No doubt his nostrils flare too.

He's pissed at me, but I'm not sure I care. Loosing a demon on one misguided human was one thing, but when millions of people's lives are on the line, nope. No way. I'm not playing.

"Now that we've reached that understanding"—his dark eyes bounce between Dante and me—"let's head to Earth and have you witness the final preparations for this long-anticipated plan. It promises to be a spectacle of devastation the likes of which neither you nor humans have ever seen."

Chapter Twenty-Seven

The unmistakable sound of demons screeching makes my heart speed as a large room with a gathering of no less than a hundred men—all wearing black or white turbans—comes into focus.

I drop Dante and Ambrielle's hands and clutch a buckle of my leathers as, from the back, I spot countless mongrels swooping about the space, the humans completely unaware. The demons at the séance didn't attack me, will I be as lucky this time?

"I am pleased to announce that preparations for the joint invasion of our enemy are complete," a uniformed man at the podium in front announces to hearty applause.

"That's Major General Mousavi, Commander in Chief of the armed forces of the Islamic Republic of Iran," Mossad informs over the roar as he pushes up the sleeves of his black sweater.

"Our land, sea, and air forces stand in readiness, awaiting only the order from our Supreme Commander and that of our brother nations." The speaker bobs his head toward an older gentleman who sits alone on a dais at the front of the room, clearly a leader of some sort.

The speaker continues, "Our submarines have just entered the Mediterranean and will be in position, along with our warships, within the week."

Several heads nod. I can't help but squirm at the sheer number of demons involved. It seems every attendee has at least one, if not more, latched on to their backs. I'd be willing to bet that supreme commander guy has several on him too, planting nefarious suggestions in his mind.

"We estimate that their Iron Dome system will neutralize the first 40 percent of our warheads, but after that, between our constant pummeling and our brothers-in-arms launching their missiles, our enemy's shield will fall. We estimate that we should clear the way for our joint ground forces to invade within three days."

Crap. Crap. Double crap.

More turbans bob.

My stomach twists. Iron Dome. That's Israel's missile intercept system.

Dante rolls his shoulders like he's completely unfazed by the speech. Ambrielle tosses her hair over a shoulder, then straightens her dress like her appearance is the most important thing in the world.

How can they be so callous?

I lean forward, careful to avoid notice by Mossad who seems to be taking in the goings on with great interest. Bethor has his meaty arms crossed, leaning back, while Nisroc sports a bored expression. My other two classmates, those females, keep whispering to each other behind cupped hands.

Dante nudges my shoulder with his arm, then leans in and whispers, "Like I said before, you need to be strategic in what you object to. Clearly you can't intervene and stop this, so chill."

My eyes go wide. Chill? When millions of people will be wiped out?

My mentor brings his hand over and makes like he's casually patting my shoulder. I wish, because his hand finds my neck at the top of my leathers and he grabs the muscle on the side and squeezes, hard.

Despite the continued squawks from the demons, my grunt draws a glance from Mossad.

"Don't squirm. Close your mouth. We're just aligning our expectations, aren't we, Trainee Scum?" His closed-mouth whisper is light, and his face remains impassive.

I'm anything but with my eyes starting to water. Rather than react, I grit my teeth. I may not be a warrior anymore, but I'm trained as one. I can handle this.

Ambrielle ignores us; the whole class does.

"Aren't we, Trainee Scum?" Dante's pinch strengthens.

I nod.

"Stop looking down your nose at all of us."

I open and close my mouth like a fish out of water.

Dante's squeeze tightens, and I grimace, unable to hide my discomfort.

"I've no doubt the demons have updated their hit list by now." My eyes go wide. "So if you can't stand here and chill, whether you agree with this human or not, you will attract their attention. I don't think you'll like the result. Am I clear, Trainee Scum?"

I search his face for signs of insincerity but spot none. Demons have a hit list? Surely not. They're dumb and stupid.

Dante forces a smile that doesn't reach his eyes. "Try me."

The pain is agonizing, but I hold his gaze for as long as I can stand it. I've no idea if he's bluffing to control me, but his stony expression never changes.

I finally raise a hand, motioning surrender.

The shooting pain vanishes in an instant, and I exhale as Dante pulls his hand back and nods toward the speaker, his message clear.

I frown.

His arm's retreat stalls and his gaze pierces me.

Control freak.

I draw a hand to my neck and start massaging the sore muscles, directing my attention to the military guy and the demons flitting about. It kills me to back down. Millions of humans will die, but there's not a darn thing I can do about it. I know Dante said to be "strategic," but it still galls me. I don't know that I have it in me when it comes to humans. Feeling powerless stinks.

"Okay, let's head to our next stop," Mossad says, a minute later.

Except for the varying dress of the all-male delegates attending, the scene repeats itself down to the swooping demons and hangers-on as we stop by Ankara, Turkey; Tripoli, Libya; and Khartoum, Sudan. My stomach has grown increasingly tight with each stop. I never knew so many nations had it out for the tiny nation of Israel, at least not enough to want to wipe it off the face of the Earth.

To a great extent, getting all of these nations in on this plan seems excessive. Or maybe that's just my wishful thinking. But with this new information, I wonder how Israel has managed to survive as long as it has. It may be the Almighty's pet, but there's a lot more animosity against it than I'd realized.

"Our last stop is Moscow and the Kremlin," Mossad announces as we join hands and everything goes dark.

I hear sirens blaring just before an artfully designed, old-world, Russian-style auditorium with an abundance of fine gold accents appears. There are only a few dozen people, and they're all talking rapidly on their cell phones, many barking orders. They rub the back of their neck or wring their hands as they head for the exits.

Mossad stiffens, his muscles going rigid.

Clearly this is as much of a surprise to him as the rest of us.

More sirens sound just outside, and Mossad says, "I want you all to pair up and gather as much intelligence as you can concerning what's happened. It's critical that you observe the ten rules, because if the Enemy sends troops, I do not want them knowing we're here."

I barely squash the grin that's begging to surface. He's concerned celestial warriors might show up. I know the probability of seeing my friends is small, but there is still a possibility. My stomach quivers. Might I see Kessien?

"Ah, yes, we have one more." Mossad sniffs. "Nisroc and Dante pair up and take the extra with you." *Thanks, just thanks, ya jerk.* "Let's all meet back outside of St. Basil's Cathedral in Red Square in three hours. That's the building with the colorful domes not far from here."

Ambrielle and Bethor disappear first, and the snooty females a second later, along with Mossad, who I assume will do whatever he does by himself.

I join hands with my partners, and the sounds of sirens grow ear-piercing seconds later as we land on the bank of a river. The air is thick with demons swooping and rising, shrieking their pleasure with all the chaos. Their calls turn shrill as a celestial warrior appears, along with the rest of his squad, parting the legions of demons, and my heart accelerates.

I don't recognize any of the squadron, but heavenly forces are on the scene, so my friends may well be close. Of course, if I spot Kessien and the others, I can't call out, not and comply with Mossad's orders to not be seen, but it will still be nice to see them.

"Let's scout on foot, so we blend in." Dante's scanning the skies as I turn my focus to him.

"Agree," Nisroc says, his attention on a car that's wrapped around the pole of a traffic signal not far away.

The wreck has backed up traffic for several blocks in one direction, but it's not the only cause of the chaos.

The celestial warriors land and approach the vehicle, but based on their body language, it seems the driver has left the vehicle. Odd considering I question whether they would have survived the crash with the car mangled so badly.

"Trainee Scum!" Dante's frustrated tone tells me he's called me a few times already, but I've been focused on the car.

"Sorry. Sorry. Yes, Dante."

"Keep your attention present, Trainee Scum. Now let's go."

Nisroc is already several steps down the sidewalk, and I hurry to catch up.

It's not long before we come upon a host of humans down and bloody in our path. People surround them like bees in a beehive, pressing clothes to wounds, and my stomach twists.

A woman is trapped under the front wheels of a silver sedan that appears to be the culprit based on the line of casualties.

"I can't believe he mowed them down."

"Did the driver have a heart attack?"

"There was no driver. Look." The woman points.

"I saw it happen, and she's right, there was no driver."

I overhear these and similar comments as we mingle with bystanders who are unaware of our presence.

Two seemingly unrelated accidents. Two missing drivers? What are the odds? What's going on?

Chapter Twenty-Eight

Over the next two hours, my stomach ties itself in knots, and my heart grows ever heavier as I follow Dante and Nisroc around Moscow. We come upon dozens more automobile accidents and three subway trains that stalled above ground. The train's occupants are trapped inside but look like they'll be fine.

Crazy enough, in every case, there's no driver. To say we're perplexed is an understatement.

Disappointment weighs heavy on my heart as we spot three more celestial squads, but none of them are the warriors I really want to see.

I blow out a breath as my boots crunch the gravel of a railway bed as Dante holds up a hand, motioning for us to stop. Ten passenger cars lie at odd angles down the embankment below where they came to rest after it appears the train skipped the track at a sharp curve, on the outskirts of the city.

The smell of death, as well as shrieking demons, is thick over the crash site as personnel from only one emergency vehicle tend to the wounded. Sounds of wailing escape several of the train cars and form a requiem accompanying their work.

I clench and unclench my fists. Survivors need rescuing. Every fiber of my being screams to go help.

I scan the area. Mossad's not around and, on the way to class, both Dante and Nisroc made it seem like they were being forced to conform to a certain way of behaving that they didn't necessarily agree with.

Or was that wishful thinking?

I'm already scum, what have I got to lose? We could save several humans if he'll let us.

"Dante."

He glances over from gazing at the horror before us.

"Can we help?" I bite my lip.

Nisroc furrows his brow on Dante's other side.

My mentor huffs loudly and rolls his eyes, and I already know that's a definite no. "Trainee Scum"—his voice is testy—"I'm going to chalk this up to it being your first day at Morningstar Academy, but that is the stupidest thing you've said yet." He shakes his head.

Nisroc just watches, his expression unreadable.

Dante continues, "I assume Headmaster Arioch informed you of our three primary objectives." He holds up a finger. "Exercise power and control over humans." He adds another finger. "Make humans suffer physically." He adds one more finger. "Make humans' lives a living hell."

I can only nod.

"Which of the three would 'helping humans' be part of?" His tone is snide.

"Never mind," I mumble.

A corner of Nisroc's mouth hitches.

"Answer the question, Trainee Scum." Dante's look is fierce despite his blond hair falling over half of his face.

I want to look away, but I resist. "It's not any of the three."

"Repeat the three objectives." He brushes his hair back.

I stumble through the three to Dante's constant correction and demands that I repeat each until I can say them all word for word. I bite back frustration at his relentlessness the more he pushes.

"It's time we head to the meeting spot," Nisroc says as he turns to Dante and adds something I can't hear. Dante gives him a long look before his expression turns stormy as he replies. But Nisroc clearly doesn't back down because he says something else, to which Dante begrudgingly nods.

Does this have anything to do with Mossad's threat that my mentor is to ensure that my perspective concerning humans shifts by the end of this field trip?

Dante's shoes crunch the gravel as he turns and takes the lead, heading back toward the city.

Nisroc falls back beside me as we follow. Several strands of his blond hair have come loose from his man bun, but I don't mention it, not with the dynamic that's played out between Dante and me. I'm just sorry he had to endure all that. My mentor is a real piece of controlling work.

I take to stepping from wooden tie to wooden tie, glad for the distance from Dante.

Nisroc lifts his gaze up from the ground and over at me, and in a low voice says, "If we had helped those humans back there, the demons would have gotten word back to the academy. They're Arioch's eyes and ears."

I miss the next railroad tie and step on the gravel between. "Oh."

"As it is, they will report back as to our whereabouts this afternoon. Do you know what happens if we're found not following what's been drilled into us?"

I swallow hard and shake my head.

"Detention. You probably haven't seen it yet, but the Hall of Correction is not a place you ever want to find yourself." His eyes go unfocused, and I wonder if he's reliving time spent there.

I roll my shoulders, then grab the back of my neck as we transition from the railroad tracks to a dirt path that runs behind a row of tenements.

"Dante may be frustrating at times"—I chuckle, which brings a warm smile to his face—"but believe it or not, he's doing you both a favor, keeping you both out of there."

I tilt my head.

He glances at Dante ahead of us, and I wonder if he's debating saying whatever he's considering, but he goes on, "Before today, Dante's been on a fast track to get out of here."

"As in leave the academy?" I clarify. Interesting.

Nisroc nods. "He appears to have conformed to whatever requirements they throw at him."

"Appears to have?"

Sidewalks appear again, and Dante continues leading the way between buildings, never looking over his shoulder to see that we're following. I have to wonder if he's steering us clear of more accidents because, while the sounds of chaos still fill the air along with swooping demons, I haven't seen more carnage, for which I am grateful. I don't think I could stand seeing more while being unable to help. Maybe that's why he's doing it, if he is.

I push the thought away, because that would make Dante caring, and he's anything but.

Nisroc waves his hands as if erasing my question. "The point is he's carefully managed his identity."

That's an interesting comment.

"I noticed he can be a real brownnoser."

Nisroc snorts. Either Dante doesn't hear him or he chooses not to react because he still doesn't look back. "But they've given him more freedom as a result."

"So he's gamed the system."

"In a manner of speaking, I guess so. They try to keep you off-balance in order to see where you stand in terms of adopting their views. Being off-balance is the quickest way for them to know if you're bluffing or not, because you'll usually default to what you really believe when you're reacting to something unexpected."

"So you give yourself away," I add, sighing.

He smiles. "Yes, if you don't happen to agree with them. You, Trainee Scum, are the latest in keeping Dante off-balance." While he uses my assigned name, there's no malice in his tone.

My mouth falls open.

"If you screw up, as his mentee, you'll both be punished. And he'll get a worse punishment than you, I can assure you."

"Seriously?"

Nisroc just raises a brow. "Seriously."

"So hence, why he's being such a jerk."

He shrugs. "If that's the way you see it."

"What's he plan to do after he gets out of here?"

We take several steps as he glances ahead, at Dante, before he finally says, "That's not for me to say."

Seems they've talked about it. But based on how Dante's treated me so far, I'm not sure I care. I'm nothing but an obstacle to him.

"So what do you suggest I do when humans are in jeopardy? I can't just stand idly by and not lift a finger. I can't." My pitch rises.

"I can't tell you what to do. It's something only you can decide. What can you stand to live with?" He locks gazes with me. "Just know that whatever you choose affects more than just you and the humans you're hoping to help. On this side, there are real consequences… and for more than just you."

My heart feels like it's shrinking. How do I make this work?

Nisroc leans toward me and, in a hushed voice, says, "For what it's worth, Dante has a softer side to him that I doubt you've seen." I roll my eyes as I look to the sky. "I think he's just reeling from having you, who he can't control—" He chuckles. "—be assigned to him out of the blue."

I match his hushed tone. "It sounds like you're enjoying seeing him stressed." I swing my arms as I step lightly over a crack in the sidewalk.

"No, I just think you may make him perhaps a little less calculating and a bit more feeling. You're not a thing to be strategized around."

"Thank you."

He bobs his head.

A more feeling Dante.

I'm still pondering what that might even look like when we reach a cobblestone plaza and the colorful domes of St. Basil's Cathedral appear.

Dante stops when we reach the wall that skirts the front of the ornate building and turns. He pulls at the sleeve of his tunic like he's uncomfortable as he catches Nisroc's attention.

"She's up to speed." Nisroc removes the band around his man bun and reorders his hair.

I'm not sure I agree. I've certainly not capitulated, but I stay quiet.

Dante sizes me up, then nods.

Did Nisroc offer to have that conversation with me because he knows Dante would mess it up and nothing but an argument would ensue? I don't mind. I wouldn't have gotten the off-the-record feedback concerning a potentially softer Dante without him.

Ambrielle and Bethor stop beside Nisroc a couple of minutes later, followed by Diniel and Dahlia shortly thereafter. The pair of females continue to scowl and refuse to so much as speak to me.

I couldn't care less. Seems I've got a couple budding friendships, and I don't need their negativity.

"What did you discover?" Mossad asks, shoving the sleeves of his black sweater up to reveal the tattoos on his arms as he joins our circle. He's late by ten minutes, but I guess that's the teacher's prerogative.

"A plane crashed in the middle of the downtown," Bethor offers. "It didn't look like any humans survived."

The ring on Mossad's pinky finger glints in the sun's lengthening rays. "Excellent news."

Mossad's eyes connect with mine in an instant, like he's just waiting to see how I'll react. A muscle in Dante's neck bulges beside me. Nothing like baiting me to see if Dante achieved the objective set for him with that threat earlier.

Several choice names for Mossad flow through my mind, but since I've no desire to visit the Hall of Correction, like a model mentee, I keep my expression neutral and don't so much as flinch no matter how long Mossad scrutinizes me.

It's a very long minute, but he finally turns his attention. "Diniel. Dahlia."

Dante's shoulders drop, and I know I just passed two tests.

Diniel reports, "A lot of graves have been broken into. We stumbled upon Vagankovo Cemetery and discovered that. We thought it odd, so we went to Vvedenskoye Cemetery and found the same thing. Novodevichy Cemetery has also been ransacked." She shakes her head.

"Were the grave markers broken?" Bethor asks, receiving a frown from Ambrielle. "What? I'm curious."

Dahlia furrows her brow, then tilts her head, considering. "Actually, no, now that you mention it." Her expression goes slack.

Dante adds our discoveries, and even Mossad is scratching his head at that because nothing adds up.

I summon my courage and ask, "Did the plane that crashed have a pilot?"

Everyone stares at me. "What? Like Bethor, I'm curious."

Bethor chuckles. Dante rolls his eyes.

"There's no way of knowing. The thing was nose down," Ambrielle offers.

What happened? Absolutely nothing makes sense.

Chapter Twenty-Nine

Kessien

Motion out of the corner of my eye draws my attention just before we follow orders, heading to third heaven's front gates. I pivot my head, beating my wings to stay aloft.

What in the universe?

Jael's head jerks back.

Aliyah's eyes go wide.

"What?" Issra points to....

I close my eyes, then open them again, disbelieving.

Against the backdrop of the starry sky, a full moon illuminates thousands of humans—men, women, children, and babies, in all colors, shapes, and sizes—all looking upward, dressed in white robes, arms outstretched as they rise. They're not slowing; it looks like their destination may well be third heaven.

The Fallen guards in front of the dragon gates below crane their necks, staring and pointing along with us.

This is the strangest thing I've ever seen. How are these humans floating?

Jael tilts his head, and Issra's mouth hangs open, both as mystified as me.

When a human dies, their spirit rises similarly, but it's fuzzy and ill-defined, more smokelike than anything, until it reforms in its final destination, at least I'm guessing that's what also happens down below if their destination isn't the third heaven. I've never seen that place, so I don't know for sure. But bottom line, it's not at all like these. No, these humans look like they just stepped out for a walk around the block—well, except for their robe getup.

Their conversations and exclamations reach us a second later. Some shout, others sing, others clap and giggle. Especially the babies, there are so many of them, far outnumbering the adults. The ones I can see are all cooing and giggling in those white robes, which are huge on them. I've never been one to dote on human babies, but I can't keep a smile from my face—they're too cute. But to a one, all of these humans are happy and excited.

Aliyah kneads her long hair, eyes wide.

I chuckle when a boy executes a forward roll, starting a number of them doing the same. A girl goes prone and extends her arms and legs fully, still rising, and shouts, "Look at me. I'm flying!"

"We best get moving." My voice startles the others, bringing them back.

Seconds later, I vanish us to the gates of third heaven.

The area just outside the set of ornate pearl gates looks nothing like normal. It's usually quiet with an orderly single file line waiting to reach whoever's looking up names in the Book of Life. Things are anything but quiet at the moment.

Several warriors are directing the arriving throng into two lines. One of them shouts, "Anyone whose spirit preceded you, please join this line." He motions toward a long line winding off to his right. "All others, please join that line." He directs them to a line that leads to the Book of Life that Gabriel, Uriel, and Jophiel are all tending at the moment. I shake my head. I've never seen so many angels working book duty at once.

"That's awesome." Issra's beaming as he looks to the front of the first line.

I follow his gaze through the gates to an open field where a thousand more souls wait. Raphael, Azrael, and Chamuel attend the front of the line that's been divided into three.

Above the crowd noise, I hear Azrael shout, "Jonathan Benjamin Schwartz, born London, England, January 10, 1674, arrived in third heaven October 12, 1722."

"Oh, that's me." A male in the middle of the crowd inside waves his gray newsboy cap. Others waiting clear a path for him to pass. Several pat him on the back as he makes his way forward, toward the gates.

When he reaches the front, a pair of guards escort him to a male dressed in a white robe who has been waiting with another guard just outside.

I do a double take as the pair hug, because they somehow blend; the robed guy vanishes, and the male in suspenders, tan knickers, and white shirt is the only one that remains. "Did I just…?" I lean over and ask Jael.

He laughs, watching spellbound. "Yes, you saw what you think you did. It happens every time."

I run a hand through my hair. First it was humans floating, rising, now this? I'm speechless. Never in my existence have I seen either. What is going on?

When the man who has just been blended with the new arrival lets out a loud whoop, I can't hold back a laugh. He fists his hat and waves it above his head. A guard escorts him toward Nanaelle, Astread's fashion-forward coworker.

She's scratching on a celestial notepad—a device that's no doubt connected to the Tree of Insight—just inside the gates, below a sign that reads INFORMATION. She's wearing a chic top, skinny jeans, and sneakers this time. Several strands of her golden locks have gone rogue from a bun and flop about.

"We should get our assignment." Aliyah bites her lip, looking a bit overwhelmed.

I don't blame her. It's bedlam.

The man stops before Nanaelle and asks, "Where do you want me to help out?"

Nanaelle consults her notepad, then directs him to the right.

Before we reach her, a white-robed woman stops before Nanaelle. "Gabriel didn't know where you have everything set up today and said to ask you for directions. Where do I go to find lodging?" She leans in.

Nanaelle points to a white building behind her, where arrival coordination is usually done. "Housing assignments are being given out in the welcome center." Not surprisingly, it has a long line out the doors.

She turns. "Thanks so much."

"Can you tell me where the newly arriving children are?" A young woman in a baggy sweater and yoga pants reaches our destination first. The fact that she's not dressed in a white robe means she's been around third heaven for some time.

"We're using the children's court as the intake area," Nanaelle says.

"Thanks so much." The young female waves as she leaves.

"How can we help?" I ask before someone else can grab Nanaelle's attention, as the squad circles up.

She blows out a breath, her stray hair bobbing. "Whew, things are a bit busy. We planned, but who knew things would be this hectic?" She shakes her head. "But you need an assignment." She consults her notepad. "We need reinforcements in the nursery as well as with unaccompanied children; with reunions, helping folks find their loved ones; we need buddies to help acclimate newly arrived with no loved ones to greet them; help in housing, escorting folks to their new quarters; as well as general crowd control, take your pick." She chuckles.

At least she's smiling.

"Astread's over at the nursery, if you're interested."

Aliyah lights up at that. Glad loves children too, but....

I clench my jaw, then bring a hand up, examining its meatiness. "I don't want to break any babies."

Nanaelle and Aliyah both laugh. My brothers don't.

"You won't," Nanaelle assures. "They're amazingly resilient."

"All the same, Aliyah, go ahead. We'll—" I grab the back of my neck.

"I agree," Jael adds, looking more uncomfortable than I've seen in ages.

"How 'bout we help with housing? We'll get to see inside all those new mansions," Issra suggests.

I shrug. "Sure, it's as good as any assignment."

"That'll be Rhamiel. He's helping coordinate that in the welcome center." Nanaelle points us toward the big, white building behind her, then makes a note on her notepad.

"See you back at the break room." Aliyah waves as we turn.

Issra waves as we head to our assignment.

We squeeze through the doors of the welcome center, past the line that stretches outside, and make our way to Rhamiel, one of eight behind the large, white counter at the front of the welcome center. It seems impossible that Astread introduced us only hours before. So much has happened since then. Judging by his skewed hair, he's as harried as Nanaelle. He's helping a dark-skinned, white-robed arrival, pointing at a map laid out between them.

We stop before Rhamiel, beside the new arrival. "We're here to help."

Rhamiel exhales loudly. "Thank goodness." Turning to the new arrival, he says, "This is Kessien. He'll help you find your accommodations. Kessien, this is Nicholas. He's at 721 Joy Street in Harmony District, beside River Vida."

"I'll see that he finds it." Turning to Jael and Issra, I say, "I'll see you back home whenever you're done."

Nicholas grabs the map and folds it as we make our way through the crowd and out the doors. I direct us right, in the general direction that Harmony District is in.

He squints, then holds the folded map up to shield his eyes from the bright light. "Thanks so much for helping me. I really appreciate it. Frankly, I'm surprised to even be here."

"Really, why's that?" I ask as we wind our way through more new arrivals, older citizens, and angelic staff.

Nicholas chuckles as he adjusts the fabric of his white robe. "You could say I made a mess of my life. I started out well enough, did well in school and all that, but my best friend—" He pauses, then swallows. "—was killed in a drive-by shooting. We'd been friends since grade school."

"I'm sorry." My heart goes out to him. Human life is never long, relatively.

The golden main road through third heaven is a lot less congested, and I direct us to the walking path that stretches along beside it.

"It never made the news. No one was ever charged, much less prosecuted." He fists his free hand. "I swore to his mother that I'd see him avenged."

I give him a long look. This is sounding very familiar, too familiar.

"It took years, but I finally found out who did it and"—he looks away—"got justice. I ended up in prison, but by then I didn't care. I'd gotten revenge."

We pass by a grassy park on the right with picnic tables.

"So…?" I'm not sure how to ask the question that leaps to mind.

He laughs. "So how did I end up here?"

"Yes."

"I only have a speculation, but I'll tell you my story."

I bob my head.

"There are lots of drugs available in prison, and I started experimenting. Nothing serious at first, but the more I took, the more I wanted. Got to the point that nothing else mattered. I attacked my cellmate two weeks ago." He looks over at me. "They threw me in the infirmary and forced me through withdrawal—seizures, vomiting, trembling, sweating, anxiety, paranoia." He gives a bitter laugh. "That's what I've been doing the last few days. I don't recommend it."

I raise an eyebrow as I look at him.

"Anyway, I had time to do a lot of thinking." His shoulders droop, and he sighs. "I was at the lowest point in my life. I had nothing to look forward to."

He's quiet for several seconds as other escorts and new arrivals pass by on the golden road.

He swallows, hard. "Two days ago, I cried out to anyone who might be listening. Figured I had nothing to lose." He waves his hands. "I apologized for the mess I'd made of my life, asked them to forgive me and fix me."

I pin him with my gaze, anxious to know what happened next.

He smiles. "That's it."

"That's it? What do you mean?"

"Exactly what I said. That's it."

He apologized and asked for forgiveness and then to be fixed. Hope bubbles up. Can Glad be restored the same way? Is that all it takes?

He tilts his head, giving me a questioning look.

I raise a hand. "I mean no disrespect."

He nods. "None taken. Yesterday, they released me from the infirmary. I went to the library to distract myself from the cravings and found a book that said that acknowledging my screwups, asking for forgiveness, and determining to live differently are the first steps in recovering."

"How do you know that's what got you here?"

He stops and clenches his jaw. "I didn't do anything to deserve this. Trust me." He brings his arms down quickly, underscoring his point, then looks around and shakes his head, still not believing. "Nothing I've done would have landed me here. Far from it."

My heart accelerates. "What book was that?"

Chapter Thirty

Until fifteen minutes ago, I had no idea how many Fallen attend Morningstar Academy, but they're here en masse this morning.

Despite being decked out in a fashionable, black leather jacket, black turtleneck, and gray slacks thanks to Ambrielle's help at The Co-Op after espionage class two days ago, sitting beside Dante in this ginormous auditorium with its black-themed décor, I feel the other students' dark looks. I don't miss the fact that they send Dante sympathetic ones, which he acknowledges with a nod or a wave—the miscreant.

Nisroc, beside him, does nothing to stop him.

Harrumph.

I run a hand over my barely fuzzy scalp, wishing my hair would grow because a shiny head seems to be the moniker for a particularly difficult new arrival from what I've gathered, and everyone I meet makes sure I don't forget.

As if that's even possible.

Shopping at The Co-Op, the place me and my hair were parted, ended up putting me in debt with the school supplies and two outfits I purchased, but what else was I to do? I rub my hands together, still loathing the fact that I have only one month to repay, either by time spent at the Hall of Correction or by having a teacher make a commendation for exemplary behavior in accordance with what they consider to be meritorious conduct—like that's ever gonna happen.

I'd been ready to buy one more outfit, but Ambrielle, with a pinched expression, advised against it until I know "what I've gotten into"—that's exactly how she said it—paying for the first two, plus supplies. My stomach twists just thinking about it.

I need a distraction.

I lean over to Bethor and Ambrielle. "Any idea what this assembly is about?" We'd been heading to history class when the announcement came over the PA to come here instead. "Not that I'm complaining, mind you, but cancelling the whole school's classes on the spur of the moment seems a bit…."

"Odd?" Ambrielle interjects, leaning forward beside him.

"Yeah. Have they ever done something like this before?"

Bethor brushes shoulder-length locks over his shoulder. "Yeah, not long ago. The Prince was celebrating the result of a victory after coordinating the release of a plague by one of Earth's nations whose leaders are warm to his suggestions. It exterminated six million humans while it raged on Earth for a couple years." My eyes go wide. That was Lucifer's doing? "They cancelled classes for the whole day. I don't remember anything similar before that though."

Before that.

Curiosity makes me want to be nosy and ask how long exactly each of them has been here, despite the past being taboo to speak of. I'm guessing they wouldn't have a problem saying, but I'm still getting to know them, and I don't want to overstep.

Nevertheless, my chest tightens. "Do you think he's celebrating something again?"

Ambrielle shrugs. "It sure would be nice. They also opened the cafeteria, free of charge, that entire day."

Food is one thing I definitely miss about the third heaven. While we don't need to eat, not like humans, I'm seriously missing me some amazing coffee, but there's no way I'm going further into debt to enjoy that simple pleasure. With my luck, it'd probably taste burnt anyway.

Zophiel, our history teacher, breezes out from one of the wings of the stage in a patterned, fuchsia, flowy blouse and skirt that matches her bright pink, bobbed hair. As with my first two days of her class, between her eccentric dress and ethereal voice, it's hard to take her seriously. Blue mascara combined with copious amounts of black eyeliner and bright red lipstick only underscore the point.

I guess we didn't miss her class today after all.

She starts bouncing when she reaches center stage, making her hair bob, and I barely stifle a snort. A glance at Bethor says he's barely keeping it together too.

"No doubt you know about the significant number of accidents that occurred on Earth three days ago."

Who wouldn't by now. I still think it's bizarre how all those drivers went missing.

Her wispy voice makes it hard to concentrate, so I scan the full auditorium, and I swear I spot Jacob, that creep who came and got some binders to run an errand for Umbrelle, Arioch's admin, my first day. I'm glad he's sitting two sections over and oblivious to me.

Several students whisper to a neighbor, not paying attention. I can't blame them.

Blind to the lack of attention the student body is giving her, Zophiel claps, excitement oozing from her. "What you may not know is that these calamities occurred all over Earth. Nary a town nor village was spared."

That gets my attention. The whisperers quiet too, and a hush falls.

I furrow my brow, and to Bethor and Ambrielle, I mouth, "Seriously?"

Ambrielle shrugs, clearly at a loss.

"Naturally, the Prince wants to understand what happened."

That makes two of us.

She draws a hand to her abundant chest. "Because of my expertise in history, the Prince himself asked me to head up the investigation of one part of this mystery, that being the many graves that have seemingly lost their occupants."

Wait. What?

Diniel and Dahlia mentioned seeing lots of graves broken into, but Zophiel says that they "lost their occupants." Is she saying the bodies are missing? I thought my two classmates meant the stuff a human was buried with had gone missing. The bodies are gone too? That's just gross. I mean, these humans were dead and decomposing.

I nudge Bethor. "Did Diniel and Dahlia actually look inside any of the graves?"

Ambrielle and Bethor both shrug. "I don't know," he says.

Dante and Nisroc are whispering when I glance over, no doubt about the same thing we are.

"With permission from our esteemed headmaster"—she dips her head to Arioch who's sitting in the front row, and I roll my eyes—"he has approved engaging our school in an investigative training mission."

Like he had a choice. Who would be crazy enough to refuse Lucifer?

She puffs out her chest. "Oh, but it gets better." She fans herself. I shake my head.

Pa-lease.

"This is a unique opportunity for our school to impress his Excellency." She titters. "And I dare say, several of you could well earn commendations from the Prince himself if you are significantly helpful."

Solving it won't hurt her at all, either, I dare say.

Murmuring erupts throughout the auditorium at the mention of commendations. This is one thing I don't mind doing. It's not harming humans in the least, so say no more. Maybe I can pay off my debt and still have a little credit to spare.

"Alas, this was a massive grave robbery, but together, we *will* figure out what happened to these bodies." Zophiel raises a clenched fist as if she's a general sounding the rallying cry for the troops before battle.

I don't care what she fancies herself, bring on the commendations.

"Form groups of four or five. You'll get your assignment as to which area of Earth your group is to investigate at the doors as you leave. Oh, and the Prince is anxious for answers, so all classes are cancelled for the next three days to give you time to solve this mystery. Good luck to you all."

With that she turns.

What had been whispers erupt into a roar.

"Classes are cancelled." Bethor gives me a high five, the dimple in his chin growing more pronounced with his broad smile. It reminds me of the ritual Astread and I shared before each mission, but I tamp down on my melancholy.

I turn to find Dante's eyes dancing. Nisroc reaches over and high-fives me.

"Ready to earn some commendations?" Dante asks, brushing back his bangs from over half his face.

It feels like it takes forever to finally reach the doors with the crush of students getting assignments, but at last we approach Umbrelle, Arioch's scantily clad admin. Three days have dramatically improved my dress. I can't say the same for her. She smiles when she spots Dante; I earn a scowl.

"Why, Dante, it's been too long." She hugs a clipboard to her generous bosom.

For an admin, she sure seems chummy with my mentor, not that I'm jealous.

"It has, hasn't it, Umbrelle?" Dante gives her a winning smile, and my stomach starts to churn from the saccharine of his brownnosing. "Perhaps we…." He glances about, making a show of being discrete despite all of us standing here. He leans in, and I can't hear what he says, but she lights up, even giggles.

Ambrielle, beside me, leans in, then points into her open mouth. Barf, indeed.

I barely stifle a snort.

Dante leans back and, in a loud whisper—clearly intentional—says, "Alas, it seems we're all being kept a bit busy for the foreseeable future. We'll have to… later." He wags his brows.

What favors is he—No, I don't want to know.

Nisroc coughs, then clears his throat, not at all subtly.

I turn around and mouth, "Thank you."

Bethor chuckles beside him.

Umbrelle frowns at Nisroc but lowers her clipboard, revealing another tight shirt, just like before. She scans down the list. "I think…." She gives Dante a wink and says, "Yes, I think Jerusalem for you. It is the capital city of the Enemy's pet. I'm sure you'll find no shortage of clues there. Perhaps a few commendations, hmm?"

I want to roll my eyes. Leave it to Dante to charm this wench.

"You're the best, Umbrelle," Dante says as we pass.

Seems we have a choice assignment, but what will we find?

Chapter Thirty-One

Ancient Jerusalem pines and Mediterranean cypress break up fields of closely spaced, above-ground crypts adorned with an abundance of ornate crosses when we land. A gentle breeze that moves the boughs adds to the calm, and I can't help but note the absence of demons swooping and screeching.

I don't spot any celestial warriors either, but I won't give up hope in finding them.

A woman's weeping from not far away interrupts the silence. She's bowed beside a crypt that the top has been slid aside.

I draw a hand to my chest, my heart going out to her.

Other groups of mourners dot the landscape amongst the plethora of similarly desecrated tombs.

"This is Mount Zion Cemetery. Let's have a look around," Dante says. "Trainee Scum, come." He bobs his head, indicating the direction we're going.

So much for exploring on my own.

I grab my notepad and a pencil from the shift. After my shopping trip with Ambrielle, she got someone to issue me a locker, and I regained the ability to shift. For such a simple thing, I've never been happier. It's definitely the little things in life that can bring the greatest joy.

I make note of the names and dates on the tops of open crypts as I traipse after Dante's toned form. Nicolai Schmidt, born 11 Oct 1839, died 28 Dec 1876; Oskar Schindler, born 28 April 1908, died 9 Oct 1974; James Leslie Starkey, born 3 Jan 1895, died 12 Jan 1938. My list goes on and on with the number of graves that have been desecrated.

We enter a tree-lined grove that's kind of quaint. A yellow and orange-brown boundary wall sets off one side of the forested area where the graves are no longer carved stone crypts but dirt plots bordered in stone with a headstone. Looks like these are the more affordable plots.

As with the other section though, no fewer mourners are in attendance. But this time, they're gathered around holes through which it seems the perpetrators made off with the bodies. I shake my head.

My heart hurts for each of these families of the missing. Human lives are short to begin with. I find it hard to fathom the depth of grief they must feel at having a loved one stolen from their final resting place. Acute. Agonizing. Excruciating. These are just a few of the words that make my heart feel like it's shrinking.

Lucifer's flummoxed, so I'll pass on holding him responsible for this. If it's humans, I've seen some pretty horrific stuff done by them, but never something like this, not so many and so widespread. Could it be demons? But if so, why all of a sudden? And what would be their motive? It's not like there'd be fear to feast on, and the sadness of mourners just doesn't excite them from everything I've seen.

I write down several more names and dates until Dante stops and puts his hands on his hips as he surveys the area. I half expect him to ask me if anything has struck me concerning the mystery we're supposed to be sleuthing.

He brushes his long bangs back, then bobs his head toward a younger couple crouched at a graveside with a gaping hole in the middle. The statue of a lamb crowns the headstone, and my stomach tenses. It's the grave of a child.

"What are our three primary objectives when it comes to humans?"

I furrow my brow. Why is he asking this?

He motions with a hand to hurry up with an answer, so I slowly recite what's been drilled into me. "Exercise power and control over them, make humans suffer physically, and make their lives a living hell. Why?"

"The next time I ask, there'd better be no hesitancy. Understood?"

I nod slowly, then glance around. The others are nowhere in sight, and there are still no demons about.

"Your performance the last two days in temptation class has been anything but acceptable."

What he fails to say is that I'm reflecting poorly on him. Tough, ya brownnoser.

I vanish my notepad and pencil, and I put my hands on my hips. "You can't seriously expect me to have made that dog bite that mail carrier or made that child lose control and ride his bike into oncoming traffic."

Despite them not being the friends I wanted, I'd never been so happy to see celestial warriors arrive to protect that child from harm. I wish they'd intervened for the mail carrier too.

My stomach clenches. He can't mean for me to practice on grieving humans.

Dante's expression is anything but jovial. "I did and I do. I told you that you need to be strategic about what you decline to do, but you're still declining anything that even remotely harms a human, and that's got to stop."

My heart picks up pace. What's he going to make me do?

"If you choose not to comply, I will not hesitate to refer you to the Hall of Correction. Perhaps it's what I should have done the first day. It might have made you more compliant to start." He frowns, and under his breath mumbles, "So much for being nice."

I only barely stifle a snort. He thinks he's been nice to me? He's delusional.

He raises his pointer finger in my face. "And if you're thinking I'll be punished too, there you're wrong. If I refer you, only you will experience a… readjustment."

I want to bite his digit, but I resist. It's probably not the best time to indulge myself, even though he deserves it.

"That couple over there." He points. "Do something to them that is consistent with our three primary objectives."

"What?" My tone rises with disbelief. "Dante, that's too much. They're grieving their child."

"Then it shouldn't be hard." He chuckles.

I stand there, my mouth opening and closing like a fish out of water.

"Oh, there you are," Nisroc says, leading Ambrielle and Bethor between the maze of graves.

Bless you, Nisroc. I exhale because I can't see Dante continuing this farce in front of them.

Ambrielle's gaze ping-pongs between Dante and me as they approach, and she furrows her brow.

"We found something interesting." Bethor adjusts his gray tunic as they stop.

"What's going on, Dante?" Ambrielle puts her hands on her hips.

Bethor and Nisroc give her curious looks.

"Nothing. Why?" Dante pushes his chest out.

"Because Trainee Scum looks like she's about to throttle you."

I cross my arms, the leather of my jacket squeaking, as the trio looks me over.

Dante huffs. "She hasn't yet learned to follow our three primary objectives. I saw an opportunity to give her some practice without spies circling."

Bethor scans the area, then holds up his hands. "You planned to have her practice on these humans? Dante, come on. They're already feeling like their lives are a living hell. You want to make it even worse?"

Brilliant response. Why didn't I think of that?

I close my eyes and throw my head back, relishing the moment.

"Dante, we know you want to break her in as quickly as possible so you feel like you're in control again, but really?" Ambrielle shakes her head.

"It's been just three days. Cut her some slack," Nisroc adds.

"You seriously need to stop being such a control freak, Dante," Bethor adds.

How I love these beings.

My mentor throws his hands up. "Fine. Fine."

Bethor clears his throat. "As I was saying, we found something interesting."

"What's that?" Dante's expression is still pinched. I know he's ticked, but he holds his tone even.

Bethor nods at the younger couple still kneeling by their child's open graveside. "Every single grave that belongs to a child has been pillaged."

My mouth drops open. "Seriously?"

Nisroc bobs his head.

"There's plenty of adults that have been taken too, but there's nothing consistent with them, not like this." Ambrielle shifts from one foot to the other.

"If I may…." I don't know if they'll welcome my suggestion, but what have I got to lose? "I think we should check out several other cemeteries to see if they've all experienced the same problem."

"Exactly what we were thinking." Ambrielle gives me a high five.

Dante rolls his eyes before closing them for several seconds. No doubt he's checking with someone telepathically who can look up where other cemeteries in Jerusalem are located. I look forward to the day when I'll have earned the privilege to have telepathic communications in second heaven. At least I'm assuming that's why I've got nothing at the moment.

"Seems there are several cemeteries in the area, so let's fly."

Everyone unfurls their gray wings, and I follow suit, grinning. Despite forfeiting two wings, it feels really good to stretch the two I have left. I can't wait to feel the wind on my face again.

Nisroc chuckles at my giddy expression as he rearranges his man bun in preparation for flight. "First time since you arrived?"

I nod as I beat my wings and ogle his mighty large and mighty fine pinions.

Dante frowns. What crawled up his behind?

"I well remember my first flight here. Takes some getting used to." Ambrielle forces a smile that doesn't reach her eyes, and I'm struck by her transparency. As well, I'm still curious to know when exactly that was.

Dante launches due west, putting the sun directly behind us as we soar up, nearly touching the fluffy, low-hanging clouds. I tuck in, between Bethor and Ambrielle, behind Nisroc who flies beside Dante, as buildings pass by below. A plethora of grassy parks punctuate the sprawling cityscape.

While I certainly don't have the mobility I had with four wings, I feel alive up here with the wind kissing my cheeks. I beat my wings, then glide on the currents.

The sounds of cars, trucks, and scooters, along with honking, drift up from the bustling city. If they experienced a similar situation with car and trains crashing and losing their drivers, any debris has been cleared away.

The Knesset, where Israel's legislature meets, and a sports stadium pass by below, not long before the white stone arches of Mount Herzl National Cemetery's entrance comes into view—at least that's what the name engraved on them says—and we vanish our wings after landing.

What will we find here?

Chapter Thirty-Two

A small, white-background-with-blue-star Israeli flag stands beside each raised, brick plot that bears a green turf blanket of sorts. The white headstones look nearly like pillows at the head of each, in the perfectly uniform field of them.

I furrow my brow. The last cemetery was nowhere near this orderly, with everything identical. Is that significant?

We fan out, but I'm relieved when Bethor lingers near Dante and me; my mentor won't be training me with the many mourners that dot the area.

I catch his eye and mouth, "Thank you."

Bethor nods and takes to ambling between the graves, and I turn and scan the sea of them. Ambrielle and Nisroc are each exploring on their own, a ways off.

There are relatively fewer graves that have been disturbed compared with Mount Zion Cemetery, but I don't know if that's important. I grab my notebook from the shift and start jotting down notes along with the names on the graves that have been ransacked, including the human's birth and death dates.

As I make my way around a large section, one thing stands out, there are no children buried here, absolutely none, which seems odd, so I make a note.

The five of us circle back up as the sun crests the sky.

"Any observations of significance?" Dante tilts his head.

I dive right in, offering my seeming oddities—especially the one about no kids—before anyone else, because why not? Maybe I can earn a few commendations as well as a reputation for something other than being ornery when it comes to harming humans.

"I read a sign somewhere that this is a cemetery for Israel's war heroes and national leaders," Nisroc offers, running a hand over his white tunic, beneath which I'm guessing is a firm chest.

Dante again frowns as my gaze lingers on my classmate's chest. He's watching me like a hawk. What is his problem? Can't I appreciate strong muscles? I loved Kessien's.

"That would explain the lack of children and the orderliness, as well as the flags everywhere." Ambrielle brings me back, tracing her upper lip with a finger, deep in thought.

Everyone else pretty much noted the same things as me, so we head to our next stop, Mount of Olives Cemetery.

It's another short flight, and as we land, the first thing I notice is the dress of the mourners scattered among the off-white stone crypts of the hillside graveyard. Every human, both male and female, is decked out in black from head to foot. The men wear flat-brimmed hats along with sidecurls, long silk coats, and black pants. The women wear a headscarf that conceals all their hair, long-sleeved blouses, skirts that extend below the knee, and stockings.

Nisroc lingers near me this time, earning a glower from Dante. I chuckle to myself. My mentor is thwarted from "training" once more, if he would even dare to consider it after the others' rebuke.

I grab my notebook from the shift and resume making note of the names and dates on desecrated graves. Like the first cemetery, children are buried here and every single one of their graves has been pilfered. But interestingly, very few of the others have been disturbed. I can only shake my head. Other than the children, there's no consistency between the three cemeteries.

I stop beside a crypt whose top has been pushed aside. Only a few of the stones that others have left to indicate they'd stopped by remain on the lid, the rest are scattered on the ground. A quick read of the inscription tells me this was a seven-year-old boy who died less than a year ago.

My heart squeezes. So young. And so recent.

I haven't verified what Zophiel, our history teacher, said about the "occupants" having "gone missing," but I feel like I should.

I tug on the cuff of my leather jacket and scan the area as I summon my courage. Seeing and smelling a decomposing human isn't exactly my idea of fun. I pray our teacher was telling the truth, so I'm spared the grossness that otherwise awaits.

After I dither long enough to annoy even myself with my cowardice, I bite my lip and dive in, passing through the partially open lid.

My heart picks up pace because the pine of what was probably the top of the wooden casket is completely splintered, like an explosive went off, and I draw a hand over my mouth.

But as I take in more, other than splinters everywhere, the bare wood inside of the casket hasn't been harmed. Dirt and a white sheet are the only things inside.

I exhale. There's no dead body.

I don't know Jewish burial customs, but if I had to guess, I'd say the boy was buried in that white shroud.

Zophiel was right, the "occupant" is missing.

So what happened to him? What happened to all of them?

I exit the crypt and continue wandering, making notes until Dante calls us all back together to share our discoveries. No one has anything new of significance to report, so it's on to the Armenian cemetery by St. James Cathedral Church, then an Arab cemetery in the Arab Quarter of the city, a Muslim cemetery just outside the eastern wall, Beit Shemesh Christian cemetery, and more.

The sun is setting on the hilltop burial ground of Mount of Rest Cemetery, the largest in Jerusalem, as we circle up at the eastern edge of the ocean of white graves to again share any insights we've gleaned.

Ambrielle brushes dirt off her pants. "I've seen more graveyards than I ever imaged existed."

"You and me both." Bethor throws an arm around her shoulders. They look wiped. We all do.

Dante runs his hands through his hair beside Nisroc, then blows out a breath, underscoring the tension that's been growing all afternoon with each successive cemetery we've visited with no further insights gleaned. "I've no idea what to think. I have absolutely no question about *what* happened. But we still don't have even a hint concerning what *caused* it." Frustration flavors his tone, and he punches the air.

I shuffle my feet beside Ambrielle.

Bethor crosses and uncrosses his arms.

"We can't go back with nothing." Nisroc rubs the sleeve of his white tunic between Bethor and Dante.

He's not wrong. I run a hand over my fuzzy scalp. "Well, what *do* we know?"

"All the children are missing, as in every single one." Ambrielle fists her hands on her hips. "Anywhere from infants on up."

I pull my notebook back out of the shift. "How old do humans consider children?"

Dante raises his open palms.

"Maybe until they hit puberty?" Nisroc shrugs.

"So that's like what, ten or twelve?" I clarify, scribbling.

"I guess, why?" My mentor furrows his brow.

"Were all the ten- to twelve-year-olds missing?"

Ambrielle shakes her head. "I only paid attention to the graves that were disturbed, not the ones that weren't."

Bethor raises his pointer finger. "I saw a couple twelve-year-old's graves that weren't ransacked. But I also saw several that were."

"Good. Good. Any younger than that, that weren't disturbed?"

We all look at each other, shaking our heads.

"So maybe all children up to like ten or eleven are gone. But…." I chew on the end of my pen, thinking.

"Wait." Dante straightens, standing taller. "Are you thinking it might be something in their bodies, like their genes, that every human starts with at birth and many, but not all, outgrow as they get older?"

"I hadn't thought of it that way, but, yes, possibly." I wave my pen.

Bethor taps the dimple in his chin with a finger. "But this has never happened before. If it had something to do with the makeup of their bodies, wouldn't it have?"

I wave my hands. "I'm just throwing out ideas."

Dante taps a lip. "The graves of the missing all look like something shredded the tops to get the bodies out."

"Or maybe...." Ambrielle catches my gaze. "Did something animate these bodies"—she waves her hands—"for whatever reason and they shredded the tops from inside?"

"And climbed out?" Nisroc's tone holds skepticism.

"So where are they? Where are all these reanimated dead humans, if that's the case?" Bethor closes his eyes. "Can you even imagine seeing decayed humans walking around?" A shiver rocks his body.

"I agree. That would be gross." I can't help squirming.

Silence again falls, as well as dusk, and the cemetery's safety lights come on as we continue noodling, searching for some plausible explanation.

I'm drained. I close my eyes as I talk to myself. "Are we making this too difficult? Do all these people share something in common? Something simple? If we could look them up...."

My eyelids fly open as I feel eyes on me.

"What?"

"Trainee Scum." Dante's tone is gentler than I've ever heard, and I perk up. "What were you writing down all day?"

I shift from one foot to the other. "Just the names, birthdates, and death dates for the missing humans. I didn't know if it might be useful at some point."

Dante smiles, and I swear my stomach quivers. What is up with that?

He looks around the circle. "Did anyone else write down any of that information?"

The other three shake their heads.

Dante rubs the back of his neck. "Seems Trainee Scum might actually have helped us out."

Bethor rolls his eyes, to which I let a corner of my mouth hitch.

It's backhanded, but wow, a compliment from my mentor? What's come over him?

"We're getting nowhere visiting more cemeteries. If Trainee Scum has that list, perhaps it's time to visit the library. What other option do we have?"

I ignore his slam and raise my eyebrows. "The library?"

"Yes, you know that place with all those books?" Dante brushes his bangs back from his face.

I roll my eyes. "I love to read. It's my most favorite place." I'd wanted to visit when I first arrived but haven't apparently earned that privilege yet.

"You're a bookworm?" Ambrielle's face lights up.

I raise a hand. "Guilty as charged."

"Me too." She leans in and squeezes my shoulder.

"I knew there was a reason I liked you."

Her voice drops to a whisper. "I'll warn you though, the books are probably a lot—" She snickers. "—spicier than you're used to. Like a lot, a lot."

Chapter Thirty-Three

I don't know if I'll ever get used to the perpetual dimness that saturates the second heaven. It's as clear as ink soup. My eyes had adjusted to the daylight and dusk of Earth, which are both brighter than this, so it's that much more obvious… and suffocating. Moments like this make me miss third heaven and my squad mates, my friends. I swallow and brush sadness aside as I climb the three steps to the library's doors.

Tension fills me as I follow Dante, beside Bethor, Ambrielle, and Nisroc. How I hope my list can give us the clue we need to figure this mystery out first—no pressure, but I really need that commendation.

A loud caw followed by a yelp greets us as Dante hauls the heavy wooden door open, and I inhale sharply.

"Okay. Okay. Stop. Please." A student cowers, hands over his head as he kneels on the runner of the dark, wood-paneled entry hall. A large onyx bird has him in its clutches, holding him in place as it flaps its wings.

The bird sounds another loud caw, and we shrink back, against the paneling as the door closes behind us.

Two black-robed males appear at the far end of the entry and stride toward us with grim expressions.

"We've got him, Corvo." The pair grab the student's arms and yank him up as the bird relents, retreating to a bench that runs the length of the opposite wall.

"You were warned about stealing books," one of the two says.

Corvo squawks, jerking its head as if miffed.

Unsurprisingly, the student remains silent.

"It's always the new ones." The other attendant shakes his head as, still grasping the student's forearms, the pair drag him back into the library. "Looks like some time in the Hall of Correction will do you good."

I throw a hand over my chest as I right myself, then swallow hard. Note to self, don't take any books, not that I'd planned to.

"Just make sure you check every book out." Ambrielle forces a smile that doesn't meet her eyes.

I nod slowly. "Got it."

"And on that note...." Dante motions for us to follow the apprehended student.

The smell of burning brimstone still lingers in my nostrils from navigating the courtyard after landing, but there's a different smell, like smoke, that hits my nose as we pass by the hulking, dark-wood front desk. A black-robed librarian looks down on the errant student from atop the elevated dais, verbally chastising him, between the pair of fuming attendants.

Good luck, whoever you are.

"Is something on fire?" I whisper to Ambrielle beside me.

She chuckles. "No, the library always smells like that."

I grimace but keep following Dante and Nisroc. The wood wall panels and dark-wood floor look well-worn, much like the rest of the school.

"Expecting a musty, stale, moldy-parchment smell?" Bethor leans in.

"Uh, kinda, yeah."

The dimple in his chin stands out as he grimaces. "I learned to stop expecting things to be what I'd always known."

"Noted."

Ambrielle points at a doorway we approach. "The Library of Alexandria is in there if you ever want to consult documents from that time."

My jaw drops. "Wait. What? But it was destroyed thousands of years ago."

Bethor chuckles. "Apparently the Prince burned it in order to bring its contents here. I guess he thought if humans continued building on their knowledge, they wouldn't be as easily influenced."

I give him a long look. "You're saying the flames didn't destroy it?"

Ambrielle nods. "Flames allow some things to be transported here. That's why many things on Earth burn."

I can only shake my head as I stare at the closed door as we pass. The Library of Alexandria is spelled out in block letters on the frosted glass of the top half, beneath the image of that dragon that seems to be everywhere.

"The entire library is in there?" My skin tingles. "There were thousands of scrolls. This building isn't that big."

"I don't know how it works, but I've been in there a few times, and it seems like it's all there, not that I'm a good judge of the space needed by that many scrolls." Ambrielle shrugs.

I can only laugh. The whole darn thing. "Unbelievable."

"This is the school's copy. At least that's how it was explained to me." Bethor furrows his brow, no doubt remembering the conversation in which he learned that.

"A copy?" My eyes go wide. "Of the whole freaking thing?"

"I guess the original as well as other copies exist in second heaven, but obviously we haven't ever left here to find out," Ambrielle adds.

Right. Right. We're all the same in that respect.

We pass by Aristotle's Library, the Library of Pergamum, the Imperial Library of Constantinople, and Bibliotecha Corviniana, the primary library during the Renaissance period on Earth.

My inner bookworm is dumbstruck. Never in my bookwormish existence did I ever dream of reading texts from any of these institutions. I know where I'll be spending my free time, if I ever get any.

We approach the end of the hall. Before us is a wall, the top half of which is fogged, but I can see things moving behind it, nearly like sharks or other fish swimming in large aquariums on Earth. Whatever room it is extends as far as I can see in both directions.

We follow Dante and Nisroc right.

"That's the Library of the Pre-Written, aka the Library of Thoughts." Ambrielle grimaces.

Bethor runs a hand down the long sleeve of his tunic. "You'll spend more time there than you care to."

"What does that even mean, the library of the pre-written? Of thoughts?"

Ambrielle waves off my question. "You'll find out soon enough."

My stomach tenses. Foreboding much?

We eventually pass what I guess is the school's own library collection with scores of books on shelves that extend up three floors. A large, high-ceilinged reading room stretches out in the middle. There are a good twenty or more tables lined up in three rows, but as with the rest of the place, only a few groups of students are around—not a surprise with everyone assigned to solving the mystery.

A couple turns later and Dante pushes open a door with Inquisition Center spelled out beneath that dragon image across the frosted glass. My stomach tenses. What am I getting myself into?

That burning smell gets significantly stronger as Ambrielle waves a hand over her nose, following Nisroc inside. "Nothing to worry about. This is where we query second heaven's history files. You can get information about both Earth as well as second heaven."

I exhale. Third heaven has a query center that serves much the same function, but what an awful name, Inquisition Center.

We turn left and head down a hall with more worn paneling on the left and several dark-wood doors, one right after the other, on the right. The only illumination comes from the flame of sconces every so often. Dante stops at the tenth door, which Nisroc opens.

It's tight in what feels like a cupboard with all five of us, but that's not what makes me inhale sharply, then start coughing with the smoke. There's no back wall to what looked like a study room. No, the back is open, and I barely hold in a shriek when a huge, emerald, plated head with long spikes above its eyes moves maybe twenty feet away from us. Its golden eyes take us in.

A dragon. There's a ginormous freaking dragon in here.

My heart races, and I grab for my celestial blade only to realize it's not there and never will be again. I brace beside Bethor as the creature eases up and makes its way toward us. The horde of gold coins, silver cups, an assortment of jewels, and other treasures it's been lying on sound a discordant chorus that accompanies the thing's raspy breathing as it approaches.

I keep one eye on the long claws at the end of its front feet and another on its wings that are tucked at the moment. I pray they stay that way.

"Trainee Scum." Dante's voice is demanding, like he's called me a few times already but I haven't heard him.

Everyone's looking at me as Bethor puts a hand on my arm and points to where Dante's waiting.

"Oh. Sorry. Sorry." My heart may beat out of my chest, but I ease forward, squeezing between the others.

"Get your notebook," Dante says when I reach him.

The dragon lets out a puff of smoke. Is it getting ticked at my delay?

I do my best to calm and do as bid as Dante turns to the beast. "Great Dragon, we need your assistance in determining if the humans whose information we will give you have anything in common."

Wait, this is what Dante and the others believe will help us figure out the mystery? A dragon? Seriously?

The dragon puffs more smoke. "What is this information worth to you? I perceive it is connected to the Prince's current quandary which, if solved, could benefit you handsomely."

The beast isn't moving its mouth, yet I definitely hear it. Seems it can speak telepathically. Interesting. I hadn't realized any being other than angels, fallen or not, possessed that ability.

Dante bobs his head. "You are as wise as ever, Great Dragon. I have something that I believe is worthy of that value, something that will make you and your riches all the greater."

I glance up at my mentor. Is he trying to sweet talk this beast?

Is he insane?

Chapter Thirty-Four

I swear the corner of the dragon's maw hitches, and it's all I can do to keep my knees locked.

"Do you now, then let's see this treasure." Amusement colors the dragon's voice.

Dread makes my stomach twist.

My mentor points to a thick, yellow line that I hadn't noticed until now. It marks the end of our space. "With your permission, Great Dragon, may I cross the line?"

"You'll have to take a chance." The beast chuckles.

I swallow hard.

"Thank you, Great Dragon." Turning away from the beast, Dante says, "Nisroc, Bethor, a little help."

I move back, beside Ambrielle and out of the way, as Dante reaches into his shift. Something gold, ornate, and carved appears, and the other males grab hold and help pull it out.

Grunts and groans along with Dante's repeated admonitions to be careful fill the cupboard-size space before the trio wrestles an enormous, gilded mirror from the shift. The thing is taller than any of the guys and must weigh a ton. Where in the universe did he get it?

The mirror blocks most of the opening, so what little light there was in the space, thanks to the glass domed roof, is banished. Nisroc and Bethor pant as they support the back of it.

Dante's breathing is labored as well. "Great Dragon, do you not agree that this is something that will make you and your riches all the greater?"

The click of talons on the wood floor draws closer. If I was Dante, stuck on the other side, I might pee my pants.

The quiet grows uncomfortable before the dragon finally speaks. "Yes. This is a fitting tribute." It comes out nearly like a purr. "I congratulate you on using more imagination than most in choosing this for payment."

"If you would permit three of us past the line, we can place it where you can most enjoy it."

"Oh, please," Nisroc murmurs. I'm getting sick on all the syrupy-sweet words, too, and nearly snort.

"Very well." The clicking recedes, and I can only assume the beast has backed off to give the males room.

It's several long minutes before the enormous mirror is wrestled into place where the dragon instructs, against a side wall. Dante has heaped on flattery the whole time.

Judging by the gleam in the dragon's golden eyes, it's furling and unfurling its wings, showing them off, and more, Dante's got the thing wrapped around his little finger.

Nisroc and Bethor scurry back over the yellow line, breathing heavily and wiping sweat from their brows. Dante follows close behind, probably not wanting to push his luck.

"Trainee Scum." Dante calls me forward again. "Please read your list."

My hand trembles as I begin, "Nicolai Schmidt, born 11 Oct 1839, died 28 Dec 1876; Oskar Schindler, born 28 April 1908, died 9 Oct 1974; James Leslie Starkey, born 3 Jan 1895, died 12 Jan 1938."

I glance between my list and the dragon as I continue reading names and dates. The creature has its emerald eyelids closed, and I wonder if it decided to take a nap, but I don't dare stop.

The dragon puffs out a particularly dense cloud of smoke, and I devolve into a coughing fit, so it's a few minutes before I manage to continue reading the last fifty or so names.

"That's all I wrote down." My tone is raspy as I try not to cough more.

The dragon opens its golden eyes. "You wish to know what, if anything, all of these humans share in common."

"That's right." Showing it respect can't hurt, so I add, "Please."

The dragon looks to the dome as if pondering.

I shift. Dante stands tall, never flinching.

"These humans do not share one commonality."

I drop my head, and three loud exhales sound behind me.

Dante plants his feet and pushes back his shoulders. "Do many of them share something?"

The dragon tilts its head as if considering answering, but then looks into the mirror. "The humans under ten years share nothing but their ages."

Dante lifts his chin. "And the others?"

I gotta give him credit. He's got tenacity.

The dragon continues admiring itself. "The older humans do share one common interest. They are all members of the Resistance."

"Every one of them?" Dante confirms.

The dragon smiles at itself in the mirror. "Yes."

I furrow my brow and whisper behind me. "What's the Resistance?"

"They're a rebel group," Nisroc murmurs.

Seriously? I've never heard of them. But all the older humans, every single one, are supposedly part of it.

Were all those missing drivers also part of that group? How do the children fit in? Where did they all disappear to?

Dante turns and taps his lips, then motions toward the door.

Ambrielle opens it, and we tiptoe out.

Out of earshot of the Inquisition Center, Dante slows when we reach the main library's wood-paneled reading area. Sconces on the end of every bookcase lend minimal light to the area. If they're going for cozy, they failed. It just makes it hard to see to read. No one's around, so we grab a table and sit.

"I've only ever gotten to ask one question before, and I didn't want to take the chance that Verdad would ask for additional payment."

"Where'd you get that mirror?" I can't help asking.

Dante smiles. "Let's just say I can be very resourceful."

I roll my eyes. It's not an answer, but we have more pressing matters to discuss, so I let it go.

"Tell me more about this resistance group." I run a hand down my jacket, leaning back in the squeaky wooden chair at the head of the table.

"They are a bunch of conspiracy theorists who consider the Enemy to be their founder." I tilt my head as Dante sweeps a hand over the worn tabletop to the right of me. "It's good they're gone. It'll make our lives easier."

Nisroc shifts beside Dante, his expression tight.

Bethor slumps in his chair across from Nisroc.

I lean in. "Conspiracy theorists? What do they believe?"

Ambrielle chews on a fingernail, worry lining her eyes, to my left.

"You'll learn more about them in history class, but among other things they believe in parting a raging river with a walking stick, lighting a shrub on fire but it not being consumed, tearing down a huge city wall by sounding a trumpet, reasoning with a stormy sea to get it to calm." Dante chuckles.

I furrow my brow. "A resistance group? It sounds like you're describing the Enemy's fans and admirers as well as events in…." I glance around to make sure we're still alone.

Bethor leans forward. "Shhh."

Ambrielle shakes her head, nearly imperceptibly, but it's enough to shut me up.

All the Almighty's fans and admirers are gone? My brain is off and running because I remember reading a prophecy a while back— never mind that I found it in the forbidden section of the library—in which, at some point, the Almighty was supposed to bring these very humans to live in the third heaven. It's what all that construction was for, to house them all. I inhale sharply. The last time I saw the mansion area, most of it was complete, along with the public squares.

I draw a hand over my mouth. Astread was reassigned to process engineering, leveraging her considerable discipline to improve efficiency in a host of areas. They were supposedly gearing up to handle a whole lot more citizens.

My brain won't quit. The prophecy mentioned that if one of those humans fell asleep, they'd still be brought to the third heaven, so they weren't in danger of missing out if they took a nap. My eyes go wide. Whoa. Wait. Had I misunderstood? Was it speaking figuratively of death and not just being asleep? Is that why all those graves were "missing their occupants"?

I can't hold back a whimper.

"What's wrong?" Nisroc asks, leaning forward.

I relay everything I've just been thinking, including the part about where I found it because this info is not common knowledge. I don't apologize for speaking about my past despite the fact we're not supposed to, and end with, "If I remember right, that prophecy supposedly happens not long before—" I check that we're still alone. "—the Enemy destroys Earth, like torches the place, as well as second heaven. It says more, but that's the most important." My voice comes out in a squeak.

I'd been reading it quickly because, well, I wasn't supposed to be looking at it, but it bothered me. All the humans who weren't taken to third heaven would die. I'd never forgotten—the imagery was just too vivid. It was no wonder it was filed in the restricted section.

Dante laughs. "*You* navigated the library's forbidden section?"

"Is that the only thing you got out of what I just shared?" I want to smack him. "I did, but that's not the important thing. What it said is."

Bethor's eyes go wide. "That's crazy."

"Not a wonder you ended up here then. Trespassing into forbidden territory." Dante snickers.

I roll my eyes.

Nisroc shakes his head and frowns at Dante, before he plants his open palms on the table as if steadying himself. "What about all those missing children?"

I shrug. "Maybe the Enemy just decided he wanted a bunch of little kids running around and took them to third heaven too?" I'm making it up. I've no idea.

"Why would… the Enemy want to destroy everything?" Ambrielle bites a lip.

I can only throw up my hands. "I don't know, but what I do know is that everything adds up with what happened to my partner, housing in third heaven, the missing humans, and empty graves. I don't remember what else that prophecy said, but if this is that, we have to find a way to stop it."

I have to save all those humans that are at risk. For that matter, I'd rather not be crispy critters if I can help it.

Dante chuckles. "Let me get this right. You're saying that the Enemy somehow grabbed all his groupies and brought them to third heaven?"

I nod, slowly. "If this is that prophecy being fulfilled."

"Why should we believe you?"

I open and close my mouth several times before finally spitting out, "Be-because it's true."

How can he not believe me?

Dante leans forward, and our gazes connect. "Prove it."

Nisroc gives Dante a hard look.

I wave my hands, disbelieving. "The book is in one of third heaven's libraries."

Dante looks to Ambrielle. "You're a bookworm. You've read a lot of the books here, haven't you?"

She leans in. "I have."

"Have you read any prophecy, like she describes, in any book in this library?"

She glances at me, then sighs. "I haven't."

"If she can't prove it, we can't get any commendations." Dante brings a hand down on the table.

My mouth drops open. "Is that the only thing you care about?"

Bethor runs a hand through his golden hair and blows out a breath.

They have to believe me. They have to.

My brain takes off at a gallop. How can I prove it? How?

A minute later, Operation Pet Poof comes to mind, and I suck in a breath. No. Really? Could it really be? I hadn't realized before, but in light of the latest events… if true, it would definitely convince them. But what if I'm wrong? No, I'm not. I feel it in my gut.

I throw up open palms. "That same prophecy mentions a *massive* attack on Israel by several foreign nations around the same time." I bite my lip as I look around the table.

Ambrielle furrows her brow.

Bethor cocks his head.

"The attack fails."

Nisroc's eyes go wide.

Dante barks in laughter. "Operation Pet Poof? You're saying it fails?"

"If this is that prophecy, that's what it says." I clench my jaw.

"That's really funny. From everything we witnessed across all those countries, there's no way it will fail. Israel's toast." Dante claps, chuckling. "That's a good one."

I don't laugh, much less clap. "Mossad said the operation was in its final stages of preparation." I lean forward, and my gaze connects with his. "If I'm right, if Israel wins, will you believe me about this prophecy?"

Dante guffaws. "You're serious." He shakes his head. "Sure, if the pet isn't utterly decimated, then I'll happily believe you."

"No." I shake my head. "Israel wins decisively."

"Fine. Whatever."

My stomach twists.

Stop doubting yourself, I reprimand myself. My gut is right, it is. I hope.

Chapter Thirty-Five

Kessien

I wipe my watery eyes; the vapor and stench of brimstone is making them burn no matter how much I blink. My sense of smell may forever be ruined too.

Despite the dim, it's clear the rest of the squad is fairing similarly.

I fail to see how the six Fallen guards patrolling not far away have become accustomed to this, but they're not wiping their eyes as they laze about in front of the hulking pair of wrought iron, dragon-accented gates that is the transfer point between second and third heaven.

It's been a month since Glad was here. The dispatcher has kept us busier than usual, per Michael's instruction, helping us "cope" with our loss. But when we're not busy, we've come here to watch for any clue as to where they might have taken her. We've tracked nearly a dozen messengers, but they've all been a bust.

"Demons." Jael nods. "Ten o'clock."

We all look that direction. There's a legion of six approaching.

Our leathers scrape against the coarse soil as the four of us scoot down, below the top of the jagged boulder we're hunkered down behind to wait until they're gone. With Glad's reputation among demons, I shudder to think what they'd do to her if she was turned over to those creatures.

My stomach twists. They wouldn't have done that, would they?

I rub the hilt of my trusty blade, unease biting into me. This is taking too long. What else can we do to find Glad?

Demons.

The single word strangles my swirling thoughts. Have I been thinking about these creatures wrong? What if…?

Issra tilts his head to the side as I sit straight up. "Demons never give up grudges, right?"

Aliyah scoots up and looks between Jael and me.

"Right…." Jael draws the word out.

"Not until they take revenge," Issra adds. "Sometimes not even then."

"What if instead of hiding from them, we grab one and see if it knows where Glad is?"

The trio exchange looks.

I raise a hand. "Hear me out. They've declared Glad a demon killer. They called what they did to Astread"—I air quote—"a down payment. Not to mention the ire she stoked by killing two more in retaliation."

Jael gives me a slow nod.

"Don't you think they'd know where their archnemesis is?"

"You think they know she's here?" Aliyah grimaces.

I nod. "I think it's a safe bet." My skin starts to tingle. "And I can't see the Fallen protecting her if they go after her."

Issra stiffens.

Ever the calm one, Jael pushes his shoulders back. "What are you suggesting?" He gives me a long look.

"I want to nab one of them and ask for directions to Glad."

"A male wants to ask for directions?" Aliyah raises an eyebrow.

I shrug.

"If we do this, we'll probably become targets too." Jael looks at each of us.

Issra flexes his fingers. "I'm okay with that if it means finding Glad."

"Me too." There's a gleam in Aliyah's eyes, like she's tempting the Enemy to try something. "But you don't have to if you don't feel comfortable, Jael."

"Just try to keep me away." He winks at Aliyah. "When I said I was all in to find Glad, I meant it."

"Then let's go hunt us some demon booty." Lightness erupts in my chest. This is so much better than waiting and hoping.

We scoot into a circle; then Jael holds up a hand, which we all join with our own. In hushed but enthusiastic whispers, we chant, "Let's do this," then bring our hands down.

I vanish us a safe distance from the transfer point so as not to be seen by those Fallen guards and unfurl my wings, keeping my celestial brightness dimmed, as do the others.

"One o'clock," Aliyah says behind me, not long after we begin a circular path around those dragon gates.

She's right. I count eight of them.

"Four per pair." Jael rubs the hilt of his sword with a thumb.

"Leave just one. It's all we should need," I say as our prey nears.

The instant the demons spot us, their pace hastens.

"Stay dimmed. No need to attract unwanted company in enemy territory," I quickly add.

Jael turns and covers my back as I draw my blade. Issra and Aliyah mimic a second later as the hideous menaces attack.

"Enemy scum," a wolfhound-sized, leathery-skinned foe hisses between protruding canine teeth, beside its mastiff-size partner.

Persuasion, my trusty blade, glows white, ready to help him realize he really doesn't want to fight us.

It takes little convincing with the wolfhound-size demon after I pierce one of its leathery wings, then find the joint between its shoulder and chest. Despite the skin's toughness, my blade cuts its hardened, black coat like butter, and it winks out of sight.

"*One*," Jael says mind-to-mind.

"*One for me, too.*"

I sneak a peek over at Aliyah and Issra. It's hard to tell how they're doing with three huge demons after them, but that mastiff-size demon is on me.

The thing takes a mighty downbeat of its wings and lunges, saliva spraying as it opens its maw.

It's a good thing I have four wings, because that peek to check on Aliyah and Issra cost me. I pump my lower wings, maneuvering to the side, out of the way, just before it slams its teeth closed on empty air.

It fully committed to that maneuver, and now it can't backpedal fast enough to avoid Persuasion's bite. My blade severs one of its pointed ears just before I find its tough neck and bring my blade down, hard. I'm rewarded with a spray of silver blood.

"*Two,*" I announce to my partner who battles another mastiff-size demon.

Aliyah and Issra have two Doberman-sized adversaries left.

It'll be easier to control a demon that size rather than the mastiff, and I communicate as much to everyone, then pivot, bringing my blade up and through the exposed abdomen of Jael's opponent. It winks out of sight, just as Aliyah's does.

"*Issra, you've got our guide. Keep it occupied. Don't wound it.*"

"*Will do,*" Issra grunts as he redirects his blade so it doesn't hit it.

Jael and I dart over to Aliyah behind the demon where it can't see us and sheath our blades. As engaged as Issra is keeping it, it never sees us coming. Aliyah and Jael each hook an arm over a leathery wing, holding them taut and immobilized. I rush forward, furling my wings so I don't hit my squad as I throw an arm around its stiff neck and pull myself even with one of its black eyes.

The thing lets out a squawk, reaching for my arm, then kicks back at me. But I'm far enough up its back that it can't reach me. I draw my legs up, relying on Aliyah and Jael to keep us aloft.

Issra brings his blade to the thing's chest and holds it there, effectively stilling its hands, although its long, bony fingers still clutch my arm.

"We're looking for information," I say into one of its pointed ears.

The thing spits, spraying Issra's arm, but it snaps its mouth shut when he moves the tip of his blade higher to right in front of its maw.

"We're looking for information," I repeat, "and you will cooperate because we can hurt you just enough to cause significant pain, but not enough to make you disappear."

I'm not a proponent of torture, but it's the only thing evil understands. And this demon is evil incarnate.

I feel its neck muscles contract as it attempts to dislodge Aliyah to no avail.

"Perhaps we cut a hole in the membrane of your wings or break the bones in one or both." I run my free hand over the taut wing membrane.

The thing tenses, fighting both Jael and Aliyah.

I nod Issra to reposition his blade below my arm, right above its heart, making the thing struggle more.

"We can do this all day," I taunt.

The creature continues fighting.

I'm not surprised. I expected nothing less from our enemy, but nothing will keep me, keep us, from finding Glad.

"Go ahead, Issra. I believe a small incision is in order."

Issra obliges, drawing silver blood, as well as a shriek.

"More?" I ask our captive. "Happy to."

The creature's struggling intensifies as Issra starts a second cut near the first, to the same result. But before he finishes, the creature pants, "Stop… I help."

I pat the creature on its bony head but don't loosen my hold on its neck. "A wise choice. The information we seek is the whereabouts of the angel Gladriel."

"Demon killer." Its tone is menacing, and a shiver runs down my back.

"Where is she?"

"School."

Issra and I exchange looks.

"Explain."

"Academy. Morningstar. Every Fallen start."

"They...." I want to say indoctrinate but rephrase. "They train newly fallen at this academy?"

"Yes."

I hate to ask this, but I have to know Glad's okay. "Have you gotten your revenge?" I hold my breath, afraid of the answer.

Issra tenses, meeting my gaze.

"No." It snarls.

I exhale.

"Forbidden... for now."

I don't even want to know what that means. All I know is sweeter words were never spoken.

"Show us this place." I draw my dagger and bring it to within a whisper of its eye. "I will not hesitate to inflict pain if you betray us. Do you understand?"

"Yes."

To the squad, I say, "Okay, release it."

Jael gives me a questioning look but does as I ask, as does Aliyah.

The creature digs its fingers under my forearm, attempting to loosen my grip around its neck as it beats its freed wings.

"Not happening." I flex my bicep. "We're happy to cut your wings more."

It huffs but stops struggling.

"I thought so. Now let's go."

The creature beats its wings. I can only hope it heads toward this school and not another legion of demons. Its gaze keeps darting to the tip of my knife. Good.

The squad flies so close that I can almost touch them as we fly over more rocky, barren soil. An occasional rust rock outcropping is all there is to break the monotony.

"Killer. School," the demon says sometime later.

I peer over the demon's shoulder and take in tall walls surrounding a number of buildings and a fire fountain behind a set of gates. A few beings stroll on walks that connect the structures.

The demon could be spinning tales. Glad may not be here, but my gut longs to believe, so I unfurl my wings and let it slip from my grip.

"Friends. Killer. Die." That's all the creature says as it beats a hasty retreat.

"Seems we won't be disappointed. We've been added to their hit list." Jael's attempt at humor falls flat.

"You sure Glad's here?" Issra asks, scanning the facility as he hovers beside me.

"No." I smile. "But I'm looking on the bright side, we know more about second heaven than we did. And we might even know her location."

"She could be in one of those buildings even now. So close." Aliyah chooses the optimistic side too.

Issra's gaze flits over the buildings as he runs a hand through his curly locks. Clearly, he's not convinced. Probably smart, but I can't help myself.

"Squadrons 427, 132, 698, 546, and 336 report for duty immediately," the heavenly dispatcher barks into my head, her words clipped. I furrow my brow. *"Israel is under siege from a number of nations bound by Lucifer's power, doing that scoundrel's bidding."*

We all ricochet glances. Under siege? Multiple nations?

"Massive aerial bombardment, enemy tanks, and troops spotted inside its borders rolling toward unknown targets. Demons and Fallen are engaging. Proceed to Israel ASAP."

The fact that she hasn't specified a code doesn't escape me. Between that and her shortness, my stomach twists. Nothing about this is usual.

Chapter Thirty-Six

Temptation class, my least favorite.

Dressed in a gray turtleneck and slacks and a black longcoat with upturned collar, Forcas leans back and runs a finger back and forth over his chiseled chin, taking in the seven of us as we take our seats.

I jiggle a foot at a desk between Ambrielle and Bethor, behind Dante and Nisroc in the dim, worn, institutional classroom. Layla and Liel have again taken the back row along with Sorath—they continue to ignore me, for which I'm thankful.

Several days have passed since my revelation in the library, and classes have resumed. No one has solved the mystery and claimed commendations. I'm still banking on that prophecy being the key. We just need to see how Operation Pet Poof turns out. When it does. I wish they'd hurry it up.

The bell sounds, and Forcas saunters forward, a grin on his face as his gaze comes to rest on me.

Crap. My stomach tenses, and I sit up straight.

"Still going by Trainee Scum?" He accents the last word. "Or have you become housebroken and earned a real name?"

I roll my eyes to myself and belt out, "My name is Trainee Scum, sir."

His gaze moves to Dante. "Making her earn it, good boy."

Dante's shoulders tense with the slight, but he raises his chin. "Thank you, Forcas. Can't make it easy or they'll never learn." He laughs, but it sounds forced.

It better be forced.

I grab hold of the side of my desk and squeeze, bracing as Forcas scans the seven of us.

What will he make me do today? Get another human to use a Ouija board or tarot cards, like yesterday and the days before? I will never, ever be okay attaching demons to and giving them control over unsuspecting humans. Anxiety, shame, guilt, and worse, demons are the originators of these thoughts in human minds. It's just wrong.

Will we attend another séance perhaps? Or will it be something much darker?

My breathing labors.

I've absolutely no doubt Forcas will force me to do even worse, utterly despicable things to humans before I'm allowed to be done with this class—if that ever happens.

I already loathe myself for not being stronger and resisting what he's already made me do.

The Hall of Correction is in my future, of that I am certain. A few commendations would be nice to postpone the inevitable though. If only we knew the outcome of the Prince's project.

Forcas draws his hands behind his back. "Several days ago, Professor Mossad gave you a taste of the Prince's secret project, Operation Pet Poof, that we've been working on." He snaps his fingers, making me jump. "It will come to fruition this very afternoon, and I cannot resist the temptation of seeing it happen, and I want you to experience it with me." He beams.

Ask and it shall be given.

Bethor coughs beside me.

"Something wrong, Bethor?" Forcus's gaze is piercing.

"No, sir." He thumps his chest with a fist.

Ambrielle reaches over and taps the corner of my desk. Yes, here we go.

At least there'll be no forcing me to do anything today. I breathe a sigh of relief. How I pray I'm right about the prophecy. Nine to ten million human lives are on the line.

Although, if I am right, more lives will be on the line if the Almighty plans to torch the Earth and second heaven. I've no idea why the Almighty would do this, but I can't think about that right now. One thing at a time.

"As students, you will take no unnecessary risks. There will be Fallen and demons fighting our Enemy's forces, but you will only observe, is that clear?" Forcas locks gazes with each of us, receiving a nod or verbal assent before he's satisfied. "Then let's go."

Several minutes later, Forcas is giddy, his smile never broader as dim daylight appears as we land. He extends his arms, palms up. "Welcome to Mount Bental in the Golan Heights." His black longcoat sways as he strides toward a wrought iron fence that lines the edge of the red gravel plateau we landed on. It's just beyond a parking lot that's behind us.

What looks like a tourist rest stop stands off to our left. Its roof is sloped with large windows to take in the sweeping views of a large sea off to the left. Our rocky outcropping of an observation spot is higher than everything around us. The lower-lying ground below is littered with shrubs and grasses and has a lushness and beauty about it.

"This should be the perfect spot to get a bird's-eye view of Israel's utter defeat." Forcas rubs his hands together.

Layla and Leil, aka L-squared as I've taken to calling them, huddle together to our left, eyes wide with the cacophony the horde of demons creates as they fly above. Sorath looks on with ambivalence. The skies are thick with them, flying in swarms, shrieking. The demons must sense what's about to happen, or they've been told. They give me the creeps and also make what should be bright skies at this time of day dark. The humans inside the rest stop only see dark clouds, but I know differently. I just hope these menaces are too preoccupied to notice or care about me.

Bethor folds his arms over his chest beside Dante.

"That's the Sea of Galilee." Forcas points to the body of water to the left. "And that's the Mediterranean." He bobs his head to the right, at the long expanse of water that I don't see an end to. "Israel's not very big, so we can see most of it from here. Do you see Jerusalem and Tel Aviv?"

"You mean that and that?" Bethor asks, pointing at two sprawling metropolitan areas as he steps forward, toward Nisroc.

I squint, following where he's indicating.

Forcas smiles. "That's right. Jerusalem is on the left and Tel Aviv on the right."

Out of our teacher's earshot, I cup my mouth and whisper into Ambrielle's ear. "Random bookworm trivia fact: Over half of the ten million Israelis live in those two cities."

A corner of her mouth hitches.

Forcas crows, "They won't exist much longer."

I pinch the skin at my throat. Not so if that prophecy is correct.

Dante bumps my shoulder, on my other side, and raises one eyebrow. He wants to know if I'm sticking with my story.

I return a sharp nod despite my angst, to which he grins.

How I pray I'm right.

Ambrielle ricochets glances between the two of us while Nisroc and Bethor survey the landscape where they stand. Nisroc's fists rest on his hips. Bethor looks no more at ease, judging by the stiffness of his body, not to mention his grip on the fence, not far from Forcas.

"Where are all the armies?" I throw the question out to no one in particular. I can't help but be curious because Mossad made such a big deal out of this, but the only soldiers I see are the five in camo fatigues toting machine guns, checking cars going through a gate in what looks like a border fence behind us, not far away. I don't see so much as one tank, much less invading soldier.

Forcas pivots and gives me more of his ultra-white teeth. "Ah, Trainee Scum, watch and learn."

I roll my eyes when he turns back around.

The demons' shrieks intensify, and they scatter as the sound of multiple airplanes streaking through the skies above…. No. Wait. I twist and squint at the now clear skies, straining to make out whatever is driving the demons off.

I hold up a hand to block the sun as I trace the white vapor trails of a good ten somethings.

My skin prickles. They're not airplanes…. They're missiles.

"And so it begins." Forcas claps as he laughs.

Sirens begin blaring, no doubt warning of the incoming barrage.

The tourists in the rest stop rush out the doors and race for their cars. One squeals his car's wheels on the pavement as they leave.

I hold my breath as I continue watching the armaments soar until they poof out of existence in multiple aerial explosions.

"That would be Israel's Iron Dome system at work, but don't worry, we'll easily overwhelm it." Forcas swings his arms, gloating at the brilliance of whatever plans he and Mossad helped the Prince hatch.

The sirens continue blaring as several more missiles appear from the Mediterranean to the right, as well as more from directly south of us.

My heart accelerates as I watch until, like the first ones, these also evaporate in aerial explosions that look small from this distance. Up close, I'm sure they're loud and terrifying. My heart goes out to the humans who are enduring this.

"Which country said it had submarines positioned in the sea?" I ask.

"That would be our very good Iranian friends." Forcas practically crows.

For a guy who's usually cool and suave, he's emoting more than I've ever seen.

It's annoying.

Dante crosses his arms and leans back, not saying a word, just taking it all in.

I cover my ears as more and more and more missiles soar overhead, coming from every direction.

Most are intercepted in the air, but a few hit something judging by the dust that billows up on the horizon. I pray the humans have taken cover someplace safe.

Mossad said they planned to overwhelm Israel's air defense system, I believe it.

"Allahu akbar."

I've been focused on the skies, but as the chorus of shouts reaches us, I study the plain and furrow my brow. A long line of shrubs move below us.

Oh, boy. I cross my arms, holding myself tightly.

Hundreds of soldiers appear from under camouflage they throw off, continuing to chant as they wave green flags with a white crescent moon and single star. If memory serves, that's the flag of Islam.

I bite a lip. What are they doing?

"Yes! Yes!" Forcas raises his fists above his head.

Bethor takes several side steps, increasing the space between him and our teacher. I don't blame him.

The soldiers disappear, and seconds later, the growl of engines starting reaches us. Tan sticks appear out of the ground and grow longer until....

I squeeze my arms tighter still—I may give myself bruises—and my stomach twists as more come into view.

Tanks. They hid tanks. There are dozens of them. And that's just here. I guarantee there are more hidden elsewhere.

Only as the long column of fighting machines fully emerges and begins rolling toward whatever destination they have, do I get a true sense of the armies that have been mobilized in this cause.

They've spared no expense. Absolutely nothing will stand in their way.

Chapter Thirty-Seven

The barrage of rockets and shells continues, roaring overhead every few seconds.

Motion on the road those tourists just fled on draws my attention. A column of camo-painted trucks comes into view. Some trucks have hard shells that probably carry supplies, some have only tarps covering the load. Mobile rocket launchers perch on several others. They're all headed toward the conflict, along with those tanks.

"The ones with tarps overtop are carrying soldiers," Nisroc calls over a shoulder. "I just saw a soldier pop his head out."

"They certainly are." Forcas bobs his head, like he can't get enough. "Several hundred thousand troops will arrive before this is over. Isn't this amazing?" He laughs, never taking his eyes off the spectacle.

It's a good thing he never looks back at us, or he'd see how stiff I am.

"You bunch of wusses are speechless." Our teacher guffaws.

As if intent to shift Forcas's assessment as any self-respecting brownnoser would, Dante calls over the roar of more rocket fire, "It's absolutely brilliant, Forcas."

My eyes go wide. I can't believe he just said that.

"It is, isn't it?" Forcas gloats.

"We have to play along," Ambrielle whispers in my ear. "Perhaps we should make a game of it?"

Forcas turns and catches my gaze. Holding up an open palm, he says, "Trainee Scum, join me. Let's enjoy this extravaganza together."

Dante stiffens beside me. It's barely noticeable, but I'm learning his tells.

I glance at Ambrielle. Make a game of it. I won't be hurting humans, just watching an evil, demented plan unfold… until it doesn't, I hope. But I still don't want to be anywhere near our teacher.

Play along.

Of course, to be next to Forcas when it all goes south… I could get into that. Definitely.

Dante takes a step forward, but Forcas holds up a hand. "No need to join us. I'll babysit your pet for a bit."

Dante holds up his hands, smiling in surrender. "Thank you, sir. Much appreciated. Just let me know when you've had enough."

I give my mentor a cold look. I know he's playing along, but he'll pay for that.

I give Ambrielle a tiny nod, then take a deep breath. I can do this.

Forcas watches as I force a smile and step forward. I swing my hands at my sides, pretending I haven't a care in the world, that standing beside my teacher is a great honor.

Arm still extended, Forcas throws it around my shoulders when I reach him and draws me into his side.

It's all I can do not to punch him. Miraculously, I manage to keep it together, despite being stiff. My heart is nearly beating out of my chest.

"So what do you think so far, Trainee Scum?" It comes out as a purr.

Play along. Play along. I force myself to relax despite the awkwardness of the situation.

"It's incredible, sir." I'm not lying.

More deafening missiles soar over us, but I'm not about to cover my ears.

Once they've passed, Forcas squeezes my shoulder. "Thank you, Trainee Scum. I appreciate that."

I focus on keeping my breathing even.

Come on, prophecy. Go, prophecy. Israel could really use a little intervention right about now.

As if on command, the first squadron of celestial warriors comes into focus, and I inhale sharply. I can't help it. Forcas notices my reaction.

"Happy to see them, are you?" His tone holds an icy edge.

He guessed it.

"Seems your owner has his work cut out for him, breaking you." His grip on my shoulder tightens, becoming more than a little uncomfortable, but I resist flinching. I won't give him the satisfaction.

To distract myself, I return my focus to the celestials. I can't deny they're a sight for sore eyes as they bat down many of the missiles, even though they aren't the squadron I'd really like to see.

Demons reassert themselves, joined by Fallen warrior angels in the skies, returning things to the previous dim state despite the continuing barrage; the missiles pass right through them.

More celestial squadrons appear and engage. But when Kessien, Jael, Issra, and Aliyah materialize in the sky not far away, I can't hold back a yip.

My heart races for a wholly different reason. How I miss them.

Forcas releases my shoulder and takes to running his fingers across my fuzzy scalp. It's invasive as I'm sure he intends, but focused as I am on those I love, I'm immune.

Jael at his back, Kessien brings his celestial blade down. I can't help but appreciate his abundant wings. Two demons vanish. How I miss watching him fight. He's a beautiful male, but even more beautiful when he's in action.

My heart aches with the love I have for him.

Forcas grunts, no doubt in frustration, and swats me away. "Get out of here. Go back to your master. I don't suffer pets that aren't housebroken."

I need no encouragement. I turn and hightail it back toward friendly territory.

"Dante. Come here." There's no humor in our teacher's tone.

My mentor scowls as I pass him. I shrug, unrepentant.

I pivot when I reach Ambrielle, locating Kessien and the others again. They continue slicing and dicing and being their all-around amazing warrior selves.

But there's so many Fallen and demons.

I scan the ground. That convoy continues to grow, stretching along the road like an overgrown snake. While I don't see more tanks, I can't help wondering how exactly this prophecy is supposed to work.

A fat raindrop splats on my cheek, followed by another at my feet. More pregnant drops start to fall. But before long, they've condensed into ice pellets that bounce as they hit the ground. Thankfully they don't hurt passing through me, but they're starting to impair visibility with their increasing pace.

I take in Issra and Aliyah as they take more demons out, and it's all I can do not to cheer them on as aerial fighting continues. They're beautiful fighting, especially Kessien. I can't take my eyes off him as he swings his blade and another demon vanishes. How I miss him.

Kessien pivots and our gazes connect. He's a good distance away and visibility stinks, but there's no mistaking it. My heart races.

"Kessien."

"Glad." He sounds winded. I inhale sharply. Am I imagining things? No, it's definitely him that I hear in my head. But how? Our telepathic connection was severed.

"Kessien. Oh—"

Before I finish the thought, he turns back to his next adversary and barely gets his blade up in time.

I draw my hands over my mouth. How did I hear him?

"Kessien."

But he doesn't respond with his attention focused on his next opponent.

"This hail is making it hard to see. Let's move." Forcas waves us toward him.

No. Every fiber of my being resists my teacher's instruction. I'm so close to Kessien and my friends. No, this can't be happening.

My gaze is fixed on the skies, making my steps slow as I amble toward our maniac teacher. I'm the last one to reach the circle and take Bethor and Nisroc's hands.

Forcas gives my mentor an icy look. "Dante, break your pet before I'm forced to break you."

"Yes, Forcas." Dante's jaw is tight as he holds eye contact with our teacher.

L-squared smiles at me from across the circle, Sorath ignores. I couldn't care less.

Ambrielle bites her lip as she catches my gaze. I don't mean to worry her, but sometimes…. I shake my head, hoping she understands my message, not to worry.

I fist a hand. So close. Kessien spoke telepathically. I know he did. I don't want to leave, but there's nothing else I can do.

Oh, Kessien. I get one last glimpse of him and my friends battling in the skies before everything goes dark.

Not more than a minute later, we land and Forcas says, "This is Mount Nebo in Jordan. We're not far from the border of Israel." His words are clipped, and he steps away from us, striding toward a knee-high, limestone wall that rings the scenic overlook.

I push back thoughts and frustration over Kessien. I'll just make myself miserable if I don't. I'll give myself time to think about and figure this out later. Definitely.

There's no precipitation here, but thunder and lightning create an ominous feel to the rain and hail falling in sheets not far away. The downpour is so thick I can't make out what's happening on the ground below.

"That's weird." Bethor points at the deluge.

"It's almost like the border is a boundary," Ambrielle adds, furrowing her brow.

Dante rounds on me and grabs my arm. He growls in my ear, "That's the last time you'll embarrass me in front of Forcas."

Before I can respond, the temperature drops dramatically and the size of the hail increases, becoming like baseballs, maybe even softballs.

"Whoa." I've never seen hail this size.

Dante loosens his grip as he pivots.

A peal of thunder claps not far away and makes my heart speed. It's nearly deafening.

"I can't see missiles being able to fly in this stuff," Nisroc remarks above the tumult.

The ground beneath my feet gives a lurch, and I grab Dante's arm to steady myself.

Layla shrieks, reaching for Liel, as more vigorous shaking ensues.

Just when it seems like nothing can make things worse, a distinct sulfur smell assaults my nose as fist-size rocks mix with the hail.

I tighten my grip on Dante's arm as the shaking intensifies.

"All we need is fire," Dante mumbles, loud enough that only I can hear him.

Sulfur's rotten egg stench that's permeating the air makes my stomach churn.

Another blinding flash of lightning streaks through the sky, chased by a deafening clap of thunder a second later.

"What's that?" Bethor cries, pointing.

My eyes go wide as I take in a blinding, pure-white streak that touches the ground on the edge of the deluge. It's not lightning; it's way too thick for that, and it stays there, standing tall a good twenty or more feet. It reminds me of a fire tornado.

More and more of the white-hot spouts descend, swaying in place despite the torrent of rain, hail, and sulfur rocks pummeling the plain. There must be hundreds of them, and that's just the ones I can see. I guarantee there's more.

"Be careful what you wish for, Dante."

Another tremor shakes our perch, and Nisroc enfolds Ambrielle and Bethor in a bear hug.

Dante brushes his bangs back as he surveys the horizon. "Nothing can survive this."

Chapter Thirty-Eight

"Nothing can survive this." Dante's words clang in my head.

I don't disagree. There's no way even the good guys will survive at this rate. Have I been completely wrong? Is this not the fulfillment of part of that prophecy?

Dante catches my gaze. Gone is the tightness of his snarl for embarrassing him in front of Forcas minutes before. Instead, he gives me a look like none he's ever given me—there's warmth in his amethyst eyes and a corner of his mouth hitches.

My breathing labors.

"I think you may have just earned us all commendations."

"The prophecy?" My voice wavers.

He nods. "Assuming the Israelis aren't harmed."

My eyes bounce back to the tumult. "You think that's even possible?"

"I thought you believed in that prophecy."

I roll my eyes, making him laugh. He actually laughs.

Nisroc and the others furrow their brows as they look our way, still huddled. D-squared ignores us, cowering as the ground gives another good shake.

Forcas is still standing by that wall. His posture is rigid, hands fisted at his sides.

I ticked him off earlier, but I guarantee he's not thinking about me right this minute. I can only imagine what's going through his head. I know what disappointment feels like, boy do I, and I almost want to feel sorry for him. Almost. But I don't.

As suddenly as the chaos began, the rain, hail, brimstone and fire tornados stop, along with the ground's shaking. It just stops. It's like someone turned off a water spigot or flipped a switch.

My jaw drops, and I step from Dante's hold, then scan the suddenly blue-again skies. I'm not alone.

Not one demon, fallen angel, or celestial warrior lingers. The sun is shining. It's utterly silent.

Bethor's eyes are wide as Nisroc drops his arms and steps back.

"What… just happened?" Dahlia asks.

Forcas flexes his fingers, then jerks on his coat sleeve. No doubt smoke would billow from his ears if it could.

I believe I'll stay as far away from him as possible.

I turn my focus to the plain. And my stomach twists.

Blackened earth, twisted tanks and trucks, bodies, and blood stretch for miles.

"Do you suppose he'd mind if we get a closer look?" I nod toward our fuming teacher's back.

Dante nods. Turning to the others, he says, "Anyone who wants to investigate, let's go, but stick together."

We all unfurl our wings.

Dante calls, "Forcas, unless you have an assignment for us, we want to have a look."

Our teacher doesn't so much as twitch for over a minute while we await his response.

Dante shrugs, then points upward, and as one, the seven of us launch.

"Nothing can survive this." Dante's words flow through my mind again as our shadows brush Jordan's dry, rocky ground. A large sea passes by below a minute later, just before we cross some line of demarcation, because the devastation begins right here.

Smoke rolls off a line of a dozen tanks whose treads are in shreds. The turret of one lays askew several yards away, along with one of those green flags. The gun of another has been bent and points at the ground. Others are completely smashed, flatter than pancakes, no doubt from the hail.

Soldiers' bodies lay at awkward angles in various states of dismemberment. No doubt many are still inside the pulverized machines.

We near the remains of a long column of supply trucks in no better shape. Every wheel has burst, and the mobile artillery batteries lay on their side, flattened. Crimson flows from the back of several of the trucks—those soldiers didn't stand a chance. No one could have survived that, exposed as they were.

A bird's caw to my right draws my attention. Several vultures fly not far off. It didn't take them long. It's a disgusting thought, but they'll feast for days from the looks of things.

Deep crevasses mar the ground everywhere, the work of all those earthquakes. While we felt rolling and rocking, we couldn't have experienced anything compared to what they did here. I wonder where the epicenter was.

I furrow my brow, then call over to Ambrielle beside me, "I didn't memorize the landscape of Israel before all the hail started, but I could have sworn it had a lot more rolling hills and valleys, or am I imagining that?"

She looks over at me, then below. "You know, I think you're right. That's so weird. All the hills are just gone."

"It's like those earthquakes flattened everything."

She bobs her head, still studying the ground.

We soar past more and more and more smoking tanks and trucks. I spot what I think are wolves and striped hyena packs already on the prowl not long after.

We approach the debris of a building. From what's left of a rounded dome, it looks like it was a mosque, but I can't be sure.

"Jerusalem straight ahead," Nisroc calls over a shoulder from beside Dante.

At this distance, the ancient city is a mound on the horizon. My stomach quivers at the possibilities of what we'll find. Was I right about the prophecy?

I strain to see as we approach. But before we've even reached it, I can tell that the entire city stands tall despite the strong quakes—not one tall spire, much less high-rise, has collapsed. Even the iconic gold dome of the Al-Aqsa Mosque atop the temple mount looks intact.

Another line of ruined tanks lies just outside the city walls, a stark contrast to the city itself.

"The walls are still standing." I point.

On my other side, Bethor's mouth drops open. "After all those shocks? That's crazy. They must really know how to build strong walls."

I spot humans coming out of hiding and moving about, and tingling erupts in my chest. Nine to ten million Israelis have been spared; I know it in my gut.

It's the prophecy. It has to be.

I tip my head back and laugh. Despite much of it being lost to the wind, Ambrielle touches my wingtip with hers. Bethor does the same on my other side.

Curiosity apparently satisfied, L-squared along with Sorath bug out, heading home, or so they say. Who knows, who cares? I'm just glad to be rid of their judgmental stuck-upness.

The thwap, thwap, thwap of helicopters and their blades join us in the air as we continue on to Tel Aviv and several smaller cities. No doubt humans are assessing the damage and necessary clean-up efforts.

These cities have been spared, but between them lays ruin and devastation, marked with those green flags. It's literally going to take months to clean up all the bodies, even with the scavengers gorging themselves. Add to that the time it will take to dispose of all the pulverized equipment.

To say that the Prince's forces were destroyed is an understatement. No, they've been utterly and completely decimated.

The sun's orange rays are stretching long across the city of Beer-Sheva as we finally set down in a grassy, manicured park near a lake. Adults stroll on walking paths toward a food pavilion, enjoying the warm weather despite the chaos the day has seen.

It's unbelievable. Humans are certainly resilient.

I glance about, expecting to hear the shouts of children, but there are none. What's more, the jungle gym stands empty, along with the swings not far away.

I hadn't been back to Earth since we investigated the desecrated graves before today, and I hadn't come in contact with families to notice other children then. Was it not just buried children who vanished? Are there no children left on the entire planet? It seems impossible, but who knows?

"I'm in a mood to celebrate. Anyone want some halva?" Dante asks, rubbing his hands together.

Halva is a fudgelike dessert made from sesame seeds. The semisweet, nutty flavor and crumbly, fluffy texture are what make it unique and delicious.

"You and your halva." Ambrielle shakes her head in mock scorn where she sits down on a concrete bench, her back to the pond. "He'd get halva even if there was nothing to celebrate. I'll take raspberry, if they have some."

"You got me there," Dante chuckles.

I've never seen my mentor so relaxed. It's nice. It seems he may actually have a personality beyond brownnosing control freak. But how long will it last?

"I'll take pistachio," Bethor says, stretching out his legs as he props himself against Ambrielle's bench.

I plop down beside Bethor on the grass and lean against a tree. "I'd like chocolate, please."

"I'll go with you," Nisroc offers.

We're all eating our sweet treats several minutes later when Dante, leaning against another shade tree, wipes his hands on the grass and clears his throat. "As I said when we arrived, I'm in a mood to celebrate."

Ambrielle and I exchange questioning looks.

"Based upon what happened today, I'm willing to grant that this prophecy of which you speak"—he bobs his head toward me—"is true and is what we've just seen unfold, as crazy as it seems." He shakes his head.

Nisroc nods, and Bethor sends a smile my way.

"That being the case, I think our trainee has earned her name."

I inhale sharply and draw a hand to my chest. He's recognizing me. Until this instant, I hadn't realized how much I loathe that other moniker. I'd sucked it up and hadn't allowed myself to dwell on it but it was a crap name.

Ambrielle tumbles off the bench and envelops me in a hug.

Bethor puts two fingers in his mouth and whistles while Nisroc claps and says, "Hear! Hear!"

Dante laughs. "So, what is your name?"

Ambrielle climbs back onto her bench.

I've no idea if those demons can trace me by my celestial name, so I decide to stick with what I first blurted out to Major Adoel, my traitorous escort to the academy.

"Call me Dree." I grin.

"I like it," Ambrielle says.

"Well, Dree, I think you will be our spokesperson to present your theory to Arioch so we can get those commendations."

My eyes go wide. "But we don't have the prophecy. How will he ever believe me?"

Dante wags his brows, his face taking on a mischievous look. "I have reason to believe Arioch was miffed when the Prince passed him over way back when for Operation Pet Poof, choosing to work directly with Mossad and Forcas instead of him."

Interesting.

"You have reason to believe…," Nisroc murmurs, chuckling as he picks at a blade of grass.

Dante holds up a hand. "What? I do."

Nisroc waves him off. "Oh, I believe you. I won't even ask how you came by this information."

I snort. I don't know much about Dante, but from what little I do, I believe it.

Dante laughs. "But back to the prophecy. I believe we can use this to our advantage. We tell him about the prophecy, and he'll send us to find it. Meanwhile we enjoy the benefits of his favor, which will extend the life of our commendations."

"Spoken as only a brownnoser could," Ambrielle says, earning laughs from everyone.

I shake my head. "You're one scary guy, Dante."

"Thank you, Dree. I'll take that as a compliment."

He's so certain. I just hope we can stop the destruction of Earth and second heaven. I've no idea how much time we have, but we've got a lot to do, and the clock is ticking.

Before I can think more on it, movement above catches my eye. I suck in a breath as Kessien and my warrior squad mates land not far away, taking ready poses, swords drawn.

Chapter Thirty-Nine

Kessien

"I knew it. I knew I sensed Glad," I crow to the others as we land. I have no idea how I sensed her location when our telepathic connection was severed, but I threw caution to the wind in the face of their skepticism and followed my gut.

My heart pounds as my gaze locks with hers. She's here. She's really here. Excitement makes my arms tremble, and I grip Persuasion's hilt more tightly.

But as I look her over, anger ignites. What have they done to her beautiful hair? It's gone. I clench my jaw. What else have they done to her?

Glad yips and scrambles up, grinning. She rushes into Aliyah's arms, then hugs Issra and Jael before stopping in front of me.

She bites her lip. My stomach quivers.

Our parting was rushed. I laid a lot on her, and while she kissed me passionately, we didn't have a chance to savor the afterglow, much less talk about what our mutual confessions might mean.

Glad. Love and longing flavor her name.

Her lips turn up in a smile, her eyes not leaving mine. I'm dying to hear what she's thinking.

A second later, she furrows her brow and frowns. "Can you not hear me in your head?"

My mouth goes slack. "No." My shoulders slump.

A corner of her mouth turns up as she closes the gap between us. "Then I guess I'll have to show you."

My heart beats wildly as she rises up on her tiptoes and brings her lips to mine.

"Oh, Glad. I missed you." I envelop her in my arms and deepen the kiss. All that longing and wishing and hoping of the last month comes pouring out in the kiss. I can't get enough of her.

"And I missed you." Her lips move on mine as she brings her arms around my neck.

I'm lost in her, but I have to know what they've done to her. *"What'd they do to your hair?"* Although she's still in my arms, I can't keep angst from my tone.

She pulls back a little, smiling. "That's what you really want to know?"

I pull her closer. *"I have to."*

Her smile fades, and she whispers, "It hasn't been easy." She looks away. "Let's just say I've earned what I've gotten because I won't do what they demand when it comes to mistreating humans."

A shiver scales my back. I fear to think what that might be. *"What else have they done to you that I can't see?"*

"Nothing, thanks to my mentor, Dante, and the rest of my new friends."

I look up, over her shoulder. I keep a hand on the small of her back as she turns to face them.

"So you're being the same selfless, frustrating, at times reckless female who follows her heart like always, no matter what rule gets in the way."

She snorts. "They're growing to love that about me… just like you. They just don't know it yet."

Jael, Issra, and Aliyah still hold their weapons at the ready, eyes fixed on Glad's four Fallen friends who stand watching us with a mix of expressions.

Glad steps forward. "While we're not supposed to talk about our past, I'd like you to meet my warrior squadron who I served with for ages."

I furrow my brow at the odd statement. Not recognizing her past?

I nod Jael and the others to stand down, and they gather around me as she makes the rounds of introductions. I can only say she looks happy with these beings. I'm not sure what to think about that.

"How did you find her?" There's no humor in Dante's voice as he shoves his overlong hair out of his face with a flick of his wrist. He takes several tight steps forward, then crosses his arms and looks us over with cold, flinty eyes.

Glad glances at Dante, then turns toward us, a furrow marring her brow.

The other two males, Bethor and Nisroc, I think she said, remain back, holding stiff postures. Ambrielle looks conflicted.

Jael's thumb caresses the hilt of his sheathed blade.

She said these Fallen have protected her. While I don't see it, I believe her despite this guy's churlishness. Perhaps a goodwill gesture might bring him around.

"During fierce fighting over Israel, Glad and I spotted each other earlier today. Despite her telepathic connections having been severed when she left third heaven, somehow I started sensing her location much like we normally do. That's what we followed. I've no idea how it happened, especially because no one else could sense her." I won't mention the grief, aka kidding, I took from Jael and the others over it.

Glad's eyes go wide.

Dante's eyebrows rise for half a second. "You came after a Fallen. That's highly irregular."

I glance at Glad. "It is." A smile mounts my lips, which she returns.

Her mentor tenses his crossed arms and frowns.

What's his deal? If I didn't know better, I'd say he's jealous. My jaw stiffens unbidden. Is that even possible? What's been going on between them? I shift. It's time to set things straight.

"I mean to find a way to reverse her sentence and restore her to third heaven."

Surprise ripples through Glad's friends.

Dante barks a laugh. "I don't believe there's any history of a banished ever being allowed back into third heaven."

"Has anyone asked?" I raise an eyebrow.

"It's possible?" Ambrielle steps forward, stopping beside Dante. She looks like she's holding her breath.

I fix my gaze on Glad. "I think I might have found a way. We need to verify."

Glad draws a hand to her chest. In a whisper she says, "You promised you'd try."

I nod as the Fallen males bandy glances about behind Dante, who lowers his arms.

It's hope I see rising in them. I understand, because if this proves correct, they all might be restored.

Dante clears his throat. "You said you're verifying."

"Yes, I have a lead. We're going to check it out. Once we confirm it, you'll be the first to know."

"If they're researching that, maybe they can get us that prophecy while they're at it since they have access to the library?" Nisroc stops beside Dante. Bethor comes even with Ambrielle on his other side.

"That's a great idea." Glad's practically bouncing, and I can't hold back a chuckle.

"A prophecy?" I rub a buckle on my leathers.

"Yes. Have significantly more humans arrived in third heaven recently?" Glad asks.

Aliyah inhales. "How'd you know?"

Glad's smile can't get any wider. She gives Dante an "I told you so" look, and I snort.

"Like how many more?" Bethor asks, brushing his hair over his shoulder.

Jael recounts the highlights of the last many days, ending with, "I've never seen so many arrive all at once."

"So this prophecy?" I move to get us back to that.

"Right, yes." Glad bobs her head. "When lots of humans went missing all of a sudden, the whole school was tasked with figuring out what happened to part of them, the ones who disappeared from all those graves."

I give Glad a long look. "Disappeared from graves? What are you talking about?"

Nisroc snorts. "You heard her right."

"Wait, you're telling me there are empty graves here? How?"

"That's what we're supposed to figure out," Dante confirms, pushing his hair back.

"The merging...," Jael murmurs.

I look over at him, brow furrowed.

Everyone follows my gaze.

"Remember those spirits who merged with the new arrivals? I'd wager that's what that was."

Issra draws a fist over his mouth, eyes wide.

My mouth opens and closes. "You think that was the reuniting of their white-robed physical bodies, like dead, in-the-grave, decayed, decomposed bodies, with their spirits who have been in third heaven for a while?"

He nods. "It makes sense." He recounts the details of watching several beings merge.

"Seriously?" Dante says, exchanging a glance with Nisroc.

I'm speechless for the second time in one day. The Almighty somehow reanimated the bodies of his dead followers? And brought them to third heaven? Unbelievable.

"If that's the case," Glad interrupts my musings, "when we were researching, I remembered a prophecy I read a while ago that talked about a time when"—she looks Dante up and down—"the Almighty would bring a lot of humans to third heaven. It sounds like that's what's happened."

Aliyah furrows her brow. "Where did you read that?"

Glad scrunches her face. She's too cute. "It was in the section reserved only for human reading—you know, the forbidden section."

Issra's brows nearly hit his hairline. "You snuck in there?"

Dante snorts, clearly unsurprised.

Glad grimaces. "I did." It comes out as a squeak. "Hey, I was curious."

My partner chuckles.

I clear my throat. "Back to this pirated prophecy."

Glad waves her hands. "Anyway, yes, among other things, it went on to talk about an attack Israel would suffer shortly after that, from several enemy nations. Against overwhelming odds, it said Israel would win, and not just win, but win *decisively*."

I jerk my head back. "You're not suggesting…."

"Really?" Issra murmurs.

Glad bobs her head. "I think that specific prophecy is unfolding." She bites her lip. "The problem is, it also says all the humans left on Earth, as well as all of second heaven, will be incinerated shortly after that. I don't know why. All I remember is that's what it said. Scared me to death when I read it."

Aliyah's eyes bulge. "No."

A chill runs up my back. "How much time?" I can't lose Glad.

Dante pulls his shoulders back. "We don't know. That's why we need you to get this prophecy, so we can determine that as well as see what else, if anything, it says. Then we can devise a plan to stop it."

Jael clenches his jaw. "When I became a celestial warrior, I swore an oath to guard and protect all that is the Almighty's, and that includes humans, but selfishly, I'd also like to find a way to save you, Glad."

"As did I, and me too," Aliyah adds, nodding sharply.

"Count me in." Issra fists his hands.

Glad and I lock gazes. "We'll do whatever we need to help."

She steps back into my arms. "We have to save those humans." There's longing in her beautiful eyes.

"I know. We will."

In a whisper, she says, "Seems you'll be needing to know where the forbidden section is."

I smile. "You're a bad influence on me."

She snickers. "It's through reading room seven." She stands on tippy toes and gives me another kiss. It's short and sweet and nowhere near long enough to suit me. Then she turns and rejoins her new friends.

Everything in me wants to hold Glad in my arms and protect her from whatever second heaven throws at her, but I can't. I have to trust someone else to, at least for now.

"We best get back before they come looking for us." Dante gives me a look that I'm not sure how to interpret.

"Keep her safe. Please." It's my only ask of her mentor.

He bobs his head. "Let us know when you confirm your understanding."

Glad gives a small wave, a pained expression on her face, as they wink out of sight.

I don't know how long we have before this prophecy is fulfilled and Earth and second heaven are obliterated, but I can't lose her.

"Let's go find this prophecy," I say as I turn to the squad.

Chapter Forty

Kessien

When things come back into focus, we drop hands in front of third heaven's majestic archives. Glad loved this place, spending as much time as she could here. Seems she also got into a bit of mischief—the same mischief we're about to repeat. But Glad's life is more than worth it.

"What's the consequence for being found in the forbidden section?" Issra asks from behind me as we mount the dozen white-marble steps.

"Reconsidering?" Aliyah asks beside me, gazing up at the imposing, sculptured pillars that grace the angels' entrance to the library.

"No way. I'm just curious."

"I suggest we not think about being found. We'll succeed." Jael's optimism encourages me.

I catch his gaze over my shoulder and give him a subtle nod.

We have to succeed.

We stroll past the overly large, white, circular circulation desk where librarians are checking out three sets of patrons. Another at the reference desk looks to be helping someone else with a question.

"Do we know where we're going?" Aliyah asks in a whisper, scanning the brightly illuminated, domed atrium with its three-stories of stacks.

"Are you suggesting we ask?" A corner of my mouth hitches.

Jael chuckles behind me.

I lean in to her. "I can hear it now. Excuse me, librarian, but could you please point us to the forbidden section?"

She slaps my shoulder playfully and rolls her eyes.

I shrug. "If you must know, Glad told me it's in reading room seven."

The scent of leather, parchment, and musty books permeates the air as I turn right and we head between towering shelves. It stands to reason that the human side of the library would be through reading room seven. That side of the library cozies up to ours against that wall.

We pass an ancient, gilded painting depicting Michael in warrior gear, wings splayed, reading from a huge scroll.

"How'd she find it anyway?" Issra asks.

"I can't say for sure, but I speculate she got distracted and her curiosity got the better of her and she started playing around and stumbled upon it."

No one debates my characterization of Glad. We know her too well.

We take three more turns, the most direct route to the back. Thankfully, no one's about way back here in the stacks. Let's hope the same can be said for the reading rooms.

A final left and we emerge into a cozy corner area with rich, acacia paneling. Seven doors are spread out, five on the back wall and two on the side. A clipboard sits atop the lone table in the middle—the sign-in sheet for the seven reading rooms, which I scan.

"Number two and three are occupied right now."

Jael bobs his head. Yes, it's a good sign.

"What exactly are we searching for?" Issra runs a hand through his curly locks.

Aliyah scribbles her name on the sign-in.

"A hidden door of some sort." I turn the doorknob, and we file in, then shut it again.

A fire crackles in a hearth against the left wall, inviting us to get comfy beneath a fuzzy throw on the tan leather couch. Slippers peek out from beneath the divan, and an empty mug invites us to order a favorite beverage.

Hot chocolate comes to mind, and the next thing I know, that's exactly what I smell beside me. Three more cups of marshmallow-rich chocolate appear.

"What?" I've never read here before.

"Looks like you were the first to think of a beverage." Aliyah pats my arm. "Hot chocolate definitely works. Good choice."

She reaches for a cup and passes it to Jael and another to Issra.

I take a sip of the piping hot goodness. It's as good as it smells.

"Watch this." Aliyah takes a sip, then looks at the back wall.

My eyes go wide, and I swallow quicker than I should. So do my brothers judging by their sputtering.

A white, sandy beach spreads out along the horizon. The smell of salt and the sounds of rolling waves and the cawing of seagulls fill the room.

Four hammocks, strung from palm trees that have appeared on either side of us, invite us to enjoy a different experience.

When I look around the room, I note that the fireplace has been replaced by an empty surf shop to complete the ambience. A tray of umbrella drinks, along with four pairs of sunglasses, sit on a counter of the shop.

"How…?" It's all I can get out.

Aliyah laughs. "Just a thought will change the room into your preferred reading experience. I've read in an evergreen forest—it smelled amazing—in a meadow with wildflowers, poolside, in a tree house, with a cat as well as a dog"—she holds up a finger—"but not at the same time."

"Seriously?" I may just learn to love reading.

My brothers' mouths hang open as they take it all in. They may be joining me at this rate. Perhaps it will become a new squadron pastime.

I take another sip of my hot chocolate, further appreciating the view.

"But where's the hidden door?" Issra puts his drink down, scanning the space.

"Right. Yes." I chuckle, a bit distracted.

Everyone puts their beverage down on the counter of the surf shack and fans out around the room. It's not that big of a space, so we finish examining every inch of the walls in short order, but no one finds a hidden door despite pushing and probing.

Jael looks up. "Should we try the ceiling?"

I shrug. "Might as well."

Four step ladders appear, and I look over at Aliyah.

"I figured it would help."

"Thank you."

Again it takes not long at all, and again we come up empty.

"What *exactly* did Glad tell you about the forbidden area's location?" Issra scratches his head.

"She said it was in reading room seven."

"I'm not doubting, but are you sure that's exactly what she said? We're missing something. Knowing now about this room and it's… interesting abilities, might she have phrased it slightly differently?" Jael raises an eyebrow.

I think back to that moment with Glad in my arms. "I told her she was a bad influence on me." Aliyah and Issra smile. "She replied that it's—wait." I raise my pointer finger. "She said it's *through* reading room seven."

"Through," Jael echoes.

"I got it." Aliyah looks at the ocean scene, and it quickly fades, becoming an acacia wood, paneled wall like the rest of the reading room area.

It's a dead end. I throw up my hands. "I've no idea."

We all stare at the wood wall, as if begging it to reveal any secrets it holds.

At length, Jael ambles forward and takes a closer look. He pushes on a section, then moves to the next, and the next with nothing happening.

I just watch, lost in worry. We have to get into the forbidden section. We have to find the prophecy.

Jael leans on the next section, the one right next to the room's left wall, and I swear the panel shifts.

Issra yips. He saw it too.

"Keep pushing." Aliyah fists her hands, cheering him on.

Seconds later, the hidden panel gives way, revealing a dark space beyond.

Silently, we creep through the opening. The light from the reading room reveals bookshelves, and my breathing eases. My chest feels light.

We found it.

"Let's find that prophecy," I whisper, leading us into forbidden territory.

We reach the first shelf, and I lean in to see what the spines might say, but the shelf is empty. I look up, discovering the same result with the shelf above; there are no books.

My heart accelerates.

"It's empty," Jael and Aliyah echo simultaneously.

"The whole place…." Surprise flavors Issra's words.

Don't Miss the Next Book in the Series
Damned, book two in the Morningstar Academy series, is available directly from LRW Lee at
https://lrwlee.com/collections/morningstar-academy-series (where it's cheaper) or at Amazon.

"Everyone who calls on the name of the Lord shall be saved."
- Joel 2:32

"For God so loved the world that he gave his one and only Son,
that whoever believes in him shall not perish but
have eternal life."
- John 3:16

What's Next?

God of Secrets

L. R. W. Lee's completed, four-book, paranormal romance series, *God of Secrets*, is a vulnerable, intimate, and gritty tale of destined lovers, potent magic, and unique, ancient Greek myth retellings.

Grab the first book, *Empire of Ash*, directly from LRW Lee at https://tinyurl.com/EoAsh. It's cheaper on her website than on Amazon.

Or **save big** and grab the four paperback bundle that's only on her website at https://tinyurl.com/GoSBundle.

Dangerous magic, a dark god, and ancient secrets.

Archaeologist Pellucid Rose discovers THE find of the century when an earthquake hits her Mycenae, Greece, dig. But before she can claim it, a dark, dangerous, and very sexy stranger steps from a swirl of shadows claiming she's loosed a sphinx on the world by translating an ancient secret on one of the scrolls.

What's more, he insists Secret Magic requires her to go with him to capture the ferocious creature.

Against better judgment, Pell teams up with the hot stranger to discover a world of magic where the impossible is reality, crooked mortals hide corrupt secrets, and mysteries older than myth can kill you. That thought alone makes her heart race, but things get even worse when she discovers he's hiding world-altering secrets, and only she has what it takes to stop him.

Empire of Ash is the first book in the enthralling God of Secrets paranormal romance series. If you like the snark of Jim Butcher's Dresden Files *and the fantasy of Holly Black's* Cruel Prince, *you'll adore USA Today Bestselling author L. R. W. Lee's vulnerable, intimate, and gritty tale of destined lovers, potent magic, and unique ancient Greek myth retellings.*

Grab *Empire of Ash* to dive into a secret affair today! Get it directly from LRW Lee's website at https://tinyurl.com/EoAsh

The Sand Maiden
L. R. W. Lee's award-winning, completed, four-book, paranormal romance series, *The Sand Maiden*, is a twisted retelling of the Sand Man mashed up with Morpheus, the god of dreams.

Buy Lullaby, book one, at https://tinyurl.com/LullabyBk1

Or save big when you buy the complete series directly from LRW Lee at https://tinyurl.com/TSMBoxSet

She's a dream weaver at odds with her king. He's a broken prince unable to love. Can they survive their nightmares to find their dreams?

Alissandra is immortal and wasn't supposed to fall in love with her human dream charge, but they share wounded pasts and he's the first to understand her pain. For his part, the prince has experienced his share of loss and betrayal and has erected barriers to protect his wounded heart--

while these barriers guard, they also prevent him from experiencing love.

No one says, no, to the king. So when Morpheus, god of dreams as well as Ali's father and sovereign, starts pressuring her to help him conquer mortal dreams making humans mindless slaves, she flees Dream Realm for Wake Realm to save the prince she loves, as well as all humans.

What Ali can't anticipate is that political opponents in the prince's kingdom will use her as a pawn in their quest to usurp power from the monarchy. Sensing the prince has more than a passing interest in the new arrival, they force her into a brutal competition that only the winner will walk away from.

If you love to hate supernatural bullies, empathize with wounded souls finding love, and cheer for the underdog you'll devour this tale of Morpheus, Greek god of dreams, by USA Today Bestselling author L. R. W. Lee. It's a slow-burn, fated mates, fantasy romance with potent sorcery and mythical intrigue.

Buy *Lullaby* to dive into a dreamy affair today! Get it now at https://tinyurl.com/LullabyBk1

Andy Smithson
Be sure to check out L. R. W. Lee's award-winning, seven-book, coming-of-age, epic fantasy series.

Download the first e-book, *Blast of the Dragon's Fury*, for FREE from Amazon now at https://tinyurl.com/GetBoDF or buy the paperback directly from L.

R. W. Lee at https://tinyurl.com/GetBoDF1

Video games can't train you to fight dragons!
800+ five-star reviews. Experience it for yourself!

Gamer Andy Smithson is whisked away to the magical land of Oomaldee, where fire-breathing dragons, giants, and deadly curses lurk around every corner. Trading his controller for a sword of legend, Andy embarks upon an epic quest to break a centuries-old curse oppressing the land.

It isn't chance that plunges him into the adventure though, for he soon discovers his ancestors are behind the curse.

Blast of the Dragon's Fury is a coming-of-age, epic fantasy adventure from USA Today Bestselling author L. R. W. Lee featuring fast-paced action, sword fights, laugh-out-loud humor, with a few life lessons thrown in. It's perfect for fans of Eragon, Fablehaven, Percy Jackson, Magemother, and Aster Wood!

Get it FREE at https://tinyurl.com/GetBoDF or buy the paperback at https://tinyurl.com/GetBoDF1

Acknowledgements

This is always my most favorite section to write of any book because writing a book is a team sport. LOL. I mean that. If not for the input of the following folks, this book would not be what it is.

First, I want to thank Debbie Turk for her quick and insightful feedback. She says she's been told she's too forthright, that she doesn't mince words, and she thinks it's a bad thing. Well, when it comes to fixing plot problems, questioning a character's arrogance (LOL) or any number of other issues, I can't ask for anyone better at pinpointing potential pitfalls. Love you Lady <3.

Next, I want to thank Denae Saidy-Daffeh for stepping up on short notice to beta read. Your enthusiasm for the story gave me more confidence that it was ready for primetime. LOL.

Then there's my amazing moderator group: Claire Manuel, Samantha Zeman, Cabiria Aquarius, Alexandra Wilkerson, Elisa Romana Kemp, Tarra Lyn Clark. You all are amazing women in your own right, and when you come together, you help make our Street Team a fun and welcoming place for booknerds to hang out. I appreciate your quirkiness, realness, vulnerability, and dedication. You all make it fun to be an author and a fellow bookworm.

———————

You can make a huge difference by leaving a review
Share your thoughts in a quick review on Amazon at: https://tinyurl.com/ReviewCursed It can be as short as one sentence! Make a difference.

———————

Facebook Fan Group
Did you have an emotional roller-coaster ride reading this book? Do you need others to talk to about it? What about having the opportunity to be the first to sign up for ARCs of her latest books? It all happens in the fan group.
Join L. R. W. Lee's Facebook group at
https://www.facebook.com/groups/LRWLeeStreetTeam
All the feels and fanning you can handle!

———————

Stay Informed!
There will always be more new books by L. R. W. Lee.
To instantly receive notice when she releases a new one or has news about other upcoming events, sign up at https://lrwlee.com/never-miss-out/

Connect with USA Today Bestselling author L. R. W. Lee

BookBub has a New Release Alert. Not only can you check out my latest deals, but you can also get an email when I release my next

book, by following me here:
https://www.bookbub.com/profile/l-r-w-lee

http://www.LRWLee.com
https://www.facebook.com/lrwlee
https://www.instagram.com/lrwlee/
https://www.pinterest.com/lindarwlee/
https://www.goodreads.com/author/show/7047233.L_R_W_Lee